ALEX MORRALL

HELEN AND THE GRANDBEES

Legend Press Ltd, 51 Gower Street, London, WC1E 6HJ
info@legendpress.co.uk | www.legendpress.co.uk

 British Library Cataloguing in Publication Data available.

Print ISBN 978-1-78955-9-910
Ebook ISBN 978-1-78955-9-903
Set in Times. Printing managed by Jellyfish Solutions Ltd
Cover design by Sarah Whittaker | www.whittakerbookdesign.com

Alex Morrall was born in Birmingham and now lives in south-east London, where her voluntary work inspired this novel. She enjoys working using both her creative and mathematical background. She has a maths degree but paints beautiful city scenes and landscapes in her spare time.

Follow Alex
@AlexPaintings

For the friends whose resilience inspired the novel, for my Mum who brought me up to write, and for my husband, Brian for his support.

CONTENTS

PROLOGUE

HELEN

We three sat together on the sofa for two. The sofa was made of bobbling grey and white threads. The foam stuck out through the gaps on the arm on April's side. The gas fire flickered with pale blue lines. Bill was sitting closest to the black and white television, so that when he leaned forwards to pick up his tea, I couldn't see the picture. But back then, I just didn't mind. We were warm. We were cosy. Nothing could ever hurt us while we sat here as a three. The bad stuff was yet to come.

The bad stuff. That's why I can't bear to call April and Bill Mum and Dad anymore.

That day, we had been to a memorial, a memorial for a little girl who had dropped out earlier than she was supposed to. I learned what people do at memorials: they go to a flat field and put daffodils next to a small stone that you shouldn't sit on. Red-eyed April told me that there would not be a baby sister for me, after all. She shivered in the wind as if the cold was curling around her bones, seeping through the gaps in her sheepskin coat and under her paisley shirt dress. I tried to wriggle my fingers away from the grip of the orange gloves that crushed too hard. And when I remember that bit, I think of her as my mum all over again.

On the way home, we took a taxi, me for the first time. In fact, we would not have fitted in the stitched leather seats if there were more of us, if there were four of us. Back in the warm, after the metallic tink tink tink of the fire being ignited, we could feel safe on the sofa for two because we all fitted, Bill and April's knees bunched up together under the *Radio Times*, my buckled shoes and white knee socks carefully propped over the edge of the fabric. We filled in all the spaces because I was still an eight-year-old girl who had had her first ride in a taxi, who wanted to sit on the memorial stone, who honestly believed it was better that there were only three. We were close. Nothing could come between us. There was never any need for there to be anybody else.

But sometimes you can be too close. Now I have grown old, I want to shout that fact back at the memory of us, the things that happened behind the gloss-painted doors. We should have left more space between us on the sofa for two. We should have let other people in.

It was wrong what happened when we were too close, and I have to blank my mind to forget about it.

So when I grew out of being that little girl, when I stretched into my teenage years and the world looked so different, I left the sofa for two. And when I left, I made sure that no one could find me and take me back.

THE HAPPY ENDING

I want to hum a tune: Beep Beep Bop. Do you like that tune? Beep Beep Bop…

I know. I was telling you a story. I was escaping my middle-aged body, trying to remember how it was to be a child all those years ago; or forget how it was. Well, I'm getting confused from the painkillers. I am trying to remember s*ome* of my childhood, but not all of it.

And when bad things bubble up, I check out. Beep Beep Bop.

People worry about me checking out. But checking out of reality is better, safer than the day the ambulance people found me walking in the middle of the pedestrianised street, crying. I felt shame then, a different sort of shame from all the days before.

After that day, I learned how to be free of what other people thought of me, stopped worrying when people winced at my Dudley accent. Could anything be worse than being found by the ambulance men, crying in the street? I dressed my long red hair, which had always flowed loose, in a green turban and I stopped trying to be thin. I wore flip-flops in the winter and not just when I took the rubbish out to the bin huts behind the fly-tipped fridges. Sometimes, when I wore flip-flops in the winter, I maybe did care a bit about what people thought about me. I was hoping they would see me and know that I was an independent lady and I didn't need a suit and a boardroom to prove it.

I don't do that so often now, though.

I check out. Then I check back in. This is a good way of living, a simple way, checked in or checked out.

But it's all fuzzy in my head right now and that makes it harder. Checked in is here, in St Thomas's fractures ward, decades after running away from home. I am in a bed chair surrounded by wires and tubes, power sockets, monitoring lines, tubes from the dosage machine, sending strange substances into my veins and the occasional beep that is not from the tune in my head. I had an accident, a slip-up. I've been feeling dizzy and tired the last few years and then I finally slipped up. I feel like I am in some science-fiction series, like *Blake's 7*, that Mum and Dad would watch on the sofa for two. I don't even like science fiction. Maybe I knew that one day I would be here like this, hooked up to the robots that control the dose that controls the pain.

Some of the beds next to me have people sitting next to them, with hand-holding and kindness. But many do not. Many have their eyes and fingers and ears hooked up to extra machines, iPads and headphones. No one seems to think it's wrong to check out of reality so long as it's with an iPad and headphones. This sort of checking out is okay. My sort of checking out has to be hidden.

Checking out isn't working so easily for me either, because with the drugs and everything, I start remembering the past, and I don't like that very much. I don't like that at all.

I spend a lot of time at St. Thomas's, even when I haven't just had a slip-up, but it's the building next door I usually visit. I'll be back there next week, waiting for the bus under the grey brick of Deptford Station and the trawl through the Old Kent Road. I will ignore the man who throws chips at the back of my chair and stare out of the window through my reflection at the old seventies offices converted to churches; Georgian houses nestling between phone shops and international supermarkets; and smashed-out discount furniture stores with chipped fascias.

And I'll reach the waiting room where I can slip in and

out of my realities. I will try to fill my checking out with a daydream of the hills with the wind blowing through my long red hair, my long red hair that I cut once to make out I wasn't mad. Or maybe the memories that will come back to me uninvited will be of the days when I had felt joy. Things have happened to me that I never expected to happen to me and, yes, some of them even brought me joy.

So, for a moment, just that thought of the wind lifting my hair behind me.

But I am already being interrupted by the commotion at the end of the ward. Some people are leaning out in their bed chairs, awakened from the hospital reveries, to take a look at what is going on. Now that I have been disturbed, I lean forwards too. I see a young black girl at the end of the ward, striding along between the beds, a hospital trolley briefly freewheeling as she pushes past it. The girl looks as if she is trying not to run. She is followed by a nurse who is trying not to look like she is chasing after her. Both are trying to look like they are not having the conversation they are having.

It's the voice I recognise first, the voice that says, so firmly, "I have a right to be here." A voice that is both a child's, but with the self-knowing of an adult. I know that voice and it's coming straight for me.

Good grief. It's Aisha.

***

But Lily arrived in my life before Aisha, and Lily was a really good thing. Truly, if I keep Beep Beep Bopping like this I will forget about the part of reality that turned out to be so beautiful.

I was fourteen when I ran away and it was not all bad when I reached London, threaded with dirty Victorian railway bridges. There were some good things: I had nail varnish that was such an unbelievable pink. A pink that could only have existed in the nuclear age. Oh yeah, a radioactive bubblegum pink that was pure plastic.

And some mornings I would wake up and search out the least chipped nail and stare, and delight in that pink in the daylight. It was so elegant, so modern. Wherever I happened to have woken up, in someone else's cluttered bedsit, or in the doorway of a neglected building, and however broken and bruised I was, that pink nail varnish was something familiar, like an old bedspread, like a friend. My comfort came with me wherever I woke up.

But there was also the day that I had stinking period pain as I sat to rest on a bench at Southwark Cathedral, like my sides were about to explode for two days, and they took me to a hospital. They gave me a bath, and they shaved me too, shaved me in private places. Then they hooked up my ankles into strange metal arms.

"Breathe like this..." said the nurse who put a syringe in my leg when I was lying down, when the pains were louder and quicker. So I breathed like that. But between the pains I stared at my pink varnished nails right until the next roaring pain would come.

The nurses looked down at me as I lay on the bed like I was a piece of dirt. And I tried to be good and I tried to be quiet through the explosions, but it was impossible to be even slightly quiet.

And eventually my insides ripped out into a beautiful brown little baby, bald and covered in blood, kicking angrily at the air.

Now, I do know my birds and my bees nowadays. It's just that the birds just aren't worth the mention.

Oh, but my little baby bee. How can I explain? She was wrinkly and whiny, but beautiful. Beautiful feet, unbelievable toes, warm black skin. I wanted to kiss every single eyelash. She was more wonderful than a hundred zillion pink nail varnishes, and with a hundred zillion different perspectives to look at her cute ears and nostrils and tear ducts and wide black eyes, and grasping fingers, and her addictive love to me.

I called her Lily.

And I could only clasp her to me all the time and feed her, and wake and feed her again. And I would get up in the middle of the night in the safe little flat they had given me, a whole train ride from London Bridge, with the rotting windows and rotting curtains. I was changing her and singing to her in the flat where I could not keep the dishes clean and cook and hold her. I loved her. It circled in the air that I loved her and that I needed to look after her. Properly.

But the time was so confusing. Was it day? Was it night? The fluorescent kitchen light would hum at me, and the clock leered at me… I knew I had to wash, but wash what? The curtains? The bee? The dishes? And she would scream at me, my beautiful little bee. Screaming bee.

And they took her away from me for good after three weeks. "They", the machine, the council, hospital, social services. The System took her to "Better parents, older parents, ones with a similar ethnic background."

"Can I say goodbye to her?" I croaked through the tears, but she was already being taken away.

I was allowed to stay in the two-bedroom council flat that they had given me with the lock on the front door. So when they sent me back alone from the hospital, I had somewhere to hide from those ones who flatter you, then trap you. I could bolt that front door if I ever needed to, even when the local teenagers left a burning car in the cul-de-sac outside. Once I even had to let a screaming girl into the stairwell as she begged for help from an attacker on the intercom. But I was too scared to let her through my front door.

And this meant that there were no more babies.

But I didn't know how to fill two bedrooms and a sitting room and a large kitchen-diner. They just made me feel lost in so much space where there was no screaming bee. I was still a little girl. I would look out of my window onto the tiny weeded gardens of little grey houses of Deptford and see more empty space. In the first week, I pushed the settee into the kitchen-diner and made that the day room. I slept in one bedroom. I never ever opened the other doors, because there was no bee inside.

My kitchen window overlooked a small playing area, with brightly coloured climbing frames and a roundabout. In the middle of each afternoon, it would fill up with lots of little girls who weren't my bee. Sometimes I would reach out my hand to the window as if I could touch their tiny images in the glass. And I would feel the cold of it.

I counted each year out, knowing what I was missing: a little girl growing into a toddler who tried to eat yellow Lego bricks; at primary school, bright-eyed over matching stationery sets; a taller preteen who would dance to Madonna with earmuffs and a hairbrush, and have the sparkly shy eyes who looked to Mummy when her friends' parents would try to talk to her. I even wanted her to be one of the bolshy teenagers who crammed into the shiny red buses in the middle of overcast afternoons, long, long after they took her away from me.

My life was a broken-up jigsaw, no roots, no branches, no sky, no ground, no horizon, but the blankness never went away. And as Deptford stonewashed its railway arches and built towering flats with intercoms and glass bricks, I thought it was the end.

Beep Beep Bop. No. It wasn't the end. Although it felt like the end at the time. My beautiful bee, she was going to come back to me. She was going to look for me. Someone who didn't want to hurt me was going to look for me.

***

This is the story of why you must never despair.

I lived the twenty years of my childless sentence locked in a prison, never talking about my bee. I got a job at the greengrocers on Deptford High Street, with doors that stayed open onto the pavement even in the winter, where the owner would tell me off for not making eye contact with the customers.

And then my phone rang and a nervous south-east London accent asked if I was Helen Kennedy. So I said I was, although you never know who might be looking for you, even now, even when they sound really nervous. And the voice said, "I'm Ingrid." I realised as Ingrid's words tumbled out over the phone line that this Ingrid was actually my Lily, my little bee. The part of me that was long lost was just a telephone line away. Could I reach down the line and hold her? But my bee was not little anymore. No, my little bee was all grown up.

And a couple of days later, the buzzer on the intercom goes, and Lily comes up the stairs wearing a sophisticated jacket over a roll-neck jumper and carrying yellow daffodils. Her hair is in long braids that have been swept up into a bun on her head. She is much darker than she was when she was a baby. You wouldn't guess that she had a white mum. If you saw her you would think that she was all black. But I know that she is mine, so who cares what anyone else thinks?

She has a big smile that says, finally I have found my real mum and we are going to be best friends.

She's pretty tall.

Even though she is a grown-up and I have missed her life, it's like a moment in a film when things are going wrong, but the people who are left over come together as friends and family and you know it's going to be all right really. I am so daft proud of this adult who is my lost Lily, I don't even know what to say to her for a while, but for the obvious things, like offering her a cup of tea, and we end up sitting at the kitchen table, where I have put the daffodils down, clasping mugs in our hands, one a freebie from Kellogg's, the other from a stationery company, and I feel like we are fixing something, building something really good. "So," she says. She seems calmer now she has sat down.

"So, finally." I look at her. I try to take her all in; her elegant hair, her elegant dress and high cheekbones. She is blinding. She is absolutely beautiful. And she must think that I am a terrible person.

She does a nervous giggle. This time, her hand goes to her mouth quickly and I catch sight of her nails, each carefully painted in deep purple. She turns back to me and lifts a hand to her forehead. "So, well… I wanted to tell you about myself…"

"Why are you called Ingrid? I called you Lily." I have been wanting to ask from the beginning, because now I see her, I know she is mine. But on the phone, I was not so sure.

"You called me Lily?" She raises her eyebrows. I wish I had not interrupted, but I still make a little disapproving noise in the back of my throat. I am not sure why. I'm not really expecting someone to change their name back after twenty years. "Did you register me as Lily?"

"I hadn't got that far," I shrug. Now I know this was a mistake. "They said the flat was unhygienic. Is it okay now, do you think?" Should I explain that since I lost my bee I would go home and start cleaning the house, every small corner, even as the rot tried to come through from the flat above? I would battle it every evening, with brushes, with white paint, and make my square flat white and safe, losing sleep over the corners that a toothbrush couldn't reach. This was all so that I would never lose a bee again, even though she had already gone and I would never get her back. I knew it.

I had known it, until now.

"I don't think that they're going to take me away this time." She says it quietly, in a way that means that I shouldn't carry on speaking about it, and seems disappointed.

"No. I suppose not."

She looks around again at my kitchen-diner through her long lashes, that must be fake, and I don't think she is checking how clean it is. Maybe she is looking for something. The light from the window highlights where she has put a subtle shimmer of make-up across her cheekbones. Even though she giggles a lot, there is something so calm and in control underneath her shyness that she reminds me a little bit of the System that took her away from me. Yes, I am sure she is looking for something. "I think that my parents named me themselves."

"Your parents?"

"Yes – Maurice and Jenny." She clasps her hands together as she explains and there is still a bit of a tremor in her voice. "They brought me up."

Of course I knew that Lily would be brought up by *someone* else, but I suppose I was pretending to myself that they didn't really make any difference to *us*.

"Mum and Dad loved adopting and fostering, so we always knew, you know, about being adopted. It wasn't a secret. And they always said that I could look up my biological mother, well, that's you," she adds with a warm smile and taps the table near me, "when I was ready."

I'm not a biological mother. I'm Lily's true mum. "They shouldn't have changed your name." I can't help it slipping out.

"They're good people who have given me everything I have," she shoots back so quickly, across my plastic white table, that her words slap me. It's as if she had already prepared her words, as if she knew I wouldn't be happy about her new name before I did.

I lean back in my seat. I see I must be careful what I say to my bee. She does not see things my way. I must stop saying some things. Otherwise I might lose my bee again.

"But we're going to be great friends, I can tell." She sounds like she is a lady who knows these things. "Can we leave it at that?"

I glow.

And even though I haven't got an important job, and even though Lily has other parents, we talk a long time, Lily and me. She says she's a PA, part of the System that gives you prescriptions and tells you off about the state of your flat. Lily has fallen on the other side. "How about you?"

I lift a hand to my mouth. "I used to work at the greengrocers in Deptford, but it closed down."

Lily waits with a listening face as if I haven't finished yet, but I have. I am only a cleaner at Asda, which isn't half as good as being a PA.

"That sounds like fun." She leans forward with an encouraging smile.

And Lily tells me that she likes my hair, which I am very proud of. I grow it long and clip it with emerald-coloured clips on either side to offset the red. I daydream that they are made of real emeralds. It turns out that Lily likes pretty things too. She is wearing a locket. She unclicks it, laying it out on the table, and shows me the colours of the stones that she keeps inside.

We finish a cup of tea, and after a while I offer her another one, and she doesn't say, "Oh no, I must be going." Instead she says, "Could I make it a coffee this time?" and I remember that I have a packet of custard creams in the cupboard and we slowly work through the whole packet, leaving golden crumbs in the ripped-up wrapping.

She stays so long and as I talk to her for longer, I start to find it easier to say the right sort of thing and say less about the past. I have been having conversations with myself for so long that to talk to a real person makes my thoughts fall into place better. I am a lady who can hold a conversation with a PA.

***

And now comes my happy ending. Our happy ending. My little bee says that there is something that she wanted to tell me. She has gone all nervous again. "Well, I've got a bit of a surprise." She almost chokes on her words. She lifts her palms up as if in disbelief as to what she is saying herself and I suddenly notice the glint of a precious stone on her ring finger. "To be honest, I'm surprising myself. I didn't think I would tell you straight away. Well..." she starts, all smiling, brimming with her news. "This is why I wanted to find you. I met a really great guy in college, called Andrew."

A nice man who looks after my Lily. Lily is so happy. This

must be a good sort of man, a different sort from the ones I've met. I save up this thought to come back to, to close my eyes and think of peaceful things.

"And, well, we're having a baby together."

A baby! For a minute I am so happy for her.

"I really want my baby to know where he or she came from," she doesn't stop as the words rush out like train carriages, "and who their relatives are and for you all to be part of their life." And her hands finally collapse into her lap as she stops talking and she looks at me, happy and helpless.

Now I am so happy for me.

Because the point is that even though my little girl came back to me as a grown-up and I was grateful but sad that I had missed all of the little-girlness, after decades of thinking everything was over, it's all going to start again, and I will get to see my little grandchild grow from baby to toddler to teen. And I am not going to get confused about the night and the day and lose them this time. Oh no I am not. And I am not going to have an unhygienic house and lose them that way. Oh no I am not.

And this is why you should never despair. Because you never would have guessed that such a good thing would happen, such a good thing that it would make all the bad disappear as if it never happened. You would never have guessed it, not in a million years.

I stand up and hug Lily and she is crying and I think this is so strange, all these tears with someone I hardly know, who I know really well. She sits back down again and wipes tears away from her face. And after a while, she calms down and talks all polite again, "So, I can't place your accent. Is it Liverpudlian?"

"No," I say, even though I think it's a little bit funny that she would think that my accent is Liverpudlian.

"Okay, it just seems Liverpudlian..."

"Well, it isn't."

We're not to discuss where I am from.

ANDREW

She came home from that first meeting smiling. You can't beat that feeling, seeing my woman smile. "Stupid block of flats stank of dustbins," she muttered, throwing off her coat, which is so Ingrid, not one to show her feelings.

I love Ingrid like crazy. When we met at college, her first words to me had been, "Anyone sitting here?" I'd seen her before, around the college corridors with her hair wrapped up high in plaits on her head, and she was kind of "Wow!" but we were in different classes. So I wasn't expecting her to charge right up to me like that, carrying a melamine tray of Maltesers and Diet Coke.

She'd taken the seat before I could reply, which was just as well, as I'd suddenly discovered a stammer now that there was a hot girl in front of me. I was wishing I hadn't dressed so quick after training and could feel snakes of sweat run down the back of my neck. "You're Andrew, right?" she said, releasing the tab from her drink. I was trying to give Darren a look, like, don't even think of coming over, while he was still in the queue. "Seen you around."

Later on, I discovered that "seen you around" meant that her best friend, Victoria, had the hots for me but had never done anything about it. Not sure they ever spoke to each other after that.

"Well, I don't have to waste time just because she did,"

Ingrid explained later and I'm not complaining. I know I'd always said that I was gonna marry at twenty-five, settled in a job and having bought a house. But it worked out well for me. I was blown away.

Ingrid didn't tell me she was adopted for ages. No reason to, I guess. I only really got how big a deal it was for her a couple of years later, after we were married. She kept buying books from glossy magazine ads with pictures of hearts or peaceful clouds: "Heritage and identity", "Researching your family tree". I figured it was just girl stuff to start with. But then followed the letters to social services.

"Are, like, Maurice and Jenny okay with that?" I asked.

She sniffed. "I just need to know who I am, have a heritage. Like how you know your mum's Scottish and your dad's from St Lucia and how they would never have met that day if the train to London hadn't been delayed." She and my parents had got on right from the first moment they met. "You have stories."

I was going to support her all the way. She deserved the best.

But when the pregnancy test came up positive, the pamphlets about meeting your biological parents, the adoption notes on how Helen Kennedy was very young and struggling to cope, disappeared from the sofa and the coffee table. I knew not to ask. The silence meant Ingrid had read enough. She was brewing, deciding on her time to act, and she didn't want to read or talk about it anymore.

"You might not find all the answers you're looking for," I whispered to her as she lay on the bed telling me she was going to make the phone call. She looked pensive. I literally could not remember any other time that she wanted to stop and "think before doing" like this.

Maybe it wasn't my business to say so, but the thought of Ingrid's disappointment was too much.

She rolled onto her side and leant her head on her hand, looking me in the eye. "I will do," she said. "I will get all the answers."

I knew she meant it.

***

We'd made enough jokes about how Ingrid's biological mum would turn out to be a horror show and I guess I was feeling bad about that by the time she was ready to talk. "You were smiling, despite the dustbins."

She shrugged. "She keeps her flat really nice inside."

"Not a total loony, then?"

Ingrid winced. "She was very… keen."

"I would be if I was meeting you for the first time."

She gave a little sigh of exasperation, like she always does when I remind her how great she is. "And she's actually not stupid when you get talking, almost fun, but seems kind of slow, like she's not spent much time with other people."

"Did she look like you?"

"Well, maybe, hard to tell really."

"Did you get the answers you wanted?"

She shook her head, but smiled, and I remembered that conversation we had. She will get the answers. Ingrid always gets what she wants.

HELEN

My next-door neighbour is an older lady called Mrs Cauldwell. She bakes cakes, fruitcakes, and we drink tea together with the fruitcake and have a good old chuckle. It isn't the same as talking to a PA like Lily though, because Mrs Cauldwell will suddenly start to act strangely. Sometimes I will go around to her kitchen for cake, which is all neatly laid out with a gingham tablecloth as if we are in a farm barn and not a concrete flat in Deptford, and we will still chatter and giggle, but there will be something a bit wrong with the cake, things in it that shouldn't be, like dental floss. So I sit there for a while looking at the cream-coloured plate, trying not to say anything and eating the cake and hiding the dental floss all at the same time. Another time there might be a paper clip in the cake. And I start to worry what else might be in there that isn't quite so easy to work out. Definitely there has been chicken stock. I am quite sure about the chicken stock.

And Mrs Cauldwell will talk to me about nice things and not worry that I don't conform to other people's ideas of how I should be, and tell me how she's learned that people are nice inside whatever they are like on the outside, and her words are sweet, like the cakes she bakes when they are good cakes.

But around about the time that the cakes get to be bad cakes again, she will start to get a bit more nervous, and then a bit more snappy. The chipped blue jug is thumped on the table, so that the milk slops out as it lands, and she won't stop to mop it up. And she thinks that the neighbours are listening in to our conversations and talking about her. To be honest, sometimes I hide from Mrs Cauldwell when the cakes start to get funny, because she is quite scary. Then she goes to hospital for quite a long time and when she comes out, she is sweet again.

They seem to put all the fruitcakes in this block of flats.

But after my bee, my Lily, has been around to meet me, I have to tell someone. It's all so big and so absolutely real that I am brimming with words that need to come out, so I knock on Mrs Cauldwell's white and splintering door.

She opens it and hovers with it, swinging lightly. She wears a blue cardigan and a long blue A-line skirt. Somehow this reminds me of the housecoats that old ladies would wear when I was little. A song is playing from a flat upstairs, and Mrs Cauldwell hates all of that loud, fast modern music, so I know I am starting off bad.

Mrs Cauldwell doesn't quite meet my eye, but is looking up, up past my head, as if there is an enormous and lively bird in my hair. This is not normally a good sign.

"Mrs Cauldwell, I have a baby."

Her eyes turn to my midriff with some interest.

"No, I mean I had a baby and she is all grown up now."

The interest dissipates immediately. I know that Mrs Cauldwell also has grown-up children, but I don't know much about them. I am not explaining myself very well.

I take a deep breath. "Mrs Cauldwell, I had a baby and they took her away from me twenty years ago, and today she came back to me. And now she has a different name."

Mrs Cauldwell's eyes swell, and her chest swells. I have overdone it. She cannot absorb all of the information. There is a long silence and I know that she is brewing something in this silence.

"You stupid, stupid child!" she yells. I have no idea if she is talking about me for losing Lily, or for accepting Lily back, or if she is talking to someone else entirely. "You stupid, stupid…"

Terrified, I scuttle back through my own front door as Mrs Cauldwell yells obscenities in the corridor. I don't really know what to do anymore. I hide in the bathroom because I can lock the door twice there, and I don't think Mrs Cauldwell can get through two locked doors. I find a coral lipstick on the sink and I apply it, creating a perfect Cupid's bow, making my lips glow against my red hair. I love putting on lipstick. I think I will wear lipstick the next time that I see Lily. I look in the mirror and start having the conversations that I will have with Lily when I see her next, ignoring the rocking of the front door as Mrs Cauldwell throws herself against it.

***

It's a week before Lily comes back. The intercom buzzer goes and I'm scared to pick it up because Mrs Cauldwell has been acting odd for the whole week. She must be covered with bruises from throwing herself around outside. On Tuesday, she pushed a photograph she had taken of my front door through the letter box that had *I know you are in there* written on the back in blue biro. *Why aren't you my friend anymore? You have deserted me! You've used me.* The writing was very hard to work out, and when I did work it out, I wished I hadn't tried. But you can't undo a thing like that. Then I wondered if it would be rude to just throw the photograph away, because even though Mrs Cauldwell is my friend, I didn't like it very much.

Lily arrives very smart, in a knitted dress, not a formal one, but it's still clear she's made the effort. I think she knows something is wrong next door because she seems more shy than she did the last time.

It makes me feel more shy too and I don't want to lose her and her baby again. She starts talking really fast about her day at work, and sometimes she uses letters instead of whole words, like "Phil the FD" and "BAU", so I don't really know what is happening, but it sounds serious.

Once she's got her tea, she stops talking and sips slowly from the mug, which makes her look smaller, more nervous, and says quietly, "So, it must be my dad who was black?"

It takes me a moment to think of who she means by her dad. And then, when I realise, I don't know what to say.

She waits, and my stomach churns. Then she shrugs her shoulders that are tighter together than usual. "Silly question, really."

I can't say anything to that. I can't agree that my little bee might be silly. My bee didn't bring flowers this time. She brought garibaldis, dead fly biscuits which I hate, but I eat them greedily from the ripped packaging on the table in case I lose her again.

"Lily, I'm so glad to be a part of this."

Her eyes flare up and her shyness suddenly disappears. "Don't call me Lily!" Her splayed fingers come down towards the table but pause before landing on it. Her hand is full of fashion rings so that the ones on her wedding finger are nearly crowded out.

She calms down and starts talking about going to Mothercare together, and I am fizzing, fizzing inside. I could not afford to go shopping for baby things when I was expecting Lily, grabbing for grotty off-pink woollies in the jumble sale at the local primary school. That was what we did in the seventies. "And when the baby's born? Can I see it then?"

"Of course," she says with a confused frown, but she forgets that I did not get to see her for long when she was born. She was taken away from me so soon, my poor bee. "But, that's partially why I'm here." She reaches down for her soft brown handbag, pulling it onto her lap by its gold chain. There is a brown envelope with pictures inside. "I went for my scan yesterday." She lays the photographs in front of me, black and white smudges in a conical shape.

"Is that the baby?"

"Yes." She looks up at me, her smile bursting from her cheeks and her eyes. "That's my little girl."

A little girl? Like the little girl Lily that I never watched grow up? Even more perfect. But I do think, I hope that she does not drop out like my little sister.

I spend a few moments trying to look interested in the fuzzy smudges, in case a baby suddenly becomes obvious in them. Sometimes you can see hidden images in magic eye pictures, that are in the newsagents, that you couldn't see before. I don't see anything new.

Lily looks around at my bare white walls. She looks happy. She says, "It's really nice to have someone actually want..." She tails off and I look over at her from the kitchen. She picks up again, "Who actually wants to share their time with me and Andrew and be so happy for us." And then she looks down at her lap as if she should not have said that, as if there really could be someone who didn't have time for Andrew and Lily, which surely couldn't be true.

She's right about one thing. I have all my love for Lily.

"It's going to be so much fun. I can bring pictures of her for your walls." So that's why she was staring at my walls. She must find my flat very cold.

"Pictures?"

"Yes... Andrew could get them framed for you. We could add them to pictures of the rest of your family."

And I know right away that this means she's worked out that there is no "rest of the family". There's me and no one else. So I'm about to change the subject quickly when there is the sound of a crashing chair from next door.

Lily flinches, staring at the wall again. "What on earth was that?" she asks, her mouth dropping.

I don't know what to say for a minute or two. I don't know how to explain about Mrs Cauldwell in case Lily thinks less of me. "My next-door neighbour is a bit," I pause and purse my lips, "under the weather."

"Okay," says Lily. She frowns, probably trying to imagine what sort of disease might end with crashing crockery.

"Let me top up your cup of tea." I try not to think of fruitcakes or garibaldi biscuits.

***

While Lily carries her little girl, I dread the phone call that she has dropped out like my little sister. Sometimes I phone Lily, just in case I have missed a call about a fallen-out baby, and a couple of times a man picks the phone up.

"Hello. I'm Helen," I say, although I really want to say, "Who are you?" or "Where is Lily?"

The man introduces himself as Andrew and I remember that Andrew is the husband, not the pretend father who adopted her.

"Is the baby okay?"

"I have to be honest with you, Helen." He lowers his voice, my stomach trips in horror. "She's been throwing a tantrum about not having her ears pierced… but Ingrid's bought her a Nintendo, so everything will be okay."

Relief floods me and I allow myself a giggle. "It's amazing how technology can improve pregnancy these days, isn't it?" We laugh together. It's a nice feeling, laughing together even though we are on the phone and have never seen each other's faces.

"You should come around for dinner sometime. Ingrid is a great cook, you know."

I watch a cockroach scuttle across the floor. The cockroach infestation started last week. I didn't even know what they were when I first noticed them climbing the cupboard doors, touching the open food with their tentacles. Probably from Mrs Cauldwell's flat. So yes, I do want to eat somewhere clean. I sense Andrew waiting for my reply on the other end of the line. "I'd like that." I couldn't have daydreamed it if I tried. Going to my little bee's house to dinner. But I won't tell Mrs Cauldwell about it this time.

INGRID

It's not that I don't like Helen. I never expected a film star or academic and I know big words aren't what make a person intelligent. Would Maurice and Jenny ever let me forget it? Social worker mentality.

Occasionally, in the middle of her drifty conversation, Helen would clasp her fingers, and pull them slowly apart, just like I'd seen myself do once in my media studies videos, and for a brief flash, it felt as if I had come home. But the flash faded so quickly, and after a couple of visits, I knew I had not found myself. I needed more. The two of us giggling over pretty nail colours and jewellery, or her quiet warm wisdoms, still seemed to be a separate part of the jigsaw piece, something detached form the big picture. She had to give me more, something bigger to belong to. But all I had to go on was that empty flat, that soulless, empty flat. A blank. Nothing to work with to find answers.

But I know how to get what I want. That's my thing. I start by working on the heartstrings. I tell Helen about my little brother, Goodness.

"Oh no," says Helen and I try to ignore the interruption. "I have to stop you there."

I wait for her to explain, but she just looks embarrassed.

"There never was a bee but Lily," she mutters under her

breath after a while and I watch her mouth her own quiet thoughts into her lap and I pretend not to see it.

"I mean my brother who Maurice and Jenny fostered straight after me." Helen pulls another face, so I carry on before she can interrupt again. "He was so irritating." I can still feel the irritation, his ugly scar and piecemeal English. "But we shared a room and I had to look after him, even though he wasn't my real... well, anyway, after a while we realised that when we were together we weren't frightened."

"Can I meet him?"

"Well..." Can she just let me get to the end of the story? "No, not really. When we were about eight or nine, he had an allergic reaction from eating peanuts at a classmate's party."

Helen looks at me wide-eyed and so I see I have to spell it out. I regret having started now.

"He died." I flick my head to make it clear that I don't want her sympathy. "And that was quite hard, because I had got used to having a little brother, just one, who was there even when I was asleep, and then suddenly he was nowhere. You see why I am telling you this?"

"I shouldn't have lost you. This would never have happened."

Oh please! I jump in to get her back on track. "Well, actually, all I mean is that if there is a lot of family, there is always someone else to talk to if something goes wrong." I look at her for a long time, so maybe she can work out what I am saying. "So, this is very important to me." I add, when none of it seems to sink in, "Meeting you, making sure that my baby has a proper family, a heritage."

She smiles warmly. This is going right over her head. Patience. I think. I just need patience.

HELEN

I arrive with tulips at the cute little house with the tiny brick porch in Thamesmead, a home beating like a heart, full of all the warm things within: Lily and the "good man" who looks after her; Lily and the baby inside of her. I am not sure that I should make them open the door to my Deptford life and the heritage I bring.

"I'm glad Andrew invited you over," Lily says as she drops a large orange pot onto on the dining table in front of us. I can see a definite bump pushing out through her long red jumper. She's more cheery than when she was telling me about her little brother. Although even then, I waited for her voice to crack, or for her to look away, like I would if I ever spoke out loud about my little sister that never was, but there was nothing. I think when Lily is calmer, it is sadder. The air is full of the smell of spices. "I've been meaning to call you, but it's been so busy with the baby and everything."

Maybe Lily thinks that this has all gone too fast. I do not want to lose my bee and her baby because I go too fast, but she's returned to the kitchen before I can think to say anything.

I smile shyly at Andrew through my eyelashes. He is also black and wears a charcoal jumper and jeans. He has the grassy smell of aftershave and I breathe in as I try to work out what to say. I have never been to anyone's house for dinner before. Sometimes there were people in the flat opposite who would invite me in for a cup of tea. Sometimes I would just not get on with them that way. This is my daughter's house, but she is really someone else's daughter.

A photo on the radiator shelf catches my eye, and I rush to it, with an "oh" and I stand there, staring into it, until Andrew comes over and passes it to me. I just want to drink in the scene. It's Lily in a strapless white dress that clings all the way down to her knees and then flares out. She's holding a bouquet of bright chrysanthemums in yellow and orange and burgundy. Next to her is Andrew in a grey top hat and a suit and striped cravat that matches the flowers.

"Our wedding," and Andrew says it with smiling wrinkles in his eyes.

In the photo, they stand looking at each other on black and white tiles. Behind them, columns hold up balconies that sweep into a staircase, against a posh green-coloured wall.

"At Woolwich Town hall," he adds. I've been past Woolwich Town Hall on the bus. I never dreamt it would be so pretty inside. "She has your eyes, doesn't she?"

Oh! I look again, and glance at the mirror hanging over the radiator. He is right. Lily's eyelids fold out from under her brows, just like mine. Her dark pupils shine from wide ovals and even her eyebrows are arched in the same way, although hers are plucked and highlighted. She is glossy and glamorous and half black but still has bits like me.

I look again, but then I notice something else. Lily is stunning, but she's surrounded by other people, and not just Andrew's parents, I think.

"They are Ingrid's real parents," I say with a nod, putting the photo back on the mantelpiece, to show that I've learned to agree with Lily about this, and I feel like Lily's photo and the laminate floor and the crocheted throws are all staring at me, because I'm so obvious, and I glance at the archway to the kitchen, even though Lily can't possibly have heard with the boiling pots and extractor fan.

"You'll be okay, you know," he pauses and smiles. "She likes you."

She likes me?

"She thought your flat was very clean," he adds with a wink.

I feel myself scrunch back into my space in a safe little ball.

***

"How did you learn to cook like this?" I ask as dinner is scooped onto primrose-coloured plates. Lily calls it "Jambalaya", which sounds like a tune, and the smell swells and swirls towards me and through my nose and throat. It's full of prawns and spices, and chilli.

"From my parents. They wanted me to learn to cook food from around the world."

Parents again. I try not to say anything. I keep trying not to say anything, but that must show on my face because I see Andrew and Lily glance at one another as Lily passes around the plates.

"I was adopted by a Caribbean family. It's a thing the social services do. They want black kids to be brought up in a black family and so on." You can see she does not really want to have to explain all this. She is not looking at me but carefully folding the green checked tea towel down by the pot, even though the tea towel does not need to be folded.

"But you're only half black, Lily."

She gives me a sharp look.

"I mean Ingrid. You are half me, half white." And all my eyes. But I don't say the last bit.

Apparently, it doesn't work like this. "I identify more with being black," she tells me as she passes me some cutlery.

Only because your adoptive parents were black, I seethe inside, but I bite my tongue. It sounds like a phrase she has used before. I've noticed that it's best not to talk about Lily's other parents. Or are the adoptive parents the real parents?

I scowl just trying to think of the right phrase. And that's because if you can't say anything nice, it's best not to say anything at all.

Andrew picks up my plate and reaches to put another scoop of rice on it. "Helen," I know I have to look at him properly now, "it's like this. I think that I am black and white when I am at home and I have dinner with my white mum and black dad. At home, it's no big deal. But when you're out amongst English people, they don't get all of that, and they just see someone different from them, so you are black."

I don't get it. I cross my arms.

"When Andrew was little, he thought that all mums were white and all dads were black," says Lily. "Until he went to school and met all the other children's parents."

I look at Andrew and I can see from his face that Lily isn't joking and that it really happened. I feel the start of a smile in the corner of my mouth and I'm not sure if this is okay or not, but Andrew snorts first and I laugh with him.

He's okay, Andrew is.

"So does that make you feel closer to your dad?" I ask suddenly and suspiciously, through mouthfuls of rice.

Lily thumps down her fork. She is not a silly bee. She knows why I am asking Andrew this.

I love my little bee, but she reminds me that even though she came from me, the other couple were the ones who kept her properly, and kept her for longer. And they were the ones who gave her a little brother called Goodness. So she belongs to them now.

My heart starts racing. I forget Andrew is here for a minute. "But I didn't mean to give you up, Ingrid. I didn't want to give you up," I blurt.

Lily raises her hands, which are full of the tea towel and ladle, as if to calm us all down. But I am calm really. I am not shouting; my voice is just a bit higher. "The thing is done now," Lily says finally and rests the ladle on the table so that she can join us in eating.

And I bite my tongue because I do not want my bee to think that I am unhappy having dinner here with her husband and her baby yet to be born. I take a sidelong glance at him to see if he's reacted to my outburst, but he doesn't seem worried.

I really want to be here all of the time, in this red-bricked house in Thamesmead with its magnolia-coloured walls. This is my daughter's house, but she is really someone else's daughter.

Lily reaches quickly for her stomach, there must have been a kick, and we all smile, even Lily's eyes soften a bit. "They were there my whole life. How would you feel about your parents who were there for you all that time?" and she looks at me.

Oh, *my* parents. The Mummy and the Daddy, the two-seater sofa for three, with so little space in between. Those parents wanted me to be theirs forever. Even Mummy with the glazed sad eyes that never saw anything, never understood what was really going on.

As my heart stirs up its panic, Lily is looking at me. She is not looking at the plate which she is eating from. She is not looking at whether her fork is scraping where there is food. Oh, she is arch, my Lily. She slipped that thing in about my parents to see what I would give away. She does that sometimes. I need to watch her.

I'm not blaming her for wanting to know. But I can't fix everything, my little bee. I cannot give you a daddy of your own, and a granny and a grandpa. You get all that from the adoptive family you're so proud of. Don't you get greedy for what you don't really want. Don't you use me to find the things you'll discover are bad to know.

***

The man from the council has come to kill the cockroaches the day that I get the phone call. He paces back and forth on top of the lino I bought to look like wooden flooring. I feel a bit sad for the cockroaches. A couple of days ago, I sprayed some insect killer at one that came too close and it went into a mad dance. I wonder if Mrs Cauldwell is going mad, being fed meds that the System says are safe, but who can really know?

The insect killer is a kind man in overalls, whose mouth doesn't work properly. The right-hand side makes the words, but the left-hand side does not follow. It's a pity that he has this job, because he seems to feel sorry for the cockroaches too. He tells me all about their habits and their behaviour and their history and their ability to survive a thing called a nuclear winter and he talks about them with a kind of admiration. "They move so fast," he says, watching as one runs to the shadows beneath my washing machine.

"I don't think they go that fast. Spiders can move faster."

"Spiders can jump. Cockroaches are different." He waves his forefinger at me, but it's in a friendly way. He's not telling me off for not knowing about cockroaches. "They emit pheromones that help them to stick together like friends."

"Friends?" I like that. They can make up their own families as they go along. It doesn't matter where they started.

He hands me an information leaflet with an enlarged sketch of a cockroach on the front, its antennae reaching out, greater than the length of its body. I shudder and quickly place the leaflet face down on the arm of the sofa.

"Are you going into number seventeen to sort them out there next?" I ask.

"Number seventeen?"

"The flat where they are all coming from. I don't think she's been cleaning properly."

"The office didn't mention anything about that." He avoids my eye.

"Do you think that you should go in anyway? They'll only come back here if they are not removed from next door."

He pulls a face, the side of the face that can move properly, as if he is thinking, but not for very long because he knows the answer anyway. "I can't really. How'd I get into the flat without the resident letting me in?"

I think that means that I am going to have cockroaches as neighbours for a long time to come. I suppose that is no worse than what I have today. But that's when the phone starts ringing. I answer it.

"Hi Helen? It's Andrew," says the crackle on the phone.

I can hear just fine from Andrew's glowing voice that there is nothing to worry about. No babies have dropped out early.

"Ingrid and me are now three," he announces. What good rhymes he does.

"Oh!" I am wordless. What do people say when this happens? "Shall I come and see you? Are you at the hospital in Woolwich?" I forget I'm supposed to be looking after the cockroach man.

Andrew clears his throat. "Actually, we left the hospital this morning. We're at home. Ingrid's parents have just left and she is sleeping now. But we wanted you to know our little girl has been born and she weighs seven pounds."

Even though I am the second grandmother to find out, and I forget to say congratulations to Andrew, I am still overwhelmed with happiness. It is all going so well, so well I can hardly breathe. Wedding photos and babies and little homes with warm sofas. A million miles from my white flat. I think about telling Mrs Cauldwell again, so much thumping pleasure charging around my life. But she scares me, does Mrs C.

***

I get to meet Lily-Ingrid's daughter the next day. The bus can't get me to Thamesmead past the rows of Victorian houses and concrete Woolwich quickly enough. Lily's daughter's name is Aisha and when I go around to see her, it's a wonderful day. She is so tiny and delicate, all wrapped up in an orange blanket. "Coddled", they say, helpless. It's as if her skin would give way if you touched it. This is what love means, and it actually hurts. Tiny Aisha coddled like a gem in a ring box, a place where my heart all looks up.

But the day starts to be a little bit less of a wonderful day when they are sat on the velvet throw on the sofa and bright-eyed Lily reaches for Andrew's hand. She turns to me while I have Aisha warm and gurgling in my arms and asks, was her daddy, Lily's daddy, there at Lily's birth?

Dear Lily, let's put the past behind us and move on, and let's look at beautiful things and remember how beautiful a thing it is for us all to be alive, us three, Lily, Aisha and me.

THE DISCONTENT

Beep Beep Bop. Red hair and green silk skirts flying in the wind. Fifteen years whistle by like leaves caught up in the breeze, and memories bring choices. The bad things can be shoved away amongst a lifetime of events, like needles in a haystack; the good ones can be played and played again. They don't have to be the things that make you who you are anymore, like the stories old people tell of the children that they used to be.

I play the happy memory of Aisha's birth over and over again as I stare at the violet-blue curtain of St Thomas's A&E treatment room. Fifteen years. I wish I could live in that past again.

Today, shadows of bossy nurses pass along the corridor between the beds with clipboards, grumpy that I cannot give the name of anyone to fetch me and my broken shoulder, to take me home. I try to explain that it was just an elderly neighbour who called the ambulance, who, when she realised she couldn't lift me to my feet, kindly turned her back on the secrets that burst out of the Quality Street tin that I had dropped on the floor as I fell.

So no, there is no one else who can take me home. No, there is no family who can help. I hold my dizzy head high against the pillow as I tell them this, but I think I sound like a failure, because after finding Lily all those years ago, I lost my Lily again, and everything she brought me. I haven't seen Aisha since she was thirteen. Broken bones are not enough to bring us all back together.

Although if they've read my medical notes about my visits

next door, they must already know that something is more wrong with me than a broken shoulder.

I try to tell them that it's okay really. I am a stronger person than I used to be. I prefer to carry my own problems and nestle in my memories: Aisha's birth; the wind lifting my hair.

And here is when the commotion starts at the end of the ward, interrupting my dreams, the commotion that I hear Aisha's voice in. I can't really believe it's her until I see her, my Aisha really here, striding towards me in a grey hoodie. It's fifteen years since I saw her as a brand new baby in Lily and Andrew's arms.

"Is this okay?" says the nurse who was chasing Aisha along the ward to my bed chair. Her ponytail is swinging behind her, so you can tell she was deliberately trying to keep up.

I feel so bad to tell you for real, but I wish Aisha weren't here. This is not how I dreamed about our reunion. No one from that memory of Lily and Andrew and Baby Aisha should be mixed in with my visits to St Thomas's. But I stare at Aisha, the confident girl-woman who has come to visit me in hospital, and I feel a little bit proud. Her green earrings nestle amongst her black curls and she's got Lily's height, blurred a bit by a teenage hunch that didn't exist last time I saw her, her fists pulling down the hoodie and its hood against her head. I wonder if someone who doesn't know us could see a family resemblance like mine and Lily's.

"Grandma?" she asks with a small choke; her mouth is half open as if she's afraid I am going to disown her.

I wince. I need to stay in the realities, even though they just aren't as sweet. I take a deep breath. "It's okay," I tell the nurse. "We're related."

Aisha doesn't say anything straight away. She's still the same earnest Aisha who I lost when I was only trying to be her friend, her wide brown eyes seeming to say that she is about to tell me exactly what substances are in the bag that is attached to my arm by a drip, as if my medical treatment is her school coursework. She lowers her voice. “So that’s why you’re in here? You just broke your shoulder?”

I ignore the tone that tells me she’s worked out about my visits to the building next door – I know she wouldn’t know how to deal with that – and I look at my cast to try and point out it’s a bit of a silly question.

She winces again, pulling down harder on her hoodie pocket, so now I’m sure she knows there’s more to it, but isn’t saying. “We’ve let you down.” Her face crumples up for a second and she looks away. I know she is thinking of the years we’ve been separated. We are a broken-up jigsaw – all of us. I’d do anything to piece us back together.

“Now, this isn’t what you’ve come to talk about, is it?”

Aisha pulls up a chair, slumping in it, and releases her head and springing curls from the hood. Her shoulders move quickly, as if she is trying to dodge something, but she composes herself, shoving her trainered feet under the chair, and leans forwards. “Do you remember Kingsley?”

I don’t answer straight away. Suddenly the occasional beep of the dosage machine seems louder, crowding out my head.

“Grandma?”

I tut and stare at the blue curtains down the ward corridor. “Do we have to talk about him?”

“Where did he go? Why did he and my mum split up?”

I put on my it’s-been-a-stressful-day and-I’m-too-tired-to-talk look and lean back in my bed chair. “Why would you ask about Kingsley, and not about your dad?”

She has a determined look on her face. One that won’t be distracted.

“It doesn’t matter anymore.”

“I know that there’s something you don’t want to tell me.”

I look out of the window which overlooks the river and the ornate sandy buildings of Westminster. The sun has gone in. Big Ben isn’t pretty without the sun.

“Everybody’s hiding stuff from me,” she says, exasperated, and there is Lily’s voice again, complaining that she does not know about her dad, her grandparents. "I'm not a kid anymore. I'm nearly sixteen."

"What does your mum say about it?"

She looks down at her trainers. "Nothing about Kingsley. Not anymore."

I'm glad of that.

"I was just thinking about the past, you know."

"Oh, you mustn't do that. It was a very long time ago." I bring my hands to my stomach and close my eyes.

She brushes a sleeve briefly against one eye as if afraid that a tear might escape without her noticing. "Even now I'm grown up, I think you say odd things sometimes." Then she looks at me and just the corner of her mouth smiles, the happy face of my beautiful grandbee who I haven't seen for so long. She knows that she can't push me to say more. I am an invalid. I can get away with anything.

But I am not the only one who isn't saying something. Behind her smile, Aisha isn't saying something too. It sits oppressively, like the pills they pour into my bloodstream, the painkillers, the anti-all-sorts. It all mixes within me. It takes away my happiness.

I am glad to see my grandbee again, but the smell of the hospital's antiseptic seems stronger, and colder. A gust of wind sends a flurry of tapping leaves against the window. I am trying not to ask Aisha why we are talking about Kingsley, but I want to. I really, really want to.

AISHA

Oh my days, Grandma did not *want me to visit her in hospital. She said, "I've missed you so much", but with that distant, faraway, not reacting look, the one she had when I was a "naughty little girl" and things had gone too far. It was sad to see her like that, so small under a hospital sheet, her hair not as bright a red as it used to be.*

Maybe she was disappointed that we haven't been around for literally ages. That was pretty bad of me to forget Grandma. It's wrong to let your family down.

Even Auntie Becca, the Tamil lady who lives downstairs from Grandma, looked surprised to see me when I knocked on her door to find out where Grandma was. "She had a fall." Auntie Becca's earrings jangled as one of the toddlers seemed to try and want to climb up her like a tree. Her graffiti-scratched door was only slightly open and I could hear one of the other kids kicking off inside. "Maybe visit her in the ward? She'd like that," she added, pushing the door closed, so I wondered if she did know that I hadn't seen Grandma for a long time. "And you don't have to call me Auntie anymore, love. I'm not that much older than you."

I could never be so rude.

We always used to be around at Grandma's when I was little. But as I grew older, we started seeing less and less of each other, and now I think that something big must have happened, something that I was too young to understand.

***

I tried asking Mum, while we were unpacking shopping from the car this afternoon. "Why don't we see Grandma these days?" It was cold, the carrier bags were fluttering in the wind, and I wanted to get back to my coursework.

"They moved away to Bath, Aisha. Don't you remember? I thought you Facebooked them sometimes."

"No, I mean Grandma Kennedy," who totally would never Facebook.

Mum didn't answer straight away. When I glanced at her, I realised that she had put the shopping down on the pathway to stand and look at me. "People change, Aisha. Things can't always stay the same." She lifted a really heavy carrier bag bursting with soft drinks and started stomping towards the front door, giving me a "don't give me attitude" glance. "Young lady, these are your drinks I am carrying, perhaps you could deign to assist?" which wasn't fair. I'm not being funny, but I always make sure to help Mum before doing my own thing.

***

But anyway, I'm kind of worried in the back of my mind that Grandma's look was nothing to do with us being away from her for so long. Maybe she had guessed what I had found out when I tried to find her in the hospital. It's just that when I asked for Grandma's name at the busy reception, initially they said that she was in the other building. The one next door.

The mental ward.

And we both know I could never ask Grandma what that was about, that she would only say something random, like, "Oh, I do pop in there from time to time," as if that's totally normal and that it would be strange to have to explain anything more.

HELEN

When Lily first brings the subject of divorce up, she looks great. She has done her hair into a perfectly smooth wave like on American TV. She is looking after herself better now that Aisha has grown into a toddler. I tell her she looks good as I make her the coffee with one sugar. She hugs the mug with her acrylic nails with diamanté studs painted to look like a night sky. The sky wrapped around the tea. She has bought me a present, a painted bowl from a trip she has made with her girlfriends to Turkey. I don't know much about Turkey. When Lily told me about her trip, I asked the man at the till of the Turkish supermarket near New Cross if Turkey was a safe place and he laughed raucously, his bearded chin raised to the ceiling, and told me it was a very safe, very wonderful country. But I still warned Lily as she left, not to get into taxis on her own, not in Turkey and not at Gatwick.

The bowl is orange around the border with curling branches of leaves painted in a thick inky black in the middle. It's beautiful. I have never seen anything like it before. I put it in the middle of the dining table, but it looks so strange and lost in my clinical white flat.

"I'm fed up with Andrew." I am staring at the bowl as Lily says it, but she says it with such vehemence that my heart drops like a stone and makes that bowl look like a cruel thing now. I've never heard her say anything like this before.

"Pardon?"

"I'm taking Aisha away."

I stare at her. Andrew must have hit her, or Aisha, or sold their house and pocketed the money while Lily was on holiday.

Or worse. Beep Beep Bop.

"What's happened?"

I expect tears, but actually what I hear is more like fury, "I'm just so fed up." One hand drops from the mug to the table. "I can't carry on like this."

I shiver, but I will be here to listen to my Lily, like no one was there for me when it was my turn.

"I'll help you," I say. "I'll do whatever you need."

"He's just so…" She searches for a word, picking absently at her pashmina with her night-sky nails, and then shakes her head. "He puts the tea towels in the washing machine along with our clothes…"

My Lily, my poor little bee. I try to think. I know that they took my bee away because my house was not clean. Is this the same sort of thing?

"And he's so clingy." She puts on a mocking Andrew voice that I have never heard before. "'Would you like a cup of tea?' or 'Would you like some hot chocolate?' and 'What can I make you for dinner?' Like he can't make any decisions of his own."

I am definitely missing something, but I need to be here and secure to help Lily.

"But what has he done, Ingrid? Why do you have to run away?" I ask, and then I regret it. I think that just as I have secrets, maybe Lily has secrets and she does not want to tell me the real things. That's why she feeds me facts from her past, not feelings. "I'll hide you from him."

"Oh, Helen," she shakes her hands, exasperated, her engagement ring catching the evening sunlight through the window, "you're not listening properly."

I don't understand.

"You don't get it." She raises her voice. "You don't know what it's like living like this."

I thought that I was trying to help. I look again at the exotic bowl on the table.

"Like what?"

"Like exactly what I am telling you. He is so annoying." She rolls her eyes as if thinking of his annoyingness again.

Offering cups of tea? Leaving the washing on the rack? What could laid-back Andrew ever do to hurt Lily?

Suddenly the fury is focussed on me. Lily grips her mug with both hands and stares at me. "You're just like Mum and Dad. Always assuming I'm the bad guy," she hisses.

Maurice and Jenny think Lily is the bad guy? I know not to talk about Maurice and Jenny because I always say something wrong. But I realise with a jolt that Andrew hasn't hurt Lily.

That is why Lily is telling me that I don't understand. She knows that I should not understand because she is in the wrong, whether I tell her so or not. Deep inside of her she knows that she is being cruel, so she is yelling at me. If I am worrying about what I have done wrong, she thinks I might not notice that she is being cruel.

This is how I find out about Lily's discontent.

I have had a beautiful couple of years babysitting Aisha, going to get her ears pierced, listening to Aisha mouth the syllables that Lily swears to me are attempts to say "Grandma" – even if it really sounded like she was saying weewee. I must have enjoyed it too much and got too lazy. I had started to believe that everything would be okay. I had started to believe that some men could be kind. I should have carried on worrying.

***

I watch our happy ending being dashed away with tea towels while Lily whisks in and out of my flat throughout the divorce. She has dyed her hair red, not like my copper red, but a real scarlet red. This is the new Lily. Lily of the discontent.

She is avoiding using the house until Andrew has found somewhere else to live, but it's all agreed that the house will stay with Lily. "My house", is what she calls it now, with a proud possessiveness, even though they both scrimped and saved to deal with the early mortgage payments. Lily all alone, one mum, one bee. It isn't good to be just one mum and one bee. I should know.

"I just wish he would hurry up and leave," she tells me, rocking her cup of tea with frustration. This time her nails are painted like a beach scene, a tiny palm tree crafted onto the nail, and a golden sun, the paradise dream that fills the glossy posters on the Tube line. Even the people who seem to be able to afford those sorts of holidays come back unhappy. It's the dream that can't be found. Lily has discontent. Not just discontent now, with Andrew, but she harbours a deep discontent that will flare up in any situation. She is looking for distraction, whatever the cost. And now the cost is Andrew, wonderful Andrew, who I adore, who knows how to calm me down. Why should he be the cost of Lily's discontent? Why should Aisha be its victim?

Something has put a dream in Lily's head. It's like she has seen a billboard advert hanging at the end of a shop that tells her that the place to find happiness is not with her childhood sweetheart anymore. She will get her hands on that dream no matter what the expense.

"Maybe he has nowhere to go."

She shoots me a sidelong glance, curling her nose knowingly. "Oh, he has friends," and she shakes her head in disgust. I feel a flash of who Lily is when she is not with me, because hidden in the sentence is a tone that she might have said to Andrew about me: "Oh, Helen has family," with the snide glance that says she knows that I am hiding the good things from her, things that should really be hers.

"I'm so glad you have the house, for Aisha."

She ignores me. "Do you know, he is trying to get Aisha

three days a week? Not just on a Saturday, but *three* days a week."

We both turn to look at Aisha, who is swirling around and around in a swinging skirt that raises into a circle as she spins. Lily and I have just bought her the skirt from Deptford market. We'd been flicking through a cold metal rail of grown-up's jumpers when we found it, both knowing straight away how perfect it was for Aisha. Aisha is unaware of the grown-up-ness that is going on around her. I wonder how Lily will explain to Aisha that Daddy is not coming home to her every day anymore.

Lily says that she's told the solicitors that it will be too confusing for Aisha to have two bedrooms and two of everything. She won't let it happen. Aisha needs stability. Then she says that Andrew has money that he's not telling the solicitors about and that matters because it all forms part of "the divorce settlement".

"He is totally lying about the money," is how she puts it, marching around the dining table with her arms folded.

There it is, the shiver again. Does she say "Helen's totally lying about where she's from"? It's not that simple, Lily.

Because underneath this rejection of Andrew, there is my other fear. That the discontent brought Lily to me and maybe the discontent will take her away from me too, like some sad thing that happens to a person who is adopted. I got on so well with Lily when she came back home and shared Aisha with me. I had a strong "real life" to blot out the past. I saw her discontent, but I thought that it came from needing to find me, her missing true mother. I have seen on the television that sad things happen if your family is not right, if your mummy leaves your daddy for instance, or if your mummy never knew your daddy, or if you never knew your mummy and daddy. Beep Beep Bop.

"All I'm saying is, if he does admit to the money, maybe we can come to some sort of arrangement about Aisha," she interrupts my thoughts.

And I know I can't point out that she has the house and it's her that's leaving him.

"That would be good. She needs to stay in touch with Andrew."

Lily doesn't seem to like this. She shuffles her shoulders as if she is trying to shrug off a bad thought before leaning against the kitchen counter. I suppose it does sound like I was trying to stick up for Andrew.

I offer her another drink and get up to take the cups over to the sink. Hopefully that will make her forget that I said anything, but she's stewing. Even without seeing her clenched fists on the table, I can feel it. I am just about to change the subject when the words come out. "Well, at least she knows who her father is. That's more of a luxury than I am allowed," she shoots at my back.

"Oh, Lily!" My hands fall into the washing-up suds.

"My name is Ingrid!"

***

I clean in Asda on the business park on Monday and Tuesday nights. I can walk there and back from where I live, through the Victorian terraces and then past the glossy clothes chains. The journey used to frighten me to start with. There are strange ghouls in the night, mostly ones with cans in their hands, or eyes with enlarged pupils, but they don't look at me, and I start to find the journey makes my heart beat and cheeks red in a good way. I used to check out on my journey and look forward to seeing Aisha and Lily at the end of the week. Now as I walk along the broken pavements, I wonder if it's wrong to hope that such a nice person as Andrew is really really bad? Because if Andrew is really really bad, then it makes sense of what my little bee is stirring up. It means my little bee is not the problem.

But if Andrew is really bad, then Lily has been hurt, and I don't want to think of Lily being hurt either.

I remember how I have seen Andrew working on the colouring in with Aisha; playing with her dolls; taking them on family outings to the London Eye. I've seen the photos of the three of them eating fresh doughnuts, the Thames reflecting the twinkling amber lights of the North Bank, beyond the railings behind them. My three bees are captured in glossy time, smiling and waving with sugary mouths and fingers, a family so golden under the trees of blue fairy lights, they should be an advert for something.

There is no terrible secret being hidden here at all.

I thought we had a happy ending. I thought we were all solved now. But Lily wants to break it all up. I tread the broken pavement, and I make silent cries as my steps fall against the paving stones.

I dream of walking through the hills in my long embroidered skirt that has tassels at the end and when I get home, I get out my scrubbing brush and start scrubbing at the grout in the tiles again.

This is all years before they found me crying in the middle of the road late at night.

***

Andrew drops Aisha off at my house on a Thursday before he goes to work. He drives a nice-looking company car. It has a colour that is really two colours when you look closely at it. There is a sheen underneath the gloss and I tell him that it looks posh and ask if it's a BMW and he laughs, mock-polishing the bonnet with his sleeve, and says, "It's all image, you know, the car isn't expensive at all."

I quite like that it doesn't matter to him.

Andrew still has to drop Aisha off at mine even as Lily unpicks their lives piece by piece. That doesn't change because Lily prefers it that way, so Andrew still has to do it. He is running late today. It is unfortunately close to Ken's rubbish bag trip. Ken, my upstairs neighbour, is clockwork predictable. He always does the same things at the same time of day, and he usually says the same things if you bump into him while he does it.

Andrew comes up the stairs one by one, holding Aisha's hand so that she can tumble and climb the steps, punching out squeals of joy, or anger. Andrew is endlessly patient. She is delivered into my arms in a puffed pink jacket and polka dot leggings, and then Andrew goes back for the pushchair. I want to say something cheerful like, "You won't have to do this much longer; she'll be too old for the pushchair." But maybe Lily will change her mind about Andrew bringing Aisha here soon, and he won't have to do this any longer anyway.

As Andrew brings the pushchair up to the door, bashing the wheels intermittently against the railings, he avoids my eye. He spends more time than usual trying to reorient himself when he has bumped into something. He has deep circles under his eyes. His natural charm and ease have run away and left him like a man without a real person inside.

I want to ask him why. Why is this happening? What have Maurice and Jenny said? Can't he change Lily's mind? But when I manage to catch his eye, I realise that he wants to say exactly the same thing to me and I don't have the answers for those questions either. He pulls his eyes away from mine.

"I don't know what to do," I yelp.

Andrew has just made it to the top of the stairs and put the pushchair down, but his shoulders drop. He looks like he is going to say something, but the shabby door of number nineteen opens and Ken gently works his way out while Andrew and I look at each other with so many unspoken words that cannot be said in front of Ken. And I hope, I hope that my thoughts are loud enough on my face that he can see that I wanted to ask the same questions that he did.

Ken is a short old man with a tremor who really likes Andrew. Normally when Andrew sees him, he takes the time to listen to Ken's ponderous sentences that twist and meander around whatever he was trying to say. Because Andrew takes a little bit of time to be patient with Ken, Ken in turn rewards him with deep appreciation. "Your son-in-law..." he would say if we would bump into each other on the landing (Ken and I do not receive each other into our houses. He is a man, even if he is an old one). "He is a very nice man, a very decent one, you know. A good person." He will take a few moments to catch his breath and push his glasses needlessly back up his nose. "The thing is, that does, even though. You know. Those racist people. Someone should tell them, they have it all wrong."

Ken is wearing a yellowed blue shirt, and the buttons have not been buttoned into the right buttonholes. He sees Andrew as he comes down the steps, closely followed by the non-regulation kitten that peers out at the great outdoors, the cemented floor and the red painted brickwork, and shivers at what she sees. Ken nearly drops his bin bag in delight. "Hello Andrew."

"Hello." Andrew slides his eyes away from mine and seems to try and shake himself into normal Andrew mode. I am glad that he is trying to be kind even when things are so bad, because Ken would not have understood if Andrew was different with him now.

"I've been listening. The thing is the birds. In the dawn. They call it the dawn choir. It's a choir because it's like loads of singing, lots of people, lots of birds. It's beautiful."

"It is very beautiful, Ken. It is very loud at this time of year."

"Yes. Loud." He laughs briefly to himself, rubbing his hand against his side. "They say, like a cacophony. A word for great and loud and beautiful. Cacophony."

"It really is a cacophony."

Ken seems contented with this exchange. "Must get on," he mutters under his breath and pulls the bin bag down the steps, those steps that Aisha has been climbing. I try to remember to wash her hands when she gets in.

We watch Ken walk down the first set of eight steps, and

then turn the corner that is obscured by the staircase above us and he is out of view.

Andrew looks back at me, and for a few seconds, the heavy metal door beeps to announce it's open and then clangs shut behind Ken.

And with the clang, Andrew releases a sob. Just the one for a moment, and then chokingly more sobs.

"Andrew, what can I do?" I want to reach out and hug him.

He shakes his head because we both know there is nothing that can be done.

I want to say sorry, but the beep of the door starts, as Ken returns and starts ascending the stairs.

Andrew waits. Ken reaches the top of the stairs. Andrew manages to clear his face from the crush of the sobbing. "Good to see you, Ken," he says almost sharply, and dashes down the stairs. There is a pause before he presses the button to open the door. "Thanks for looking after Aisha, Helen," he calls as if the tears had never been. "Bye bye, Aisha."

Aisha's tiny hand forms a wave into the thin air. The response she has been taught to give to a "Bye bye", but there is no one in front of her to receive the wave.

I'm sorry. I'm sorry, I'm so, so sorry, I want to call after Andrew, the cacophony of our unsaid words crowding out the stairwell.

***

I start to feel lonely again, even with Aisha asleep in the box room. For the first time since Lily came back, I think about Beep Beep Bopping again. I think about being with Lily, but leaving her in my head. Is it wrong to daydream about the days when there was a nice man to look after my Lily, as if they had never gone away? Here in my head, there's no need for a divorce, or unhappy Andrew, or fatherless Aisha. But it's difficult to imagine there is no bad stuff at the same time as keeping all the good stuff in my head.

Lily has strangely been asking me to look after Aisha for whole nights recently. When I ask her if the council is keeping her really busy, she doesn't answer me with words and folds her arms that tinkle with extra gold jewellery, staring out into the distance until I pretend to forget I asked. I peer into Aisha's bedroom, where she is curled up in a little mermaid onesie, so defenceless. I wish she had a little brother like Lily did. I whisper to Aisha that we will be okay, but I am not sure if we will be. I am not even sure what it means to be okay, because things are wrong, but no wronger than they are for other people. The shards of broken families are scattered all over south-east London, and sometimes the shards prick people outside of their families too.

All these things and my heart thumps inside me. And I worry. I worry.

***

"Ingrid, can you hear me? I can't have Aisha tonight."

"Oh, I heard you." Lily's voice is so clear, icy clear over the phone, that I'm embarrassed that I suggested that the line was broken. It's not just her look, her voice has also changed a little lately. I don't think of my bee in the same way these days, and I don't think her extra gold jewellery helps.

I hear the sound of crashing glass outside, shriller glass than Lily's glassy clearness. I duck my head down, even though I know that glass can't break through the walls of the flat. There will be damage to the front door, though, splintered wood growing from my green paint. But that's not so bad, is it? It's not like damage to yourself.

"So what exactly is the problem?"

"I'm err..." I couldn't lie if I wanted to. Lily knows that I would not be meeting anyone else. "I have a shift at Asda."

"No you don't. We checked your diary when we arranged this."

Now a high-pitched screeching starts up in the hallway. I

cannot stand all these noises: Lily's clear voice in one ear, the sound of a human alarm outside.

"*What* is that noise?"

"Nothing." I bite my lip, but then I hear a massive thump against the door and I let out a whimper.

"What's happening?" She's suddenly less angry, but still a bit disapproving.

I try to tell her, I have to now, but nothing comes out of my throat, which has clenched up, no matter how hard I try to unclench it.

"Helen?"

"I think she's thrown herself against the door." It comes out so high, that I know Mrs Cauldwell will have heard me talking about her, and that will make her madder. I bring the phone into the hallway to see if the front-door hinges are still holding. That one at the top, with rust around the nails from the leak upstairs a couple of years ago, it holds loose. The letter box clatters again with another thump and I rush back into the living room.

"Your next-door neighbour?"

I nod, even though I know Lily can't see me. But Lily is clever and she knows the answer anyway. She probably even knows that I am nodding. It's no good, her cleverness. I don't want Lily to know all about Mrs Cauldwell and to stop my grandbee from visiting.

"Have you called the police?"

The police are part of the System. I can't call the police. They look down on you and laugh at you and if you phone an ambulance, they will take your little bee away.

"Did you hear me? I said…"

All the noises make it so hard to come up with excuses to tell Lily, for bruised Mrs Cauldwell on my straw doormat. No police, no police, no police.

"I'm coming right over, now, okay? I just have to sort a couple of things at my house."

"My house." I let an annoyed breath run out of my mouth.

INGRID

Everyone thinks that it's okay to tell me what to do.

Like Maurice and Jenny: "This is a cruel way to treat your husband after everything he's done for you, insisting on the house when you both worked so hard on it."

Cruel. They really used that word. Like they loved him more than they loved me.

And Andrew was no better himself – back when we were still together. "Do you think you could be a bit kinder to Helen? She's not had it that easy, you know." What does he know? Does he have to visit Helen with me when I take Aisha babysitting in that cold soulless flat?

Cruel. Everyone's buzz word for Evil Ingrid. Don't they understand I'm just trying to keep things afloat? I am trying to be happy. Everyone deserves to be happy.

"So why are you leaving the father of your child?" demands Jenny. That's typical Jenny speak. Manipulative. I can't answer that question now, not when they already said what they think about me leaving. The fact is, Andrew used to be fun. Or maybe it was just fun to snatch him out from under Victoria's nose. After all, she deserved it. She did nothing about that crush but apply extra lip gloss and gaze through the common-room window, having stupid Andrew daydreams instead of finishing her psychology essays. I get now that none of that made him my soulmate. He'd make me stick to sensible

budgets so we could pay off the mortgage, when all I really want to do is dress up and go dancing, and visit spas like the ones in the back of the magazines I read. I've never been to a spa.

Fortunately, I was dressed up when I met Kingsley and he came to the bar and offered me champagne. I knew he couldn't be part of the work crowd with an offer like that. In fact, I thought, here it is. Here is where my life is changing. And then he took me dancing, way into the night, took my mind off things, off my missing family, off the stepping stones of gaps that lead up to Ingrid. I texted Andrew and said I would be home late, so I don't know why I had three missed calls to check if I was okay. That was the final straw, really.

I want to stay "dressed up" for Kingsley. So Helen's mad neighbour and the dustbin flats is the last thing I need. There's nothing glamorous going on there. How do I broach the subject of Helen? How do I explain why I keep hanging on, hoping to hear a snippet of family, something more to build my identity on, something to back me up if I start losing any more family?

I tell Kingsley that I have to go to visit a friend, and that if we don't, I'll lose the night's babysitting. Do you know he actually says that he's busy with clients, and it was only Bluewater we were headed for, after all? I can hear him thinking that maybe he will just go and do his own thing if I can't make it. But I really wanted to join Dave and Petra for drinks and hear about their new house this evening, so I manage to talk him around.

At the flat, Helen tells me not to bring Aisha all the way up. "I'm still trying to clear up glass. I don't want her to hurt herself."

I leave Aisha in the stairwell and walk carefully through the debris. "What happened?"

Helen's trying to get at the broken glass under the mat with her broom. She doesn't meet my eye. "The police took Mrs Cauldwell away."

"Good."

"I don't even know what the police were doing here. Did you call them?"

I nod and then she looks at me properly, and I know that look. Yet another person thinks Ingrid is cruel. But then the look falls away quickly.

"Does that mean that they arrested her?"

"They've probably sectioned her. Didn't the police explain?"

She doesn't answer and concentrates the broom on one corner of the stairwell. I bet she never even answered the door to the police.

"They can make her stay in hospital. It's called sectioned because it's a section of the law that says they can do that."

She shivers. Honestly, this is what you get for doing someone a favour, but then she says, "You're so clever knowing all of this, like the lawyers on the television."

I look at her scratched and battered door. "It's to stop her hurting someone, or herself." The door definitely looks like someone could have got hurt. It's propped open, which gives me an idea, and I reach out for Helen's broom. "Let me finish this bit while you go down and pick up Aisha."

She gives me a grateful smile. I know how much she likes Aisha

I work quickly, just enough to be safe. "Just getting the dustpan," I call down and walk through the front door, towards the kitchen. As there often is, a pile of opened mail sits on the counter next to the kettle. I can hear my heart in my ears. This is so exciting. I have to be quick, to see if there is anything. Bank statement, invitation for a flu jab, it's all so mundane and I don't know exactly what I am looking for anyway – anything that will help me find my empty past. But Helen is already at the door and I have no more time, pulling away from the grey mottled counter quickly. "Not sure where you leave the dustpan?" I ask and see that she is holding it in her hand.

She looks so innocent, I know I have not been caught

out. That's the one thing about Helen. She looks at me with such love that it's actually confusing. Maurice and Jenny were never like that. I mean they had hugs and things, which actually Helen has less of, looking ever so slightly scared as if she's not really allowed to hug me. But they never had the other thing, the thing that makes you save all of your kid's daft finger paintings and put them on the fridge, that makes you believe your kids can do no wrong. Helen has so much of that I don't know what to do with it. I'm sorry if I get a little snappy with her sometimes, but I really don't know what to do with all that love.

There is a long beep outside the flat. I mustn't keep him waiting. "I have to rush off. Next time, I will leave a little something to cover the cost of a new front door."

HELEN

She has never said anything like this before. Was that why she was sitting so near to my pile of bills with a frown like she was trying to work something out? I don't want to take money off Lily. She is my bee, to be looked after by me, not the other way around. Where would she get extra money from? Did Andrew really have a secret bank account after all?

I go to the bedroom window which looks out onto the road, and I see Lily climb into a posh car that I don't recognise. It is one of those big four-by-fours that no one can park properly. In fact, it sits a good two feet away from the kerb right now. And it's the passenger seat that Lily gets into after throwing her bag in the back. The car revs and storms up the hill out of sight.

It was the passenger seat.

***

Jess and Chloe who clean with me at Asda seem to say that meeting the parents of a boyfriend or a girlfriend is a really big deal. They don't say this to me. They don't really talk to me unless they catch me re-mopping a bit of floor they didn't do properly. Then Jess will say, "I've done that bit," as if I'm stupid, or Chloe might say, "Oh yeah. Sorry. I wasn't concentrating. Thanks."

I hold onto the things that Jess and Chloe say about boyfriends because I won't learn these things anywhere else, and maybe I will have to help someone with this information one day. Jess is in her late twenties and Chloe is still a teenager and they both give each other advice. Here is one piece of advice that I hear a lot when they have paused for a break and I am sweeping behind the deli counter. "He wants you to meet his parents? He must really be serious about the relationship." This piece of information, along with the fact that you don't go on a special trip to buy sexy underwear as soon as you meet a man (although it sounds like they always do), is all saved up for when Aisha grows up. I was too late for Lily.

Here's what I'm thinking: either Lily does have a new beau and she is hiding me from him, or he doesn't want to meet me. Which on the one hand is a bit insulting, but it also means that one of them isn't so keen on the other. So if the driver of the four-by-four is a new beau, maybe he won't last. Maybe Aisha and Lily and Andrew could become a family again sometime soon.

***

I'm almost glad when it's Andrew in his smart jeans and shirt, but looking thinner, who drops off Aisha next, rather than Lily.

Now that Andrew's moved, he comes here less often. "Andrew, where are you living?" Are you okay?

He meets my eye these days, but the look is cold. He has no jokes for me anymore.

"I'm renting a place in Elephant and Castle."

I've bussed past Elephant and Castle. It's full of tower blocks overlooking a huge pink corrugated metal building, a castle, I suppose. But instead of kings and queens, it has shops in it, good deals on fake leather sandals.

"Just a one-bed for now, so Aisha is sleeping in the front room until I can get things together and find some space for her," he says, paying attention to Aisha's suitcase instead of me.

They probably won't let him keep Aisha for three days a week if he can't even afford a bedroom for her. I want to say sorry to Andrew again. In the olden days, if I didn't understand something Lily was doing, I would ask Andrew, if we got a quiet moment. He would explain the possible reasons for late nights and changed look and the four-by-four, and it would turn out to be nothing really.

But Andrew and I have started to separate too. It seems like just yesterday when he and I sat around the circle of my plastic dining table watching Aisha pressing buttons on her brightly coloured cat-noise-making toy, joking about which of the three noises it was going to make next, blaming each other for buying such a noisy toy. Aisha in her braids and multicoloured hair clips continuing to look newly delighted by every repeated noise.

And while I'd talked to him about Lily's trip to Turkey, I'd been careful the whole time to call Lily Ingrid.

Now, our easy friendship is over. It feels wrong to talk about anything other than Aisha. As the divorce progresses, we are beyond the stage of giving each other sorry moments. We drift to each side of our families and we cannot have the friendship or sympathy that we once had. Only Aisha links us now, and this child cannot even keep her parents together. "I'm sure you'll find something bigger soon." And I close the door like a stranger, not even thinking to mention that Lily got into a passenger seat of a four-by-four. I turn to Aisha, who is gripping a half-dressed Barbie with one stiletto and hair that says Mummy thought it was a good idea to try putting her in the washing machine.

***

In the end, I decide to ask Lily outright. We are walking around the tarmacked park, watching Aisha try to push the roundabout. She's too small, but she's having fun, climbing up and down the stationary frame. Grey and white flats overlook us. They are covered with scaffolding. I think the council are putting in double glazing. "Where did Andrew go?" I ask as innocently as I can, to hide the fact that I worry about Andrew; that I worry about how Lily will cope alone with Aisha. If she was on a family outing now with Aisha, it would just be the two of them climbing onto the blue, green and white train carriages that smell of dust and urine. Or climbing into a taxi. And that could be worse.

But I know I've told Lily enough times not to get into taxis that she will wince if I say it again. "Who cares?" says Lily. She doesn't realise that Andrew is the family that she is yearning for, that she's the only one around here who's doing things that lose family.

Just as Lily lifts Aisha from the roundabout, I go for the question I have been hanging onto, "Who is he, Lily?"

I thought she might be angry with me, but she replaces her moody look and beams right away. "Kingsley," she says. "Have you seen how posh his car is? He has such an important business."

"Doing what?"

"Well," she frowns. I can see she knows what it is, but doesn't think I will understand. "It's kind of hard to send money abroad. People make money here to send back to their families in Africa, but it's hard to do safely and quickly. It's not like going on holiday. Kingsley makes that happen."

I don't get what the new boyfriend's job and car are supposed to tell me about him. "So it's a job helping people?"

She laughs gently to herself. "Well, it kind of makes money too."

"Will he make you happy?" I wish I hadn't said this, because this is the thing that I want more than anything in the world. But Lily doesn't seem to mind.

"He's fun, so much fun. Nothing is ever the same. He knows people who throw great parties, and he has enough money to buy proper quality things."

There's a pause while I take in her happy face. I won't ask the hard questions. Even though I have already rejected Kingsley in my heart, I know he is the key to hers. "Can I meet him?"

***

There are other bad mothers. Not just me. There is the bad mother who I ran away from, burning everything from my old life to set me free. It didn't start off bad, but the heat built up in small ways: sitting in the kitchen at the fake farmhouse dining table, trembling over margarined, thin toast, burnt at the corners, trying to work out how to ask Mummy what is happening. Can you make it stop? But when I looked up at Mummy, she was staring out of the metal-framed window with the clutter of grubby and faded Schwartz herb bottles on the chipped tiles. She was looking out of the window as if my lost sister was out there, still a baby, kicking and gurgling and lively and waiting to be loved, in a phantom pram just outside of the garden gate, a love that I would not understand until later.

There was a photo of us over the gas fire in the front room. A photo of all three of us and my one-eyed elephant, Ajax, in my arms. I never liked to look at it.

These are the only things that I did not throw away when I left: the birth certificate hidden in a Quality Street tin under my bed and Ajax who was with me for the longest. But even he had to go. I lit a match on him in a dustbin, watching him burn up, leaving only his remaining eye in the ashes. I wanted to pick it up as one last memory, but I knew it would burn my fingers – it would keep me back from my new life.

So, I am very, very glad that Lily is not like me. Lily has run away, but she has a good job and a good house, and Andrew will let her keep it all. And she has a good baby and someone who picks her up in a four-by-four. Even though she is running away, she is still loved, my bee.

And when my Lily-Bee is changing partners, it stops her

doing her Lily-thing. She stops wandering around my dining room between sentences and sips of tea from the Kellogg's mug, gently touching the bare walls with her fingertips when she thinks I'm not looking. She stops pretending that she's not ticking, blinking her large curled eyelashes and arching her well-groomed brows at the white plaster, as if the family pictures that don't exist might somehow emerge, pop out from the walls just because she was willing them.

Although it would be Kingsley that would change her from curious to furious.

***

I first see Kingsley in a photograph at Lily's house, so cosy and homely, and I have to remind myself that this is the cosy home of Lily, Kingsley and Aisha now.

Sorry. I mean Ingrid.

Lily pours red wine at the dining table, the one I met Andrew at, while I sit nervously on the sofa wearing a yellow cardigan and brown eyeshadow. I've made the effort to look nice to meet the man with the four-by-four, Kingsley, because Lily loves him so much and I study the photo of Lily, Kingsley and Aisha all posing as a happy family in a large canvas picture over the fake fireplace.

Kingsley's ringed fingers rest lightly on Aisha's shoulder as Aisha beams up at Lily, half-grown teeth all on display. Kingsley's tightly short hair and goatee make a sort of square around his face. They are surrounded by an ornate silver frame against the big embossed flowers of the wallpaper. The camera rests on Lily's wide oval eyes, sharpened in black eyeliner. I want to believe the photograph, believe that there is a happy family here, but who knows if that is true or not? There was once a picture with me like that and it looked like a happy family. And I was not in a happy family.

Lily brings the wine over, leaving one glass and the bottle

of red wine, the cork lying on the side with a purply-red colour on the end.

"He's been held up." Her hair is long and wavy today and gathered into a ponytail with amber highlights snaking through it. She takes a seat. "But being busy is how he affords all of this." She gestures at the huge TV in the corner and all the blinking gadgets filed underneath it with trailing black cables. It looks like it's in charge of the living room.

I sip my wine, but I hold it like it will bite me. I don't want to get drunk and tell Lily all my secrets. Just because she is tired and drinking, doesn't mean she won't spot it if I let a small bit of the past slip out by accident. I smile at her while she bubbles over with details of Kingsley's money transfer business, which has two whole branches, one in Lewisham, one in Catford. She doesn't know why I'm smiling.

She leans forward to refill her glass, talking faster, about "what Kingsley says about technology" and "what Kingsley says about perfume". Then, after a while, Lily's phone starts to buzz. "Oh, I hope that's not him calling to say he'll be late."

I look at the clock. It's nine-thirty. "He is really late," but I know when I've said it that I shouldn't have said anything so negative. Or obvious.

She looks at a loss for a minute and then turns to me. "Stop gawping like a goldfish, Helen. I did say he was busy. I don't own him," before standing and turning through the kitchen arch to answer the phone.

I think it's the wine making her sound so irritated.

"What?" she calls into the phone, her hand closing one ear. "You're saying what?" She is by the sink with her back to me. "When?"

I can hear the voice crackling over the phone, but not what it is saying. Lily's voice is getting high and angry. I'm starting to get scared. I don't think she is talking to Kingsley after all. "I can tell you for a fact that's not true, I've been to his business, and I've seen…"

The other side of the phone must have cut her off, and

whatever it says leaves her quieter, as if she has been told off for being angry. "But what do I have to do?" she whispers. She doesn't look like she's in control anymore.

When she has finished, she comes back into the room, and tosses the phone onto the sofa. Her eyes are slightly red, but she would not be Lily if she cried in front of me.

"What's wrong, Ingrid?" I whisper.

"It's Kingsley, he..."

She doesn't end the sentence and it feels wrong to ask.

Eventually she sits down next to me. "I can't lose him when I have only just found him," she says and I look into her deep, dark eyes full of worry, a look she wouldn't normally share with me. I loved Andrew, but Lily's face is wearing a feeling I know so well. Loss. And I don't want my Lily-Bee to have to feel loss too.

"What's happened? Has there been an accident?"

Lily pulls her honest eyes away from me and clears her throat. "I can't believe it," she stares down at the rings on her fingers. "He's been taken in for questioning by the police," she says. "He's actually with the police right now."

"What? Why?"

"I'm going over there." She snaps her wine down on the coffee table.

"Where?"

"To the station, to give them a piece of my mind. This is nothing but intimidation." She goes to look in the mirror as if she is preparing her angry face.

I stand up after her. "You shouldn't shout at the police..."

But Lily's fire is back, she looks at me contemptuously through slanted eyes. "I'll do what I want."

***

Ken is in the stairwell when I get home, still hungry because dinner was cancelled. He's wearing a zipped khaki jacket over his usual blue shirt and makes me jump at first. The new neighbour has made me nervous again. You do have to be careful of men. I will never forget that. "Ken, I haven't seen you for so long," I say. I wish I hadn't said it like that because I think I sound like I am his mother and I am no one's mother, not really.

I don't know if it's possible for him to tremble more than he does normally, but he seems to, his eyes glowing with near tears, and then tells me that his kitten died, despite him not paying the rent money so he could pay a vet. He looks around the stairwell wide-eyed, as if he is imagining himself when he found Kitty's lump, desperate to find out what to do about her. "So, Kitty was my friend, see. It's lonely without Kitty and I don't want to replace her, because she was my friend and I don't think that... well, it seems wrong. And it wasn't fair for her because she was only a kitten. She hadn't, you know, grown. It goes round and round my head, poor Kitty, so little, still a kitten. So, my family. They're in Gravesend. They said stay with them."

"That's sad." But I realise when I say it that Ken is richer than me. Ken has a family that would say "stay with us", when he lost something he loved. And he has time to cry over lost things. Is this what I should offer Lily if she loses Kingsley? I just don't think she would want it. "There's a horrible man in the flat now," I tell Ken, but I don't know how to explain what I mean.

He nods sadly and then thinks of something and smiles. "But what about your Andrew? Before I left, I checked the calendar, you know, because it was definitely summer before. It really was summer, but I have not seen your Andrew for a very long time."

"Ingrid's left him."

"Ah," he seems to understand this. Strangely, he seems to calm a little, and his crossed arms unwind. "Poor Andrew. But you must tell him from me; my wife left me and I cried and cried for ages and I did not understand why she did it and why she said such cruel things and I missed waking up with her in the mornings. But sort of she shouted. I mean she shouted even before leaving, long before leaving. And see, I couldn't make her happy. It was all wrong, whatever I did for her, and I tried and I cried. But after she went, it was quieter, and I could make my cup of tea and no one complained. And I got a little cat, not my little one, not Kitty, but another one, who died properly of old age, and I must tell you a secret, it was not nice when she left, but I am glad she did. Life is a little bit less, well it's kind of. The fact is, life is sort of smooth now. Less scary."

I haven't got the heart to remind Ken that Andrew is not my son, but my son-in-law, and that means it's my daughter who is doing the leaving. And I cannot imagine agreeing with him that Andrew will be better off without my Lily. Will Lily be better off? Now even Kingsley is being taken away from her.

"But you look nice," Ken says and it's good he knows I don't want to talk about Andrew or Lily anymore.

KINGSLEY

I wish I never did meet Kingsley, that horrible man. Why did Aisha have to remind me of him when she came to the hospital? He should be long gone. But now, because I am half awake and half asleep, every time I raise my drugged head, it is like I am living back then when Aisha was a toddler and Kingsley was still in our lives. My heart beats faster when I think he is still around. It is racing with lists of thoughts about how I have to try and keep everyone safe, and make all of the lists interlink and fit in. I have pictures of him in my head that probably aren't really like him at all, all inflated and pompous.

Lily had been frantic for days after his arrest. She had run away from a safe marriage to Kingsley. And maybe Kingsley was going to let her drop in the space in between, the space where there was no one to pick her up. She'd met Andrew when she was seventeen. I don't think she even knew about the space between until then.

It was money laundering he had been arrested for. "They didn't charge him, they just questioned him for hours like it was his fault they didn't have enough evidence," said Lily.

"You said he worked with money?"

She looked guilty at first, as if she also thought this all made too much sense, then she looked defensive, more than if I were to talk about Maurice and Jenny, so I shut up.

***

I am vaguely aware that I am still on the sofa in my flat. I must have fallen asleep here, what with all these new painkillers for my broken bones and the other drugs. Maybe they should not have been mixed, maybe the side effects should have said, "Warning: this cocktail will bring up the past"; this cocktail will remind you of Kingsley."

When I eventually met Kingsley, he was swinging Aisha around by her arms in Canary Wharf, by the river, as if to impress upon me that he can be Aisha's new dad, but I just wanted him to get his hands off Andrew's daughter. And Aisha looked kind of put out too, like this was too scary a game for her, her fun shrieks starting to sound more like scared shrieks.

Kingsley had brought lilies – orange lilies – for me as they met me by the Tube to take me to Pizza Express. I don't think he knew about Lily's real name, though. Even if he was clever enough to know, he would not have cared enough. He cared about Lily, I respect that. But he didn't care for Lily's mum. When he came with the flowers, I thought maybe he was quite nice, but I was really just giving Lily the benefit of the doubt.

I am drifting all these years later, because sometimes when I lift my head, I think I can see the orange lilies that he left in a vase on the dining table. They were next to the orange bowl from Turkey, which also flashes into my mind. I remind myself that the lilies couldn't be on the table because I didn't keep the lilies for long after he left. Kingsley didn't take long to convince me he was a dislikeable person.

The orange lilies are here in my living room again. I am sure they are. It does not seem to be enough to remind myself that I threw them away. They sit upright on the dining table. And maybe Kingsley is here too, in the shadows, in one of his moods. Now that I have thought of it, there are noises I can't explain. My heart is racing.

The weird thing is, I know it is night-time because I am asleep, but actually it seems to be daytime. There is light pouring through the windows and the tinny sound of "Popeye the Sailor Man" from an ice cream van. The light is so strong I cannot shut it out by closing my eyes, and when I close them, I see Kingsley. My head is so full of him. Why would Aisha have to talk about him when she only knew him as a toddler? What is going on?

I sit up sharply and my head spins. I'll go outside for some fresh air, even though my hair must be standing on end, and my clothes are all mismatched.

As soon as I get outside, I find myself retching against the broken slabs. Then my head clears and the bright blur around me sharpens up. I can see the ice cream van now, but I must be hallucinating, because I can see grown-up Aisha too, just walking away from it.

Aisha sees me too, but that's when the stones start coming. I hear a rattle and I don't understand what the noise is at first, maybe the squirrels I have seen them throw things out of trees as if they are trying to get you to go away, but Aisha is looking towards one of the blocks of bin cupboards, and when I look where she is looking, there's a group of three boys and girls, probably not much older than her, laughing, throwing stones or something, each more confidently than the last, definitely aiming and calling at Aisha.

Aisha tries not to look at me, but when she sees that I have seen, she looks more awkward, like half of her is trying to walk faster and the other half is trying not to look like she's walking faster, and I think she is doing well, until one stone lands against the ice cream, throwing Mr Whippy against her spaghetti-strapped T-shirt. Then she lets both cones drop to the floor against her feet, more ice cream on her socks. She stares down at them, her hands agitated, and I know that she doesn't know what to do now.

She looks at me and I see in her face a look that says, please don't be part of this. But they have hurt my bee. I charge down the steps towards them.

"Get away," I yell down the road, and they don't hear me at first, so I start staggering closer. "You get away from my granddaughter." This time they hear me, or at least a couple of them do, and try to get the attention of the third, tugging at the back of his T-shirt.

I wonder if there will be the stabbing of a mad old lady in Deptford now. I wonder what I have begun. At least I know that Aisha will get away. But the teenagers look at me open-mouthed, still not moving. I am so furious with their ignorant acned faces for not moving that I go to shake them away, forgetting my broken arm and shoulder, which makes me wince, and I call out in pain, which I suppose must sound like I am screaming at them, with my lined face and my cranky hair, waving my purse.

They don't even pretend not to be a bit scared as they scatter, just the one boy, the last to see me, calling "loony" as they flee along the road under the feet of a red Mini which beeps wildly at them. They settle for swearing at him, forgetting us, their voices disappearing beyond the next block of flats along.

Aisha is still in the same spot, looking better at keeping her cool than a minute ago. She is trying to scrape ice cream off one sock with the other foot. I come up and put one arm on her shoulder, just one. I don't want to make a big fuss. "I have wet wipes upstairs, we can clean that up," I point to her T-shirt.

She nods at me, with downcast eyes. "I wanted to come and surprise you, and then I saw the van, and I thought it would be nice to get you an ice cream too." I can't help but smile, looking at the teenager who has started to look like Ingrid when I met her as a grown-up, but in a more relaxed, less made-up way. She's come back even though she found out about my visits to the mental ward next door; even though I've missed so much of her teenage years and I fell out with her mum. It's not just that she wants to know about Kingsley. Aisha wants to know me, not just the things I can tell her about the past.

"It's okay to cry, you know," I risk saying, just in case I have assumed too much that she is just like my never flustered Lily.

A small smile creeps out in one corner of her mouth and she says, "Same to you," and for some reason that means that

I do let just one tear slip from the inside of my eye and brush it away before she can tell for sure.

"Do you know them?" I ask as we make our way back to my flat.

She nods. "They must have followed me here."

"From school?"

She shakes her head. "From our estate. It's not so..." She searches for the word and I don't want to say it for her, because I don't want to acknowledge the problem at all. I just hate to see her struggle too.

"It's very white, your estate," and she nods. And I think again of the sinking injustice of how Lily had to battle not being black enough, and now Aisha is battling being too black, and it's impossible to explain to the whole world that when you have a family that is mixed race, that it's not just bad to be racist, it's daft to be racist, because you're all just family and you all share all your features, it's just looks. So many daft people causing so much trouble. "But throwing stones!"

"I think they were conkers, not stones," she adds and then catches my eye as I pull my "does that make any difference" face and almost laughs at herself, pulling her hands against her nose as if to clear away an absent tear.

"Does your mum know?" I say that because I know Lily would know what to do about this and really do it. Not like me.

Aisha shakes her head.

"Aisha," I say to her, "either you tell your mum, or I do." She nods, her eyes floating out to the road behind her. I sigh. She's not going to tell her mum and I have no idea how I could ever speak to Lily again.

***

It's weeks after the night Kingsley was taken in for questioning before we all finally sit down at Pizza Express, Kingsley who's treating us, and Lily who loves him, and toddler Aisha who hides behind Lily.

He had tried speaking to me as we joined each other at the Tube entrance, "So, Helen," he'd called out, hanging on to my name as if trying to work out what to say. "What's Liverpool like?" He was looking over at the pubs and bars we were heading towards, rather than at me.

I didn't want Kingsley to feel bad for thinking I'm from Liverpool when I'm not, so I said that Liverpool was full of tower blocks and left it at that. I sensed Lily perk up behind the shadows of her eyes at the possibility that she might hear a story from my past, but I'm not even from Liverpool and I've told her that before, so I don't know what she expected. We all went quiet, Aisha hovering on her mum's side and me not from Liverpool, until Kingsley got bored of pretending to be fun.

I choose the first pizza on the menu and think about telling Kingsley that Ingrid's real name is Lily, like the flowers that he brought me which are sitting on the table. I try really hard to say something to this man that my daughter loves so much that she's turned her life upside down, something that's not about being arrested, but it's all I can really think of.

Kingsley's arm rests on the back of Lily's chair and every now and then, he mixes his fingers with her highlighted hair and smiles like he doesn't mean it.

Eventually, while Aisha spoons vanilla ice cream from a sundae glass, he frowns over his Cobra and says, "Why are you staring?" and I can't help it, it spills out.

"Have you been to prison?"

For the first time he glances at me properly, just for a few seconds. Then he carefully lays the drink back onto the table, looking away again as if he just remembered he doesn't want to be here. In the corner of my eye, I see Lily's head fall into her hands.

I think he is going to say something, when his phone starts buzzing. He grabs at it while I wait silently. Perhaps he will pretend he never heard me. That might be best all round. After a couple of seconds of staring at the screen, he sighs and slams the phone to the table. "The police are wasting my time. My business is none of their business, and this is certainly none of yours." He pushes the phone to one side, but it skates over the table before tumbling off the edge, taking a table knife with it.

I reach to pick it up.

"Leave it!" He lifts his fingers from the table, as if throwing out an order.

Redness starts to creep up my face in case the other diners have heard his tone. Lily has moved a tiny bit away from him.

"I'm sorry..." I begin.

Kingsley stands up and his chair wobbles, but doesn't fall. He turns to Lily. "I can't be dealing with *loonies* in my busy life."

Who told him I was loony? I grit my teeth. At least one other diner is looking over at us, looking at me being called a loony. I will not cry. I've had lots of practice.

Kingsley marches to the door, the medallion round his neck swinging, the Cobra in his hand spills as he leaves. I watch him through the window, standing in front of the smokers' tables.

I turn to look at Lily. "I know I shouldn't have—"

She cuts me off. "It's been tough, you know," she says biting her lip and taking her napkin from her lap and placing it on the table. "Please try not to upset him," she adds with a frown, almost as if she is begging.

The beg in her voice makes me take a second glance, but she's standing to follow him before I can see into her eyes. Aisha is looking up at her loony grandma, her tiny pigtails shaking with the motion. I don't know what to say to her. A waiter picks up Kingsley's phone from the floor, placing it quietly next to my plate as if he knows it is all my fault really but just shouldn't say.

Lily and Kingsley stand talking on the terrace, their backs to us. Lily's gesturing gently towards Kingsley's stiff frame. Lily has always been the icy one, but now she's turned into someone else, someone who can calm Kingsley down.

After a while they come back through the glass doors, looking at Aisha so that they don't have to look at me. Kingsley is confident in his own body, walking with fluid movements to his blazer on the back of his chair. He gathers his wallet. "Here, Helen, don't go straight home after lunch. Buy yourself something nice. Get yourself a cab." He offers me two notes. Like the flowers, they are pinky-orange, scrunched up, waiting to be admired.

Lily smiles at me. "Isn't that sweet?" she says, but her face says "*Please* agree". "I'll point out the taxi rank."

"Is he going to prison?" I whisper when Kingsley goes for a toilet break. "Is that why he's so angry?"

She points with her eyes towards Aisha, but Aisha is focused on her colouring in, with the expression of someone solving a complicated mathematics puzzle, so Lily shakes her head. I wait until she finishes her glass of wine. "They had no real evidence. He thinks it's an old business partner he fell out with, trying to cause him trouble."

I look at her a little longer. She still won't look at me properly and I don't think that's because of the arrest, or that a few days ago she thought she'd lost him. She knows what I have seen, that she has changed somehow with Kingsley. Maybe Kingsley is stressed and angry because of the arrest. But Lily has changed. Kingsley has changed Lily. How did he do that?

I don't wave back as they send me shopping under the cold towers of Canary Wharf. He loves Lily, I tell myself. That should be enough for it all to be okay. He doesn't need to like me to keep my Lily happy.

KINGSLEY

To be honest, I get confused about Ing's family. Only found out about her other mum when I had to drive her over there after she had trouble with her next-door neighbour. I thought Ing's parents moved to Bath. Sanctimonious bunch as far as I could tell. We sat in the Rangie outside the other one's flat, and I was like, "You want me to come in and say hi or something?"

"I dunno. She's a bit off the wall. I just suppose I feel sorry for her. She's living in this dive, and she does help out quite a bit with Aisha."

"So she's a crazy."

Ing went a bit quiet. "Don't talk like that." First time she stopped being fun. Although she has been more clingy since the arrest.

But later on, when we started talking about moving in together, Ing was all out with the thumb screws. "You've got to meet her."

"We tried that. It's not my fault Jep tried to get me in trouble with the law." Jep, Jep. That guy's made me furious. He lost his share in the business when I bought him out of his bad debt and now he's stuck with some stupid vendetta against me. Why did Ing have to bring that up? "I am so going to find that guy and break a few bones."

Ing winced and after a while she rested a hand on my arm.

"What?"

"We could try seeing Helen again? She keeps asking."

"I thought you weren't bothered."

She went quiet.

"All right. Look, we'll treat her, take her out in Canary Wharf, spoil her with Cava or something."

"I can't imagine her in a restaurant."

"Babe, you are not making this one easy."

"Yep, okay. Let's try that. She wants to meet you. Let's just try that."

***

And I mean, seriously, Ing didn't tell me the half of it. Her mum was about fortyish, with faded red hair, and a little bit of make-up, like she was one of those women who doesn't care about how she looks, and she just stared at me for the first half of the pizza, which kills pizza for sure. Then, when she eventually spoke, she started going on about being arrested and I had to put her right about that. Would you believe, Ing followed me out of the restaurant, telling me to be nice, as if I'm the one with the problem?

"Two-hundred quid that little incident cost me," I hiss to Ing as we walk away from her bio-mum. Ing's walking too slowly because her kid is holding us up. It's not just annoying me, you can see all the suits are like, why is a kid here during work hours? "And a soulless hour of my life I can never get back. Why did you even tell her about the Jep stuff?"

"You know she was there when it happened."

"And you just blurted it all out? To a crazy?"

I wait for the normal whinge, but it doesn't happen. She looks away from me, which is what she normally does when I explain why I'm right. "I was worried about you," she says huskily.

"Don't expect me to hang out with her just because she's your mum."

HELEN

Then, Lily gets quieter. She still comes around with Aisha and has cups of tea with me, but there's a silent pool underneath her stories of designer clothes and the flat-screen TV purchase.

"Is it because you're scared you nearly lost him?" I lost my bee once, so I can understand that the thought of losing him to prison when she only just got to know him was all too much.

"Is it because of what?" She scowls, so after a while I say that Aisha's new gloves are really pretty and where did she get them from, so she tells me about TK Maxx with resentful one-word answers as if she is talking about TK Maxx but really thinking of the great silent pool underneath.

Or maybe it's because she knows I really wanted her to stay with Andrew.

When she visits, she doesn't talk about Kingsley, and maybe it's just as well, because if Kingsley loves Lily and hates me, I don't know how he feels about Aisha. That's something I could get very annoyed about.

I try to see the good. Maybe Kingsley is so unpredictable, Lily hasn't got the chance to get bored like she did with Andrew. Just because I really liked Andrew doesn't mean that Lily couldn't settle down now, and at least I wouldn't have to worry about how Aisha will be provided for.

I stop thinking about Andrew. Maybe things will be okay after all.

But it's not okay. Not really.

Lily goes very quiet on me for a very long time. I play with Aisha, the little girl I never saw Lily be, so earnest and beautifully young that that's enough for me, until Lily phones a few months after I have met Kingsley, and she says, "I had an accident. I can't drive."

"Oh, no. What's happened?"

"Listen, I can come and fetch Aisha on Saturdays coming on the bus, but I don't have time to drop her off. Would it be okay for you to come and pick her up?" She sighs and then adds, "Or maybe even stay here with her until I get back?" There is an anxiety in her voice. She is not used to asking me for favours.

"Yes, of course. What's happened?"

"I fell down the stupid stairs."

"Stupid stairs," I echo in sympathy.

"Oh, it was my fault, I had dropped some washing when I was trying to put Aisha to bed and there was one of Kingsley's shirts on a couple of the steps. And the phone rang so I went down the stairs too quickly while still looking back to see if Aisha was all right, and I slid all the way down."

What a long explanation. I try to picture Kingsley's shirts, and remember, I have only met him once, and I really wasn't very interested in his shirts. I picture the sort of cufflinks he might have. Dollar signs.

"And now my arm is in a cast."

"Oh no."

Lily starts crying.

"Ingrid?"

"I'm sorry. It's these stupid painkillers the hospital gave me. They make me tired and weepy."

This does not sound like Lily. Each year I seem to discover a new side to her. "Aren't you off work?"

"Only for a couple of days. I'm back in on Friday. Could you come then?"

The System. The council. They call the shots even when you're part of them, even when you work for them.

***

Lily is frowning when I reach the house. She is already dressed in her coat with her keys in the hand that is not plastered up and in the sling. It is a really smart burgundy coat, nipped in at the waist, with military pockets and buttons. "Sorry, I have to go right away. It takes ages to get to work in the cast." She looks like she is in pain, but that it would hurt her more if I reached out and said it will all be okay.

She gives me a warning glance as if I really might risk touching her.

"Right, see you," she says and marches swiftly through the front door, already commuting, closing it sharply behind her, rather than let me wave her goodbye. I know there is something wrong in the way that she is avoiding my eye, but I don't know what to do about it.

***

I'm okay looking after Aisha in the daytime (although we nearly killed her goldfish and I had to rescue it with water in the lid of a flask), but at twilight, I always feel scared. It's worse here, now that Aisha has been put to bed, than in my Deptford flat where I have got used to dealing with the fear, whispering to myself that there is no one coming for me anymore. Except sometimes the fear creeps back in my dreams, in the dark, sometimes then.

I hear a scraping at the front door and I can hardly breathe. But I hear a faint voice under the scrabbling and realise it's Lily struggling to use her door key one-handed. I rush to help her in. The strap of her handbag drapes to one side as she walks through the front door into the living room tentatively. She looks tired. "Is Kingsley back yet?"

"No." I pause for a moment as she slips off her shoes. I hadn't even thought he might be the first home, and what I would say to him if he was.

"I hate travelling by bus. You know, no one would give me a seat even with this cast? I went flying every time he braked."

I nod sympathetically. I don't want to bother her when she has just got in, but my thoughts are crowding out in my head, and popping around me so that I cannot stand still.

"I've cleaned up the kitchen."

She glances through the kitchen arch, frowning. "Oh, thanks." She turns to hang up her coat. She takes her time putting her one green leather glove in the pocket of her coat and she doesn't turn around when she has finished. She leans one hand against the wall while her back is still towards me. Then she says in a very sandy voice, "Listen, I wanted to ask you something, something important."

I wait and she turns to face me.

"I need to know, was my dad African or West Indian?"

I am so used to dealing with the passing comments, the sly digs for information, that the full-on question takes me by surprise, and I cannot say a thing.

She seems to think that being quiet means that I don't want to talk. She starts to look angry. For the first time she is more than just discontent. "I have a right to know."

I don't know what to do now because she sounds so right, it's hard to explain why she isn't. I feel like Aisha's goldfish out of water, gasping for oxygen, my mouth in a hopeless 'o' and my little fins flapping and not getting me to safety.

"Why won't you tell me?" She starts to get more high-pitched. "You're hiding me from my real family."

I feel crushed. "I thought I was your real family."

"Why would you separate us? You want me all for yourself." It is the first time that I have seen it like this, that Lily is not just mine. I've always known that her heart was with Maurice and Jenny. But I had never realised she belongs to the parts of the family that I have run away from. I never knew she thought of them like that. She always felt like mine. "You're all condescending about Aisha not having her real dad with her, but you can't even give me my real dad."

"I don't know, Lily. I just don't know."

"Ingrid!" She slaps the wall with her good hand. And you can see that she thinks that I should know with just that correction that I have failed, I have lost, because I do not even know my little bee's real name. It's not even bad enough that I can't bring more family, like her little brother, Goodness.

She doesn't understand that Lily is her real name, her name from her real mum. It's just that no one told her in time.

She makes her way to one of the dining chairs and sighs, trying to calm down. She puts one hand to her head, tapping her forehead with her palm as if she is trying to think really hard, trying to be as reasonable as possible. "Okay, I get that you might not know much about him. It happens. But you must know something that can help me find him. A name? A place?"

A place? No No. Nooo. Beep Beep Bop. I know nothing, nothing at all. Haziness mists me up. I start to fall back.

***

When I come round, I am on the sofa. Lily looks calmed down, her coat is lying on one of the dining chairs, but she hasn't joined me on the sofa. She has pulled over another dining chair and sits on it to one side so that she does not have her back to me. "You fainted," she explains. She is stirring a cup of hot chocolate and looking at the steam. There is also a cup of hot chocolate on the coffee table in front of me. "Drink up. It will make you feel better." She sounds defeated.

I do as she asks because this is something that I can do for her, even if I cannot produce her real family. I would like to. I would like to go and buy her packets of families like Aisha's Sylvanian dolls where rabbits are married to mice and have cat babies so there are daddies and grannies and brothers, a complete set, unlike Lily and Aisha; unlike me and the nothingness that came before me. Lily could unpack them and keep them in her little Thamesmead house with her flat-packed furniture and her fake wooden floors.

If I concentrate on thinking about the past as Sylvanian Families, I won't have to look behind me and see the real past, even when Lily pushes me for more information.

"What I really need is a glass of wine." She looks longingly at the kitchen door. To begin with, I wonder why she doesn't just get a glass of wine and then I think of a possible reason. I look at Lily again and I notice that her curves are bigger and maybe that it isn't just that she's had less exercise with the broken arm.

She watches me sip the hot chocolate from a big green mug. It is too hot and scalds my tongue, but I know that she wants me to take in some sugar because of the fainting. I have not fainted for a very long time, but I remember that they want you to have sugar when you faint.

"It's Kingsley," she says.

She's still scared he will go to prison?

"He yells at me that I'm not even properly black and he's ashamed of me if he takes me to his parties. And I can't defend myself," she shakes her head desperately, "if I don't know who I am."

Kingsley has made her sad, and because she is not used to being sad, she is also furious. Something inside me twists up, that he should dislike what Lily is, what I am, something that we cannot change for him. And then I feel real anger. Instead of being a real breathing person, I have been boxed for what I am. Maybe this is why he was so uninterested in his girlfriend's mother.

Maybe Lily has even been pretending that I don't exist.

Lily lets her head fall to her hands, clasping her ears with fingernails painted blue like the sky.

I watch her for a few moments, not knowing what to do. I wonder if I should give out some fake fact about her family to give Lily what she desperately needs. What would be the best thing for Kingsley to discover? "Kingsley's Zimbabwean?"

She looks up a couple of inches, curling her hands and shaking them. "He's Nigerian. It's obvious. It's a completely different place. Can't you remember anything?"

I don't think that I can pretend that Lily's dad is Nigerian. I'd tried to read a book about Nigeria from the library on the way to meeting him for the first time and I still can't even remember the name of the place. There will be other facts I would be supposed to know and I would not be able to fill in the gaps. It's not as if I know anything about Zimbabwe either. In the list of un-great ideas, Helen Kennedy, this was a particularly un-great idea.

It's more important that she knows that Kingsley does not have the right to yell at her about these things, to imply that somehow this is her fault for not knowing who she is and she should fix it. Who is this man, Kingsley? Now I wonder, Lily, where did you get that broken arm?

"Ingrid..." I ask quietly, looking over at a pile of half-folded pants from the laundry basket on the other end of the dining table.

She raises one eyebrow.

"Money laundering, is it..." I've started, but I don't know how to ask.

Her face steams up. "Is it what?"

"Is it a violent crime?" I don't want to ask, but it's the only thing that makes sense of what I have seen here today.

Lily doesn't answer. She looks at her hands in her lap. And she looks guilty. Then she recovers herself. "No, it's a white-collar crime, a crime to do with what you do with money." Then after a while, she adds, "He didn't do it anyway."

"So it's just that he's unhappy about where you're from?"

And she looks back at her hands again.

"I think it's better anyway," I tell her in the end.

"What's better?" she asks me, staring blankly at the dining table.

"To be both. To be half and half."

"What do you mean?"

"To share," I pause, wondering how to explain what I mean, "to share differences, in one family, in a way… so that the differences don't really matter." I think that this is something maybe that I learned from Andrew, but I know I shouldn't mention his name, just like I shouldn't talk about biological parents. "Better was the wrong word, I suppose."

She gives me a faint smile and squeezes my arm. I realise with alarm that this is the first time I feel that I liked my little bee since she left Andrew. I have always loved her, but tonight I like her again too.

"It shouldn't matter," I tell her, leaning properly around from the sofa. "Otherwise what's the point of all those news stories where racist people go to prison, all those human rights things? And films are always about how we're all equal really. Everyone thinks that they are good films and they agree with them."

She looks away. Because it shouldn't matter, but it's true to say, here and now for Lily-Bee, it does. But she hasn't stopped craving my forgotten family just because she stopped talking about it. I can tell.

***

I can smell alcohol and cigarettes clouding up the stairwell when I get back home and I know exactly what that is: my new neighbour, Dylan, who has replaced Mrs Cauldwell. I should not have stayed out so late. I think about turning back. Maybe I could buy some chips on the High Street until he falls asleep. I hold the banister for a good few seconds, trying to make my mind up, but he's on the landing and he's seen me already.

Beep Beep Bop. The bad is rising to my front door like the dust that has always crept up from the stairwell before I mop it all away.

Forgetting your past is one thing, but living with your present is entirely different.

"Heeelllo, Helen luvvie," he drawls, pulling at the earring in one ear. "I was looking for you. Where you bin?" He comes down a couple of steps towards me so that I cannot easily reach my door. He is holding a slim green can in one hand. His reddish-brown beard is a different colour from the hair on his head.

"You're not allowed to smoke in here." His door is open. I can see that Mrs Cauldwell's nice wallpaper has been yellowed up with smoke.

"Oh, luvvie, you're so uptight. You need to loosen up. I do great massages. Come into my flat and I will give you a good massage."

I look at his stained fingers with uncut nails. The nails have been left alone for so long that they have curved into his fingers and are more like bark. I've spent so long trying not to be rude and scared at the same time that I don't care about being rude anymore. I hold my breath as I pass his face and avoid his leer, and when I have reached the top of the stairs, I back away from him in case he tries to grab out at me.

"I have a girlfriend, anyway," he growls. "I don't know what you are thinking making eyes at me and then sneaking off." He releases a loud burp. I think this is a good sign and he will forget about me soon.

"Good night, Dylan."

***

And then, a few months later, there is another phone call from Lily: "I'm sorry, Helen." I have never heard Lily say anything like that before. After knowing her again for a couple of years, I am only just finding out a thousand different ways that she can be. Who are all these different Lilys? "Don't go over to the house to pick up Aisha today." Is her voice hoarse, or is it just the phone line?

"Where is she? Will you bring her here?"

"She's with her dad." With Andrew. I let his relaxed happy face come back to mind and let myself wonder how it would be if Lily and Andrew got back together again, look lovingly at one another in the hallway of Woolwich Town Hall. Recently Lily has started to tell me about the rows that she and Kingsley have had. Would it be okay now to go back to where we were before? Now it's me who wants to play Sylvanian Families.

"Okay." I am still not sure why she is sorry, but I know that something is very very wrong. "Are you okay?"

"Don't start on me…" Although she is obviously not okay, I am a little glad to hear the fighting spirit back. "Me and Aisha have left the house for a while. Just until things cool down."

"Cool down? So where are you?"

There is a shuffle and unease. "I'm staying in a women's refuge. I can't tell you where."

"A refuge?" I can only picture castles in the mountains, or maybe fortresses carved in the rock. Aren't they what a refuge is?

"Helen!" she hisses, exasperated. "It's a place where people, women, come to be safe, if their partners are causing trouble."

"What? I knew it!"

"He just got to be a bit difficult, that's all." She says it in a different way from how she would talk about Andrew, an irritated, don't talk to me tone. She doesn't want to talk about it, so I know that Kingsley is a really bad person.

"You said, cool down. Are you going back to him?"

She starts sobbing. "I don't know. It's complicated. I love him. I really, really love him."

I cannot think why. I suppose things are just more exciting there, with things changing all the time, even the drama of his arrest. Or is she used to the people who love her being distracted, like Maurice and Jenny?

I should be a mum right now, but I have absolutely no idea

what to do. I am scared if I say, "How can you love a man who breaks your arm?" that Lily will hate me and never call me again. But it's the thought of Aisha that makes me speak out. "You can't ever, ever take Aisha back to him," I hiss. "Never. You would have to let Andrew keep her." I cannot believe what has tumbled out of my mouth. I think that I have lost her now. She will not put up with her not-real mum telling her what to do about this.

But she sobs some more, and says, "I know that now," as if she would really consider it, letting Andrew keep Aisha, so that she can return to Kingsley.

"What do you mean, you know that now? What exactly has happened?"

She sniffs. Can you hear an admission in the silence over a phone line?

"He broke your arm, didn't he?" I say it like I am telling Lily off, but really I am angry with him. Or maybe I am angry with her for leaving Andrew for him.

She doesn't answer. But I notice that she doesn't deny it either. And what I also know is that Lily's arm was broken months ago, so what's changed?

"Was it that that made you leave now?"

And there is no reply, just a silence. She must be holding her breath to stop the tears. "Do you have a phone number for Andrew?" I ask. "He must need help with the babysitting too." As if that convinces either of us why I need to have his number.

She reads the number over the phone haltingly, but she has stopped crying. I write it out slowly with a broken green biro. I feel bad. I wonder if I am supposed to comfort her and tell her it will all be okay, and ask if she needs me to bring anything around. But I don't have anything to bring, and I don't have any comfort to give until I know that Aisha is safe.

***

I phone Andrew and ask if I can come round. He answers the phone sounding exhausted. He does not want to talk to me, I can tell. And he does not want me to visit, but I think that he knows he can't stop me. How things have changed between us. How things have changed even more since the childless time. Life seems to be more like layers than good things and bad things, layers of different types of worries that colour how you think.

***

There is no intercom on the way to Andrew's door and the flats are open onto their little alleyways, some filled with groups of teenagers, or even grown-ups hanging out washing on the lines on the balconies – in the night! I hunch under my Primark coat and pull it tighter around me so that no one will guess that I am still wearing my pyjamas underneath because I left the house angry. I have not learned to be angry before. I don't know if I have learned to be angry from Lily, or if this is the first time I have had anyone to be angry about.

Andrew's door has been painted since the last time I came here, and there is a brass door knocker. I knock and Andrew opens. He does not say hello. He just gives me a look and leads me to the living room. To start with, I wonder if I should take my shoes off like in Thamesmead, but I realise that the floor tiles are bare, so I don't even ask. The living room is dark, half lit by a street light coming through the thin curtains, and as my eyes wake up to the shadows, I see that there is one of those big leather sofas that forms a corner, and on the shorter end is a tiny little girl, fully clothed, sleeping under a blanket. Her lace-edged socks peek out from underneath.

I feel better immediately. Seeing Aisha is like coming home.

I do not want to wake her by walking all the way in, and I hover in the hallway instead. In the silence, I can hear the rush of passing cars on the roads outside.

"I don't really know what you want to do here," says Andrew.

"Is she okay?"

"Ingrid left her here and went off quick." He turns his nose up as he says the word "quick", like it's a shameful thing. "She gave me an envelope and when I opened it, I found instructions about what to look for with someone who has had a bump on their head."

"No!" I turn again to look at her sleeping figure.

"Not just that." He shakes his head slowly to each side, looking at the bare floor. "Aisha's in pain in her body, so I took her back to A&E and they say she's probably got a fractured rib, and gave her some more painkillers."

I catch my breath and stare at the floor. Fractured rib? I feel more fury rise up. But I don't show it. Andrew hasn't even realised that Lily hadn't told me that Aisha was hurt. I'm not going to give it away by asking for more details.

Andrew looks at my non-reaction for a few moments, and then turns to the floor, suppressing a pained scowl that flits across his face, and I realise he understands what I am feeling right now even if we are not going to talk about it.

I know what I thought before and now I know for sure. Aisha was the reason Lily finally left. Kingsley had moved from hitting Lily to hitting Aisha. Beep Beep Bop, but I cannot drown out this information. I have to look after poor Aisha. "It's Kingsley that changed her," I tell him.

"No," he makes a soft laugh to himself. "She was the same when we met at college. She's just going to do what she's going to do, no matter what. I thought that was fun at the time. Then after a while…" He glances at me and tails off.

"Has Aisha got her toys?"

"I have no idea. She has toys here." He gestures at a pink plastic castle sitting underneath a two-seater dining table that's squashed in behind the sofa. Two pastel-coloured horses with rainbow manes poke out from the turrets. "She's not going back there just for toys, that's for certain."

"I'm sorry."

He softens. "Don't be. This is my fault; I should have seen this coming."

We both stand in the uncarpeted hallway for a while, not really saying anything to each other. I notice as I look around that there is a woman's beret on the coat hook. I know it's a woman's hat because there is a brooch on it, and it's a grown-up woman's hat, not Aisha's. He sees me looking and he does not look sorry or embarrassed. It is too late, then, for the clock to go back. I suppose that is okay, because if the clock went all the way back, it would not be good for any of us.

"How are you going to get home at this hour?"

"I'll catch the bus."

"I don't want you to go alone in the dark, but I can't leave Aisha." He looks awkwardly about the flat as if it might somehow sprout another room. "There's room on the sofa next to her if you like?"

I would really like. I am drawn by the comfort that I can be there for Aisha.

He motions me back into the semi-dark room and I perch on the edge of the sofa, waiting as my eyes adjust to the curve of her sleeping cheek and eyelashes. Andrew comes back in with a pillow and a picnic blanket and a bathrobe. "They're clean," he whispers. "Will they be enough to sleep with?"

I take them gratefully and remove my coat.

As he goes to walk away, he looks back. "Helen?"

I look at him.

"Are you wearing your pyjamas already?"

"Yes." And we are both too upset to laugh, but for a moment I see in his face the Andrew I knew before. Andrew my son-in-law, my friend.

***

Whose fault is all this? I wonder, as I try to stay lying on the bathrobe and not the sticky leather of the sofa. Andrew says it's his. I don't know why he thinks that. I suppose he also thinks it's all because of Lily and I have to remind myself not to agree. Maybe Lily even thinks it is her fault for not being the right person for Kingsley. Really, it's Kingsley who has ruined everything, but everyone else is left playing a merry-go-round trying to work out who to blame.

Andrew said he will call the police, but there are no concrete facts, because Lily won't tell them and Aisha isn't able. That's everybody's fault.

But I am the one who has made Lily into a person who runs from safety to danger because I couldn't keep the house clean when she was a little bee. Lily's discontent has led her to this dangerous dark place when she should have known that she had happiness with Andrew and kept it. And she's moving from discontent to anger because nothing's going right. I wonder if Andrew has seen that too.

Maybe the discontent was something that had been passed on from me, running away from my life.

***

By the time that Ryan is born, we have decided to forget Kingsley.

I have lots of practice with forgetting. There were things to forget about long before Kingsley was around: There never was a seventies gas fire, no sofa for three, and now there was also not a man with a medallion and a temper that cracked without warning. I think we do well forgetting Kingsley. But I should probably warn Lily that you must keep forgetting under control. Too much forgetting and there's also no anchor, no story to tell, no reason for living.

Sometimes I would curl into a little ball under my bed because of the things that weren't, a little ball with my hands clutching my head and my chin against my knees, with my back to the Quality Street tin with my past trapped in it.

But it's okay really because we can think about Ryan now. I don't get to see the photographs of Ryan's scan – it can't be exciting anymore to have a biological grandmother to share these things with, so I meet Ryan back in Thamesmead a week after he is born. He's on Lily's lap and I perch behind the sofa so that I can see his face and try to get his tiny hand to clasp my finger like a Venus flytrap. His black eyes sometimes seem to see my fingers and sometimes seem to see nothing. I feel the thousand glossy pink nail varnish blast of love. He is just as exciting as Aisha and Lily were when they were new. But: "Is he Kingsley's?"

"Of course he's Kingsley's," Lily says to the fireplace. She has been breastfeeding him, and the tiny towel goes over her shoulder ready for him to cough it all back out at her again. It's not often I see her just in jogging bottoms and a T-shirt. Instead of a glossy hairstyle, she wears just the natural fizz of her short dark hair. The house is a little bit tidier than last time I was here, or maybe just emptier, because Kingsley has taken his hi-fi and computer and I don't know what else with wires.

I look at the dimples above Ryan's elbows as his crazy small arms wave over Lily's shoulder. I have never loved a boy before.

"Does that mean he has to see Kingsley?"

Lily throws me a look as she jiggles Ryan up and down. I don't like it either, says the look, so you'd better shut up. She always knows her own power. Lily has a power over me because I cannot tell her who her father is.

But this Kingsley thing is different from when she split up with Andrew. Lily is not in control this time. I am angry for my bee. And with Kingsley gone, Lily's hunger for the heritage I can't give her has become stronger, hungrier and angrier, now that Kingsley has put the things about race into her head. It's as if she thinks they would still be together if it weren't for my secrets. As if that could be a good thing.

"But how does Kingsley know about Ryan?"

"Oh, don't be so stupid. It takes nine months to make a baby. He knew before we split."

But that would mean…

I sit with this truth spinning through my head for a few minutes while Ryan, as we predicted, throws up his supper and Lily has to dab at his mouth and patches of her T-shirt, rocking him all the time.

"Well, so he must have… when he knew you were expecting…"

"He must have what, Helen?" She leans back in the sofa and looks at me, daring me to explain what I mean, because she knows that neither of us will say what Kingsley did, what Kingsley did *more than once*. She's proud like that. If I said to her, "You remember that day that we were shopping for Aisha's pyjamas in BHS and you had a broken arm," and nothing at all about how her arm was broken, she'd get defensive and wouldn't remember having a broken arm. Even if she suddenly remembered having a broken arm, she would have to remember how she broke it, then she might even have to admit to me how it was broken.

But I don't know why I can't mention it.

She has told me about the refuge she went to that night I went to Andrew's. It sounds quite nice. There was somewhere for Aisha to play. Now that I know that a refuge is not a castle I picture instead the Sylvanian doll's house, with mummy mouse and baby badger in one room, and mummy squirrel with the tabby cat in the other. Aisha is baby badger, and suddenly Lily is mummy mouse.

I have never thought of Lily as a mouse before.

We both look at Ryan, whose eyes are falling gently closed, and he looks perfect. So whatever Kingsley did when he hurt Lily's arm, Ryan is okay.

Lily has been telling me that Maurice and Jenny have fostered some twins with learning difficulties.

"Wow, they're such good people."

Lily's face does not alter, but she says, "I don't see much of them these days." I don't say anything for a while, pulling Aisha up to sit on my knee as she brushes past, and Lily adds,

"They just love children. I'm not children anymore," even though she holds a brand new baby in her arms.

It comes across like a confession because she defended them so much before. I cannot believe that they have no interest in her now. I look at her, but she won't meet my eye. Then something behind her catches my eye: fresh flowers in the Thamesmead house.

***

"I think she's seeing someone," I can only whisper it in the stairwell to Andrew, as I don't even want the neighbours to hear. It's not just the flowers. I've been observing the hints of dating with the extra babysitting requested and, for some reason, a much tidier house. I haven't commented. I don't know how I would react if Lily admitted that Kingsley was coming back. Maybe Lily doesn't know how I would react either. I had never shouted at Lily until the women's refuge day. I never knew I could.

Andrew looks older these days, tired, more irritable. Now his unshaven jaw juts out. "What?" he asks, a dark mood underneath the croak.

"I don't mean," I pause. "I don't mean, it's definitely *him*. But there's someone and she hasn't mentioned him to me yet."

He looks down at the doormat outside of my front door, and I look down at the doormat inside of my front door.

"Do you think that we should go over there?" It's the sort of silly thing that I could never say to Lily, talk about "us" doing anything, but even though he's changed, I know it's okay with Andrew. He even breaks a smile, even though he's still looking at the doormat.

"Like spies?" he asks and I do a little giggle. I hope it's okay that I giggle with Lily's ex-husband. Ryan stirs in his fancy baby carrier. We look at him, and we look at Aisha, who is reaching out to us with pure innocent children's fingers as if she knows we are worrying about her. But then Aisha beams and it makes me beam inside.

Andrew sighs, half shaking his head. "You know what, maybe it would be safer to just double-check."

***

Andrew pulls up the car at the end of Lily's road, right in front of the neat street sign that says *Pine Walk*. We can see the house, but we are at an angle, so you would only just see us from inside the house if you were deliberately looking out beyond the scraggy plants on the front driveway. He doesn't say anything. I look at his tired face, and wonder what he is thinking, seeing this old life of his being lived without him.

"You can't tell anything from the outside," I say.

"We need an excuse or something."

"She'll know." It only makes me feel a little bit bad to side with Andrew against my daughter like this.

"Yes. She will."

We all have to turn up at the door. All of us, because we can't lock Ryan and Aisha in the car. Aisha holds my hand, and Andrew holds Ryan's cot. It's only when I see him balance the carrier against his charcoal jeans that I think how good it is of Andrew to babysit both bees as if they are both his.

When he rings the bell, I feel my heart sink. This is something that I would never do alone, and now I am wishing I hadn't even come.

Lily doesn't take long to reach the door. She opens the door and stands there in a long mauve cardigan without reacting at what she sees. "Hello."

"Sorry," Andrew's apology is quick and breezy, like it's not a "sorry" at all. "I know you weren't expecting us, but Aisha doesn't seem to have any socks packed."

"Right," she says. "Socks." She scans our faces. "A four-person mission to pick up socks. I suppose you'd better step in, then."

But there is no one in the living room as we stand there hearing Lily rummage upstairs. I look at Andrew, hoping that he can see that I'm sorry that he has had a wasted trip, but Andrew is looking out to Lily's back garden. Among the discarded hula hoops in the overgrown blades of grass, a man is building a brick barbecue, each brick slowly and methodically laid over carefully iced mortar. It's definitely not Kingsley. He has fair hair which has been left uncut for too long, at that stage where you can see that there had been a smart haircut there, a few months back.

"His name's Dragos," Lily says dismissively as she reaches us and we pretend we weren't looking. "Working on some project," she sighs, and hands Andrew a Sainsbury's bag. "Here are the *socks*."

The back door suddenly clicks open and Dragos wanders through the kitchen into the living room, having no idea that everyone's here to see him. We all stand there.

Lily introduces us casually as if we are all an irrelevance. Even Dragos seems to be an irrelevance, so as we exchange "hellos" I almost wonder if I have misunderstood, and Dragos is just hired for handyman work. But then he lifts Ryan from the carrycot, and mutters to him in Romanian until Ryan gurgles at him happily. He lifts a toy elephant from the sideboard to him. I wince for a second, remembering my own toy elephant, one-eyed Ajax.

"Ryan might grow up speaking Romanian," I smile, forgetting Andrew is there for a moment.

Lily snorts and lifts two mugs from the coffee table to take them through to the kitchen. Then, halfway to the kitchen, she says, "Well, I suppose Ryan needed some sort of cultural identity. You and me aren't offering him anything."

It takes me by surprise, hearing Lily's old dig about my past. For a second, I think of the past, and a little chip of white plaster comes away, sharp and painful, and I glimpse my secrets underneath. It's too awful to look at and I look away.

Lily returns from the archway of the kitchen and turns to

Andrew, "So, have you got what you came for?" Her voice is sour like the violent fizz of the fluorescent light that kept me awake when she was a baby. Her arms are crossed. When I hear that fizz, I know that my dreams of Andrew and Lily returning to the way things were, maybe Andrew realising the lady who left the beret in his flat does not compare to Lily, will never happen.

Andrew gives Lily such a charming smile. You wouldn't know the things that have happened between these two people from that smile. "Thanks, Ingrid, we're all good now." He turns to me. "Lift home, Helen?"

I turn to Ryan to find Dragos tucking him back into the cot, harbouring his head, and pulling up the little white crocheted blanket. I can see straight away that he does not have Kingsley's temper. It's almost as if Lily was looking for someone who was the opposite of Kingsley, someone who would not remind her of him, to get him out of her head.

Because I don't think that Kingsley is out of her head yet. Behind her vacant, post-trauma, post-split, post-baby look, there is another look that says that Kingsley is still there. I wish he wasn't.

I know I should go with Andrew, but I want to get to know this new son-in-law, and I can only stare hopelessly at Dragos and Ryan. Lily waves a hand to one side. "Oh, let her stay."

"He should know better," Lily mutters under her breath as she waves her bees away. It's strange to hear her more angry at him, than she is at me. She turns to me. "I'm just trying to make sure they have a proper dad. Aisha and Ryan, I mean. It matters, it makes a difference," she adds, but when I glance over at her, she tries to cancel out the desperate note in her voice by moving over to the coffee table and flicking through a glossy magazine that was left there.

Don't be desperate, Lily. Bad things happen when you are desperate.

Dragos says nothing. It's probably too much effort to translate all this talking in his mind. I feel rude not talking to him, even though Lily looks happy to just ignore him. She has found a two-page spread of pictures of fashionable raincoats in her magazine.

I point to the barbecue. "It looks like chocolate biscuits," I say to Dragos, thinking of the slab of mortar like the slab of chocolate cream in the middle of a bourbon biscuit.

"No. We barbecue meat, not biscuits," he says, looking outside and his accent means I can't tell if he is joking or not. "You come and have barbecue with us in the summer. Maybe we have steak; maybe I get bored of babysitting the children and we barbecue them."

I smile, but I'm trying to work out why Lily is already getting him to babysit while she goes out without him, so I suppose Dragos thinks I'm the one without a sense of humour.

Dragos seems to get absorbed in the bricks again. "After this, maybe I build a pizza oven," he says to the spirit level and makes his way back to the garden.

I can't think of a joke about what to cook on a pizza oven, so I let him go without comment. I am not sure that Dragos really minds.

"Are you going to have lots of parties?" I ask Lily.

Dragos carries on, calmly, applying and checking, all in a pale green short-sleeved T-shirt over sculpted biceps. The breeze lifts the strands of his hair. He looks like he should be cold.

I see Lily's eyes flash. "Parties?"

"With the barbecue."

Lily lets the magazine drop to her lap and peers outside, her interest suddenly flared. "Oh yes, I never really thought of that."

"He seems nice."

"He's all right." She puts her feet back on the coffee table. I can tell already Lily won't be talking about Dragos much, not with the same sneaking admiration that she spoke of Kingsley. Already there is less talk of money, and Dragos doesn't seem the type to be interested in the thought of going out. It's quite sweet that he likes to have projects in the garden, to want be in the breezy outdoor silence making things out of bricks and wood.

But even now, with calmer Dragos looking after my Lily, I don't think I can quite relax. The ship may have steadied, but I know it can't stay under this grey sky, because there is nothing to look forward to. There is something uncomfortable under the surface look of calm. Lily looks at me in a different way. She has done since the conversation we had that day with the broken arm, even though it can't be Kingsley anymore who makes her resent who she is.

"You're a natural father," I tell Dragos as he comes back indoors after a while and steadies the blind which rocked as he closed the door.

He kind of smiles as I remember that he is not a father at all. He has just moved into this ready-made family like all of the others. I'm just a mess at this whole thing. Dragos smiles at me apologetically. He is sorry that I am a mess too.

KICKING UP GRAVES

In the hospital waiting room, in the building "next door" to St Thomas's, years after Dragos has left – some falling out over babysitting – I try to think of the names of all of Lily's men. It's easier if I remember to put Andrew at the beginning, but it's not likely that I would really forget him. Andrew, Kingsley, Dragos, Adam, Frank. Frank had a farm they invited me to, but I thought it would be so beautiful I might die of happiness. Or if I didn't die of happiness it would just have hurt more when Lily moved on and I wouldn't be able to go anymore.

After Frank came Mr Laterly (to call Mr Laterly "Chester" just feels wrong. That's not just because Chester is a silly first name for a man, but because he is Aisha's drama teacher, so he has to be a "Mr"). Sometimes I think I should use one of those memory rhymes to remember them by that Aisha told me about from her English classes, but I would just come up with a good sentence, when another name would have to be added.

I feel drowsy with painkillers and anti-anxiety meds and all of the rest. My misty mind creates a perfect memory rhyme: *A kindness denied always for my Lily.* I hope for a "b" (maybe a Ben?) for 'but' that will take the sentence somewhere else more positive next.

I still can't work out how Lily met so many boyfriends. Much later on, when Marnie, the little old lady who now lives in the flat opposite mine, and Becca my neighbour from downstairs got together for tea, we had a talk about it and

Becca said that it might be from internet dating, which is where you can find boyfriends on the computer.

Becca wanted me to put a photo of myself onto internet dating. Well, she said she would do it for me. I don't have any photos, I said. "Oh, that's not a problem," she said cheerily. "We should do you a makeover, and take a photo." (Since then I have discovered that having a makeover is basically Becca's reason for living.)

I know. Why bother remembering Lily's men? Does Aisha remember them? She's the one who had to live with all of these different dads, one stranger on the black leather sofa in front of Kingsley's flat-screen TV, a different stranger to make her sandwiches in the glossy white kitchen through the archway. But each boyfriend brings a flavour to the layer cake of life, the stages that you wish you could pick one and say: "I like this, I like this stage here, this layer of raspberry jam. Let me stay here, please." Or there are the stages when you find dental floss and chicken stock in the cake, when you think that the world may as well end right then and there. You forget those stages might also move on. Like seasons, but with less certainty about what comes next.

And specifically, I need to remember Kingsley, the man who wandered around Canary Wharf with the orange lilies, orange money and shoes that he has to tell me are from Crocket and Jones, sadly, because he is not just the father of Lily's growing fury, but he is Ryan's father. And that really means no escape, doesn't it? Because you can't escape from your biological family, no matter how hard you try. Ryan is my biological grandson, and Kingsley's biological son.

I stare out of the window that overlooks south London, all trees and grey blocks, wondering what I would say if Aisha were to find me in this half of the hospital. "How did you end up here?" she might ask again, if she had decided she had learnt all she could from me about Kingsley by now. And I would have to explain, it was because of that day we all went swimming.

***

Swimming was what I did when they took Lily away the first time. The chlorine smell would get everywhere: my hair, my skin, my clothes. It was comforting. I knew it would kill all the germs from the flat that could hurt my bee.

How was I to know that swimming would lead to me being found by the ambulance men crying in Deptford High Street?

I take them to Wavelengths at the back of the High Street. Ryan is eight, and Aisha is twelve. I try to swim widths as they play, ignoring the hints in the bees' conversations of whoever Lily is or isn't living with now. Before I met my grandbees, I would swim adult lengths back and forth, back and forth, like a rocking chair, soothing myself away from the bad thoughts, hiding in clear water. But now that the grandbees are here, I cannot leave them unaccompanied. I have to look after them as they try to climb onto huge floats and fall off in the attempt. You can't keep your old ways, your old daydreams, when you have family. But they are worth it. "Grandbees, bee-have," I tell them.

"Why do you call us grandbees, Grandma?" The rah-rah skirt around the waist of Aisha's swimming costume floats on the ripples.

"Why do you call me grandma, grandbee?" I ask. And then as an afterthought, "But don't tell your mum," who wouldn't really understand that she is my little bee and it could just get a bit difficult.

Aisha looks at me shocked, with her arms on the float as it rocks with the waves of other children jumping into the pool.

"I don't mean lie to your mum. I mean don't confuse her."

She relaxes a little uncertainly, leaning down on one arm until Ryan throws one of his armbands into her face and she shrieks and swims after him.

"Ryan, put the armband back on," I call. But I see that he doesn't have to. He is confidently charging up the lanes in his Finding Nemo swimming trunks until the lifeguard whistles him back beyond the red line of "too deep". He turns resentfully back until the lifeguard is distracted, and Ryan swims a loop that makes sure he both heads back to us, and crosses the red line. I try to give him a stern look, but he makes me laugh. He still has dimples on his elbows. But I would never tell him. Aisha gives him a stern look so that I don't have to.

The water is alive with their little arms and legs scattering into the air and waves and their cries of delight or upset at where the water falls. Swimming with the bees is even better than just swimming lengths.

"Daddy has a swimming pool in Jamaica," Aisha tells me as she swims around in circles with a green float that is the shape of a lily pad.

"Jamaica?"

"In the big house that he is building for Cilia, and Brooke, Benjy and Paulie." She splashes at me. But she does not explain. I catch the shadow of a scowl on her face, a disappointment that I don't know already. "Jamaica isn't even in this country, and it takes six hours to get to on an airplane."

"Six hours?"

"Or maybe it was more. I forgot exactly." She rests her chin on the top of the float, her big eyes staring into the blue ripples.

Andrew is going even further away from my grandbee?

Aisha stops kicking the lily pad into circles for a second. "Daddy says he is half Jamaican. What am I half of?"

The question hangs in the chlorine-drenched air. Lily is planting these questions through the bees, using them to chip away at the past I'll never let her see. When Aisha is grown up, is she going to want the answers to Lily's questions too? And Ryan? I look at the bees, bright and happy in the blue water; I know it is impossible to let them go. "Let's play sharks!" I call instead.

Even though Aisha knows that it's me in a swimming pool with a single palm straight up above my head, she seems frightened of my shark impression, asking me to do it and then squealing.

Also, it's a bit exhausting to keep trying the same move.

A whistle echoes over the children's shouts and splashes. At the deep end, a lifeguard is running from his post, looking nervously dramatic. I am glad that Aisha is here with me, and I look around to check where Ryan is.

And then with more urgency, where is Ryan? I lift Aisha onto the poolside without a second thought and start swimming front crawl to the deep end. It doesn't seem to work. I push and pull at the water, but I cannot get there fast enough.

The lifeguard has not gone into the water. He is kneeling, peering into the chlorine. If he cannot get Ryan out, I will have to. We cannot lose any more babies. That would be the end.

I drag myself through the water, and finally I can see Ryan's short black hair bob out over the top of the water, unsupported, holding something up with one hand while he comfortably treads water.

The last few metres kill me. But who cares now I know he is safe? I wrap my arms around him. "Grandma," he says pushing himself away from me with his feet against my knees, "I picked the locker key off the floor of the deep end."

I look up into the face of the lifeguard. He's just a teenager. His watery blue eyes stand shocked out of his pale face. We are in so much trouble. We will definitely be expelled for letting an eight-year-old make everyone think he is drowning.

Please just don't tell Lily-Bee on me.

He looks past me and towards someone at the end of the pool. "Call an ambulance," he calls and he reaches down to me. I feel heavy as lead, like the water is sucking into my heavy skin and pulling me down into it, beneath the silver rail that you would think you could hold yourself up with.

I don't understand. I am good in water. I have been swimming in the water when the rest of the world has sucked me right down.

"My name's Josh," says the teenager as he helps me

stagger onto the coffee-coloured tiles. He's wearing a fleece and joggers. It would be unfair to expect him to jump in the pool to rescue one of us when he's dressed like that.

But we know Ryan is all right. I saw him treading water with one hand. That is good water skills. Am I missing something? Has something terrible made me check out and imagine him alive and well? I start to shiver and as I start to shiver, I feel huge shooting pains in my chest, almost throwing me back against the shiny walls.

***

I am wrapped in a foil blanket, in an office behind the swimming pool reception in a large swivelling leather chair that must be for someone important and there is a man in a green uniform with pockets and badges taking my pulse and looking at his watch. My greying hair is long and damp against my back. I am cold, which seems to prove that foil blankets are just as silly an idea as they looked all along. Lily is here. Aisha is crying, but Lily has her arm around me, which is quite unusual really.

"I wasn't drowning," insists Ryan through gritted teeth. "I was just deep underwater."

"But you might not have come back up," Aisha wails. She is clutching her own plastic chair in the absence of being able to clutch at her mum. Poor Aisha. I look at her and I realise that twenty minutes ago she was the only survivor amongst a supposedly drowning brother and fitful grandmother. She is dressed, but quite clearly soaking wet under her clothes as if she knew that she had to get changed when the grown-ups said, but needed to do it as quickly as possible so that she could come back and look after us all properly. She starts to hug herself around her pink padded jacket. She has the look of a twelve-year-old who thinks that we are her responsibility and I feel a different sort of tenderness from the love I had for her as a toddler.

"But lots of divers go very deep and they come back up. I *do know* not to breathe underwater, you know."

"Those divers are not eight years old." Lily is dressed up for going out. A patterned silk scarf peeks out of her black sheepskin coat and gold hoop earrings frame her face, so the glare she gives him looks all the more icy.

"I was just rescuing the locker key. It has Aisha's trainers in it." He stares at her accusingly and Aisha's face falls, as if it has been discovered to be her fault all along.

"Look at your grandma, Ryan. Is it worth making her unwell for a locker key?"

Ryan looks at me and stops rocking his feet. "Sorry, Grandma."

I turn to tell him that it's okay really, when the man who is taking my pulse interrupts. "We'd like to take you into the hospital for some tests."

"But I want to go home." I want to dry my hair with the loud, hot hairdryer. And when I have brushed my hair, I want to put in my emerald hair clips and have a nice cup of tea and a custard cream.

Lily reaches an arm out to me, and I forget about custard creams for a brief moment, turning away because I don't want her to know how close I am to crying. She speaks as though she is my mum, "You should go get the tests done, you know. Just to be safe."

It feels like she cares. I look at her, her face unusually close to mine. I am almost afraid to see the soft concern filling up her eyes, but she is smiling kindly. "Don't worry. I'll take the kids. And listen, if you let me have your keys, I'll pick up some home comforts and bring them to the hospital."

I swallow back my tears. It's so kind of Lily to offer when she could have been angry with me for spoiling her evening. It's not like Lily to be quite so kind.

INGRID

I often thought of visiting Dudley before, but now I'm here, I'm glad that I didn't. I'm glad I was patient. Dull little town. Its roads swirl through the hills of dark remote tower blocks, all spread out as if the builders hadn't a clue what to do with so much space. If I didn't know where I was headed, this would have been a pointless trip.

But now I know where I'm going. Thank you panic attack. Oh, I don't mean that in a mean way. But it's taken me years to finally get into Helen's flat on my own, and I had to be ready for it, regardless of what emergency was going on at the time. Birth certificate in a Quality Street tin. It was nestling in her underwear drawer and I took photos of all the key information with my phone, which gave me a name and a broad location to go on. Annette at work used to be a librarian and showed me how to hunt through old local papers until I found a reference to the name. Better than a name, a photo. Then, after paying a cheap subscription to 192.com, where everyone not ex-directory is listed, I found April's address.

***

Today I have arrived at a door of squares of amber glass in a criss-cross green frame and I knock the letter box.

This isn't something I want to do. Helen has forced me to do this. How could she lie about who she really is?

A short lady comes to the door, washed out and bitter-looking. Her hair is cropped grey and her bare arms are covered with liver spots. She's frowning that I have disturbed her peace. I catch my breath at the sight of her before I can say a word. I put on my sweetest voice, the voice I'd use with Kingsley. "Good afternoon, my name is Sandra Patterson and I'm researching, well, to be honest, I'm researching sad news stories from the past to find out what happened to the victims, for a sensitive article..."

She falters. I have to suppress a smile because now I know that I have the right place. "You mean Linda," she says and I nod with commiseration.

Her shoulders tumble and her frown clears. I can see straight away that she wants to talk about the past. She wants to unburden herself.

"You'd better come in." She falls back into the dark hallway and I step through the door to a house that still smells of the seventies and am shown into a room with a worn brown velvet sofa. "Sit down," she says.

The first thing I notice is that this room is nothing like Helen's. Not because of the oppressive central heating, or the orange swirls of the carpet. It's the pictures. The room is full of family pictures. There's one on the coffee table, a faded history captured in a rectangle. A man and a woman looking like they have fallen out of the past, posing with a little girl hugging a toy elephant, gazing shyly at the camera under a red fringe of unruly curls.

"That's her," says the lady, April. "That's Linda, and the one with the hand on her shoulder, that's my Bill."

HELEN

Lily and the bees bunch up in my hallway, as if they need to check that I am definitely okay after my suspected heart attack. I don't know what to say to them as they look up at me wide-eyed. "They said I didn't have a heart attack. I'm not old enough to have a heart attack. It was sudden stress," although I have already explained this to Lily on the phone.

The thing is, it's all quite embarrassing to have that fuss about nothing. The doctor gave me a leaflet on stress disorders. Lily had come all that way to pick up my things just for an illness that could be treated with a leaflet.

After a minute or two, Aisha breaks the silence, reaching up to me with a postcard of a hammock hanging from a palm tree, her padded pink coat wrinkling at the elbow. It's taken at a funny angle so that different triangles criss-cross the perfectly blue sky. In jolly red lettering in the top right, the card says *Jamaica*. I turn it around and the back of the card is full of stamps and postmarks. It looks slightly romantic, the story of the card's travels. The postcard says, *Dear Aisha and Ryan, having a great time in Jamaica. Come and see us soon.*

I try to picture paradise. "He's gone already? Aisha only mentioned it last week."

"Yeah, he commissioned the builders ages ago," Lily says, nodding Aisha and Ryan into the living room, her long earrings shaking. "I can't really keep up with them and all the babies, to be honest."

I feel Andrew take even more steps away from us. I have a flashback to the happy Andrew who used to tease me at Lily's house. A new country, a new house, a new family, a new mother-in-law.

I read from the postcard again, *Come and see us soon.* Please don't replace my Aisha, Andrew.

Lily watches me reading and tuts. "Like we can afford to do that." She takes off her coat, revealing another shapely roll-neck jumper in a sort of mink colour, before turning to me. "We had to climb over your new neighbour moving in downstairs. Indian lady?"

"I haven't met her yet."

"There's someone new in the block?" asks Ryan, bobbing back into the hallway in his red hoodie, the pulls of the hood dangling down his chest.

"Maybe," I say.

"Stop interrupting. Grown-ups talking," says Lily.

"Who's moving in? Do you think that there will be a boy I can play with?"

"I haven't seen any boys."

"Well, it is a bit early for the boy to come in now. They might still be moving. It wouldn't be safe to come when he is moving," he says optimistically.

"Maybe, or maybe there isn't a boy," Lily says with a dismissive shake of the head.

Ryan doesn't seem too bothered by this. He marches confidently into my living room. He walks everywhere like he owns the place these days. He is slightly wide. I do mean wide and not fat. And it seems to give him confidence that he takes up more space. "When can we have our sweets?" he whines when he has sat down.

"Ryan, stop bugging Mummy, or there'll be no PlayStation this week." Lily always threatens Ryan the same way.

Sometimes it's reduced to a hissed "PlayStation!" and Ryan always knows what that means.

Ryan mutters exasperated-sounding Romanian that he picked up as a toddler while Dragos was still around. I go and put the kettle on for Lily.

"And speak English!" she snaps after him. I am proud of my half-African, quarter-white, Romanian-speaking grandson.

I smile at Lily who is still shooting evils at Ryan as she pulls up a seat at the dining table, bangles clinking. "Do you remember Dragos?" I ask her, thinking of Dragos's gentleness, and how good he was with Ryan, a different man's son, when he was a baby.

"Of course I do." She still looks like she is thinking of not having enough money to go to Jamaica. Changing the subject to Dragos doesn't seem to help. Lily narrows her eyes above her mug.

"He was ever so helpful, he fixed the boiler when it was broken."

"Yeah, I'd forgotten." She has a distant, faraway look, but also a slight scowl as if remembering a bad memory. "He was a plumber."

"You didn't like that very much, did you?"

"Err… Nope."

"But you stuck with him for a long time."

She shrugs and sips at her tea. "He wasn't fun," she says. "Not like Kingsley."

We watch Ryan take his iPhone out of his rucksack and settle down on the sofa at the opposite end of Aisha.

Then a look crosses Lily's face as if she just thought of something. She looks back at me. "Maybe I felt an affinity with Dragos being a plumber, because of my grandfather being a plumber too."

"Really?" I ask. What a coincidence. "Was that Maurice's or Jenny's dad?"

"Neither," she says meaningfully and looks me in the eye. "I'm talking about Bill."

I can't believe that she's said what she said at first, but then it starts sinking in. It sinks all the way through me, and then it rises back up in a shudder like kicked-up dust. "Someone walked over your grave", someone might say, which always sounded silly because I am not dead yet. But now that Lily has made me shudder, I realise people don't mean dead-and-turned-into-a-corpse. They mean the grave of parts of your life that have been put down and that something is walking over the grave of forgotten things, kicking up the soil and weeds, exposing bare roots. They mean that something makes it feel like your dead parts are still alive.

Lily knows about Bill? She is walking on my grave, kicking up dead things. She's kicking up Bill, exposing him from the soil. She is still looking at me with her arms folded across her mink-coloured jumper. Lily and her chic clothes need to get right off of there before things go really wrong, before bad things happen.

And she looks so smug, a smile hovering in just one corner of her lipsticked mouth. It is not a good smile, though. She has no idea what she has just begun. She thinks that she has got one over on me, that I have been trying to hide a good thing from her just to hurt her; and now she's won because she found it – as if this was one of Ryan's beeping, droning computer games.

She doesn't understand I would never hurt her. Beep Beep Bop. Lily, I told you I couldn't give you happy families. I told you that you should be content with what you have. Every phone call, and every strange car in the street, I thought it might be coming to take me back. I never thought I was going to be taken back by Lily in elegant nails and cashmere. What have you done Lily? What have you done?

"Are you going to say anything to me, Helen?"

Lily's nails are painted ruby red. Just that, no pattern or diamanté. Just ruby red, blood red, and they are filed into points. They look violent against the softness of her jumper. She sips from her drink, looking square at me.

How could Lily know anything at all about Bill? I know she is sly, but I have sewn up every loose thread and tied it down. What thread could she have found to unravel?

Bill must have tried to find me. He must have tried to find me and he won after all this time, and worse, he has found my daughter, my weak spot, the only way to control me again.

Beep Beep Bop.

But if Bill was here, would Lily really sound so proud of herself?

I glance up and the look Lily is giving me explains it all. Lily has worked it out for herself. She took advantage of my heart attack that wasn't, offering to come to the house and returning to the hospital with my Primark dressing gown, which reminded me of safe places. I should have known her game. I thought she was being kind.

Why did I let my guard down? A panic attack is no good reason to let out your secrets. I should have mopped up every last dust particle of the past. A monster could come and kick at the soil around that grave. Maybe not even a monster, maybe just my Lily-Bee.

Life had seemed so good when Lily came and brought me her bees. Lily has betrayed me. These bad times have been brewing since Lily left Andrew and now I think, was there ever really a good time, or more of a good flash in bad clouds? I have found the flash of happiness so great that it blinded me to the fact that everything was still bleak. It had let me believe that they were better days.

Lily is losing her cool at my ongoing silence.

I want her to know I'm not stupid. "You found the birth certificate under the bed." One measly scrap of paper in a rusting sweet tin nestling amongst my socks and knickers, and my grave has been overturned.

Lily unfolds her arms to start waving a ruby-tipped finger at me. "Just admit it. I've caught you out. You were hiding my family from me. Just you admit it." Her voice has gone colder, and more shrill.

"That's an invasion of privacy." Out of the corner of my eye, I see Aisha's head tip up sharply at my tone, a ponytail of braids bobbing with her. I am not going to try and appease Lily today. She's picked the only thing I will not let her win. This is my day to win the argument.

"It's not privacy. It's my family. You'd no right. You'd no right to make me a half person, not knowing who I am and where I am from. And I still…" Her eyes close briefly before she breaks off, but I know what she is thinking. She is thinking that she has still found no clues about her own father at all. That is a different matter altogether. "I thought I was starting to find my home when I found you," she starts again, and she doesn't seem so smug now. "All that time growing up, thinking that there should be *more*, that there would be more when I was old enough to work hard and find out. But you've blocked me at every step."

She has to stop. She has to stop speaking now. Somewhere inside of her is what happened after she found out my real name. Did she just stop there, hoping that I would give in when confronted with my past? But she knows more. I cannot let her say anything else. I rush into the hallway and stare at the bees' coats on the coat hooks. But Lily is in my kitchen, and this is my safe place. Lily is in my safe place and pushing me out of it.

But I love Lily.

She comes over to the door and folds her arms, looking at me.

"You have…" I begin and struggle to finish. I am angry now and I feel my eyes bob violently. There are so many reasons that Lily is so wrong to do this that I can't say any of them, because all the reasons want to rush in at once, squeezing their arguments in with each other, pushing in when the first reason hasn't made its case. She should not even be arguing with me about this. That she has crossed this one boundary should be the end. "… Crossed too many lines, Lily. Get out of my life."

When the words come out, I see how they could be construed. I meant to say keep out of my past life, Lily. Not get out of my present life. How do I take the words back without pretending I'm not angry?

Lily seems to think that this is her day to win the argument. She goes back to the dining chair to pick up her handbag, flicking her braids over one shoulder and hisses, "That's exactly what I plan to do."

I can't bear watching her gather her bees together. How do I stop her leaving? Doesn't she see that we are only having this fight because of what she has done, and all she needs to do is stop pushing to find out about the secrets she has no right to? I come back in the kitchen to see Ryan looking at us both. Aisha's flowery exercise book is in her hand, and Ryan's robot dinosaur is held suspended in mid-air.

"Come on, Aisha, Ryan. It's time to go." Lily marches to the door and waits while they struggle to catch up with her, gathering their toys, the iPhone, and grabbing for their coats. Aisha is struggling with the buckle on the belt of her puffed jacket, and Lily grabs her hand to indicate she should leave it.

"No, please, Lily."

She doesn't even bother correcting me.

Ryan's duffel coat isn't on at all, just resting on his head by its fur-lined hood. I can't seem to find the right words to explain I wasn't telling Lily to leave, so I come back to the hallway to try to smile at the bees, because it's not their fault. I look down at them so that I can avoid looking at Lily's steamed-up face, but my smile is not coming out right, weighed down by everything that is happening. The bees look kind of frightened.

Lily pushes the bees through the door ahead of her. She will turn back, I think, before she follows. I take a breath to say something. I don't even know what it is I will say. "I..." I say to begin, but it's a croak, I don't think Lily can hear. She doesn't turn back. She doesn't even pause. She walks through the door and it closes behind her.

I slump at the dining table with my head in my arms and face against the table. She disappeared on me so easily – like dropping from a cliff, almost too quickly to get shocked.

But my safe place is quiet again, clean of what has just happened. Maybe now Lily's left, the opened-up memories are just a bad smell that can be aired out with open windows, and there's some comfort in that.

Lily hates me.

Bill is back in my life.

***

The walks started a few weeks ago now. I follow the Thames pathway, amongst cyclists, lone and intense, who cycle past in bright yellow staring straight ahead.

All hours of the day are contaminated: in the night-time, it is Bill thudding up my stairs, coming from the sinister screams from late-night black and white TV and the visiting friends that I'd hoped might distract him. And in the daytime, the phone is ringing, ringing, ringing and I know it's her, I know it's Lily. So I escape the flat early each morning, getting away from the phone and from Bill who lurks behind me and getting away from the birth certificate under my bed that awakened him.

I thought I had put him away. Why would Lily finding out his name make any difference to that? But it does. I grit my teeth. How dare Lily wake him up just because she wants to know where she comes from? And then march off, like it's all my fault, taking my grandbees with her.

I will do what I did with my other life. I will forget that she exists and replace her with daydreams of summer days, like destroying Ajax, burning him in the bin until there's just one button eye left. Now it's time to separate from Lily, too, I think, with a nod.

But when I look at anything that reminds me of her, I realise that she is impossible to wipe out. I thought Lily was beautiful when she arrived on my doorstep, beautiful and mine, and nothing to do with our pasts, and she was not a daydream. She was real. Even at work, I find myself in the security office watching the grainy CCTV stills of the Asda aisles, trying to work out if Lily is there, hunting me out.

Do I have to choose between my family and my secrets?

Can I forget that she had pictures of my birth certificate with my so-called parents' names on it?

My walk takes me past the O2 dome to the unpaved section of bleak empty warehouses. I spot old men chatting, their cold fingers around pint glasses outside the Anchor and Hope pub. Their cheeks are red with cold or drink, and they enjoy hearty laughter and warm huddles. They make friendship look so easy. But if you make friends with a person, you agree to spend time out of your daydreams even though the daydreams make you happy, and you open up your heart, although they won't believe they have your whole heart because they haven't got all of your secrets. In return, they will go and meddle in the bits that you thought you could pretend weren't there. They will see all the way inside.

I don't stare too hard at the men on the riverside benches, but they still go quiet as they see me march past, my hands shoved into my pockets, walking nowhere very fast. I don't like old men very much anyway. Bill would be old now.

It keeps coming back to him. I look across the Thames to the slim chimney turrets and silos of the corrugated castle of the Tate and Lyle factory. If I plunged into the steel-grey waves and out onto the north bank, could there somehow be another life there, to start over, a different white flat with bolts on the only door? But this time, if the new flat was just as clean and square, full of no photographs, even that would bring back memories: biological parents, discontent daughters, lost bees.

I have to go home in the evening, because the nights are drawing in and dusk is my most scared time. Before I even take my coat off and have all of my safe bright lights switched on, I hear knocking at the door. I don't bother checking the spyhole. I can tell it's Dylan from the way he knocks. And if I'm wrong, if it's Lily, I'm ready for a fight. I swing it open, and Dylan magnifies himself into the door frame, him and his stench of alcohol.

"Hello darlin', can I take you out for a drink?"

"Go away," I scream at him. "Go awaaaaay."

He stands there like he has been caught in a blast of wind, too scared to move. Somewhere inside me, a calm woman thinks: How could I have known he would be so easy to control after months of being intimidated by him?

"Get out of here, Dylan. Leave me alone."

He flaps his arms. "There's no need to be like that."

"LEAVE ME ALONE," I blast, my hurricane best, but I'm not even trying. I am all hurricane now.

"Shut up," yells a voice from the railings above. The voice doesn't tell the madwoman to leave the drunk, nor the drunk to stop harassing the madwoman. It's all fine with him if we throw each other down the stairs, so long as we don't disturb his peace.

I walk back in and slam the door. I have no idea how long Dylan takes to leave. I pace the floors, trying to distract myself by finding more mess to clear up.

What does she know? What does my Lily-Bee know? What has she told them? They cannot come and get me back now that I am grown up, can they?

***

Eventually I see Lily at work. Well, actually on the CCTV at work, as I look through the reinforced-glass panels of the security office. The CCTV is focused on the soup aisle, the tins of all sorts of vegetables in salty water, and there is a woman captured mid-stride on the screen: black, statuesque, with perfect hair and not holding a shopping basket. I'm sure it's her.

As I lean against the cold wall in the back corridors of Asda, the camera flicks off to look at the bakery aisle, where a pushchair loaded with children's coats has been left near the party cakes, and you can just make out the knees of a booted woman, kneeling down behind the pushchair, checking the price of cake on the lower shelf.

I can't stop staring at the patch of the screen where Lily was, even though it's the wrong aisle now, and the scene flicks to yet another view. And there is Lily again. It makes my eyes hurt, but I'm even more certain this time. Her face appears from the front, with just the hint of the curve of her eyelashes emerging from the silhouette of her profile, just the hint that it's a really elegant face. She's two aisles along from the tinned veg already, so she must be walking quite fast.

I know what Lily is doing.

Because what she's not doing is shopping, she is not pushing a trolley or looking at the shelves. Her head is in a pose that says she is looking around her. She is looking for me, but I am safe here in the staff area, behind the scenes. She is dressed in an angular coat, with shiny black boots. She carries no rustling carrier bags, just her shiny padded black leather handbag with the chain, without so much room as to pack a tangerine. So I know she's here for me, trying to find ways through the walls I've been building up.

***

I don't want to see her. I don't want to hear her stories of my past. I don't even want to remember her after what she's done. But it's my Lily-Bee I'm trying to ignore, and I can't stay away from her, even if it means talking to the past. My legs are taking me out into the public area of the supermarket. I am running through the corridors. I am trying to get to her and I reach her as she enters the sunlight with the sliding doors closing behind.

She has her back to me, and I can't bring myself to call

out as I follow her through the doors. She must guess that I am there in my Asda uniform, she must sense the closeness of her biological mother, because she turns just as I think I have lost her and she stares for a while, before saying, "All my life I felt like there was a missing piece of me, not knowing who my parents were, losing my adopted little brother when I tried to look forwards, not backwards. But when I find you, you're just the first part of the puzzle that doesn't go any further."

That sounds bad, so bad that I don't think that she can be talking about us for a moment. But when I understand what she's trying to say about me, I think it's better than the opposite. It's better than having to share my past.

"It was like my entire life stopped with you, and you didn't want us to know any different."

I want to remind her that she wasn't so angry before Kingsley came and started breaking everybody.

Lily looks around her at the pedestrians clicking their keys at their cars twinkling in the sunlight and swings around to the side of Asda's where the smokers stand. I know I have to follow her.

She's already turned around to face me, arms folded. "At school, I never knew how to explain why I was clearly a different colour from my parents."

"You're black, Lily. You said so yourself."

"Everyone can see I'm half white," she snaps, flashing the eyes that are so like my eyes. She scrunches her fists until she calms back down to her shaking voice. "But it was easy to make people like me, even though it hurt inside that I didn't even know who I was making them like, and I was always thinking, when I am old enough, I am going to find my true parents and it's all going to make sense."

She takes a few gulps of air, and tries to steady herself, folding her arms in her angular coat. "You know, that kid at home with Maurice and Jenny, my 'brother', Goodness. He had this massive scar from the back of his ear to his forehead where the hair wouldn't grow properly. His eyes couldn't look where he focused. He told me he was related to Zulu royalty." She snorts. "His noble family just 'forgot' to rescue him in time to stop whatever happened to his head… Oh, but they were coming soon, and they were rich and kind," she adds with a knowing nod.

Goodness was a boy who Beep Beep Bopped like me.

"I wasn't so stupid, Helen. I knew that I had been taken away from you by social services. And, sure enough, when I found you, you were a weird and lonely old lady. You had more blackouts in the middle of conversations than those deserted kids. But I thought I was part of you, and I had to get to know you to know who I really am. I had more real family than my 'brothers and sisters' from home who only had their fantasies."

"You're right. You do have a real family. Who loves you," I try to tell her, because it feels like she is about to tell me that she doesn't. And it's okay that she thinks that I'm a weird and lonely old lady. It's okay, because all of this is better than uncovering the past.

"But like everyone who I should ever consider as a parent, you've let me down. You're the one who's betrayed me the most." Her voice is cracking. She turns to one side, and leans both of her palms onto a concrete bollard. Oh, the poor thing will pick up germs doing that.

I step towards her and reach for one shoulder, to comfort her, to say sorry that I have lost my past, to tell her I love her. But she swings back towards me, and I know that means I am not allowed to touch her.

Instead, she opens her handbag, and tears out a colour-photocopied piece of paper as if it's a weapon. I peer at it, confused. I know she wants me to be hurt by it. "It's you, Helen," Lily whispers, pushing it towards me.

In my hands, I see that it's me, a little girl in a dress of brown and orange flowers holding Ajax the elephant, with his sharply U-shaped trunk pointing out to the camera. "I knew it was you as soon as I saw it. Your hair was nearly that red when we first met."

My lovely red hair.

"Do you remember when we first met? I've been trying to find out who I am… All. That. Time."

But I never thought that she would go sneaking through my stuff to find it.

Underneath the picture, it says in bold capital letters, *Parents Heartbroken as Hunt For Missing Girl Extends to Reservoir.* It's from the *Dudley Herald*. Dudley. She has found out a lot. She doesn't think I'm from Liverpool anymore.

"Remember that time you were babysitting Aisha and Ryan for the whole weekend?"

That was when I still thought Lily was so kind.

"That's when I went to visit your mum and dad."

I have taken a few steps away from Lily. She does not want me to touch her and I don't want to touch her anymore either. "They are not really my mum and dad," I say in a low voice. Because those names mean something safe. Bill and April were only my biological mum and dad, just as for Lily I am only her biological mother. I think I am going to be sick.

"I went to Dudley to your family's home. Do you remember that house, Helen? I guess it's hardly changed."

Don't knock at that front door, Lily. This is not something that is good to do.

"Scared I'd tell them your secrets?"

They can't come and get me anymore, can they?

She pauses as if enjoying my fear. Why would she be so cruel? "Well, lucky you… I was too scared to say who I was. I got too scared to talk to my own grandmother. That's how much damage you've done to me."

Even though she didn't tell them where to find me, I know things are only going to get worse from here.

"I told the mousy lady who came to the door, who looked like someone had ruined her life too, that I was a reporter looking up old stories from the papers – to see how the lives of the people within them have turned out. I said that I knew that they lost a little girl in the late seventies dressed in an autumnal dress with a white lace collar and bow, a little girl named Linda. I bet they never heard the name Helen before."

I wonder if Lily regretted starting this as she stood there on a doorstep in Dudley.

"April," I say. The woman's name is April. April and Bill. "And how was the tea?" I don't hide my sarcasm because Lily already hates me now and she's done some pretty bad things to me today. "She is ever so proud of those second-hand Royal Albert teacups that she found in Sue Ryder," because April can convince herself sometimes, amongst the doilies, that she is not living in a dinky council house amongst a lot of broken and burnt-out cars. That is April for you, a woman who can turn a blind eye to the worst of things. She won't have told Lily the worst of things.

But she pretended to Lily that she was telling her the worst of things. I can picture her now, sitting there in her beige cardigan buttoned over shapeless breasts, the opposite of Lily in every way. "She showed me a picture of herself and Bill and baby Linda. Her hands shook as she passed it to me. I felt so awful for this woman. I wanted to tell her that I know how much this missing part of you hurts too."

I remember that photo, everybody smiling in their sepia kipper-tied, miniskirted lives. Pretending. Just like Kingsley and Ingrid in the photo above the fake mantelpiece. That was the snapshot of history that counted, the moment that everyone smiled for the camera, not what happened when everyone finished saying "cheese".

"I can see you get your red hair from Bill."

It counts for nothing, your biology, Lily. Haven't we covered that ground already? "She was lying to you," I try to say softly.

"Lying?" Lily spits out, but not at April. "Tell me, please, what part of this story isn't true?"

"Well, not lying exactly…" I tail off. It's that there are bits missing, important bits, but I don't want to explain them.

Lily isn't listening anyway, shaking her head with a scowl on her face. "That poor woman is so alone now. There was nothing good left for her, the childless mother now widowed."

I was a childless mother, too, Lily. Don't you remember?

Now widowed?

"Bill had a stroke five years ago, and then, very soon afterwards, he had another stroke and died in his wife's arms, never knowing what had happened to his little girl."

Bill has died in the beep beep of the hospital, under a clinical blanket with the arm of his good April around him and one hand holding her other hand. I'm sure April wiped away a tear and choked a little on her grey tea as she told Lily this, perched on the brown velvet sofa.

I stare at the weeds in the cracks in the concrete. Dead. Dead means that he cannot come and take me back anymore.

Lily reaches out and shakes my arm, so that I have to look at her instead. "Are you sure you didn't kill him, Helen? Are you sure that he wouldn't be alive right now if it wasn't for what you had done? The stress probably took years off his life."

And if I had killed him, would I care?

There's too much information to take in. I look back at the weeds and wonder how these tiny plants can push out through the weight of so much concrete. I try to look up, but everything except the green leaves is spinning: Asda, the pathway, the sky, as if they are telling me that I don't belong here in the real world anymore. Bill is dead?

Lily pushes my arm out of her hand in contempt. "Have you nothing to say? How many more people are you going to hurt before you realise how selfish you are being?"

I blink. I blink upwards to the blue sky. Bill is dead.

Lily is getting angrier. I suppose she is trying to bring me back down to earth, back to reality, but she's taken things too far, pushing my past in front of me with a colour photo. It's not possible to stay in the real world now. It's serious times like this that checking out is for. Beep Beep Bop. "Are you listening to me?" she yells.

I turn the newspaper cutting over in my hand, and I see that all of this story has been written on the back, written in blue biro on printer paper, with angry lines that slant down, the pen pressing harder, the letters scrunched up and falling into the bottom right-hand corner of the page.

"Argh," Lily's hands fall into the thin air. She turns around to face the wall. She turns back again. Maureen my supervisor is smoking just outside the side entrance, but Lily doesn't seem to care about onlookers anymore. She throws herself against the wall, and makes that small scream noise again. She stays there, her face against the cold brick, for a few moments. Perhaps I could reach out to her again, because she seems to have stopped talking about Bill. But she turns back suddenly and starts to stagger away from me down the alleyway, somehow unsteady on her feet. "You're evil to deprive Aisha and Ryan of their heritage," she shouts over her shoulder. "I may as well have a scar from my ear across my head." She doesn't stop walking as she says it.

She wants heritage.

I put the newspaper article calmly in my trouser pocket. Lily has no idea what heritage she is trying to open up.

I have destroyed so many things through my life. But I will keep the photocopied news story and its bitter diagonal lines.

I want to run away, but I walk. I put one step in front of another so that I can concentrate on my feet, not on what is broken. I walk and walk until it's night.

This is the time they find me crying in the street. It is Deptford High Street.

***

Lily hitting herself on the wall by Asda.

April, still real and alive in Dudley.

I don't know where I have been all evening, but now I am

outside Woolworths. My past lies on my hallway floor in a colour photocopy, my father's hand on my shoulder. Don't think about that hand, the thin gold wedding band, the whisper of wiry red hairs on the fingers, the trimmed nails. Don't think about the hand.

I don't want to lose my Lily-Bee, I don't want to hurt my Lily-Bee, but if I tell my Lily-Bee I will go with her to Dudley and I tell her about Bill, will it really make it as if she hadn't hit the wall in Asda? The only way to unhurt her is through this seventies picture of me with a one-eyed teddy with a trunk, being held by that hand, this past that just cannot be.

Lily has unzipped my past. How could she do this to me, throwing me down a deep well? I am in that fake farmhouse kitchen again, lined with crumbs and dust in corners, because April is too sad to clean up and I can hear Bill breathing next door.

Breathing.

But Bill is dead. Lily said so. That should be good, but it comes crashing back down because it is a bad thing to think that your dad is dead. So what do I tell Lily? I'm glad my dad is dead?

I have come to Woolworths because it always has clever cleaning equipment, but Woolworths has gone. I forgot that they closed it down. And anyway, it's night-time so it wouldn't even be open now if it did still exist. And anyway, I am crying too hard to be able to clean anything properly.

Bill is dead and Bill is bad. It should be good that Bill is dead, but it is bad to think that it is good that people are dead. Sometimes it's good to think that bad people are dead. But it's always bad to think that it's good that your dad is dead.

And who is going to make it all better now? Who is going to say sorry now?

I just want someone to rescue me as I stagger on the cobbles, opposite the glowing newsagent coated in Western Union yellow. But I've never ever found anyone who'd do that, not since I wanted rescuing at the beginning, not since I was fourteen and hiding in railway arches. Nothing's going to change. All I've ever found is pretty colours that you can lose yourself in. But the pink nail varnish and bowls from Turkey aren't enough for me now.

I slam my fists against the glass of the old Woolworths. I shout at my ugly reflection because it's just making things worse, looking at me like that.

DYLAN

So me and Gav and Sal, we have a good night over by the stone anchor on the end of the High Street. Changed round here, it has, all late-night barbers, fried chicken and halal butchers in Jane Austen houses, open all night, but I like that bit. We have great nights so long as there's no shoving. Sometimes there's shoving, but it's all good later on the next day. Got to look after ourselves, no one else is gonna look after us.

Gav's like, "Something going on down the road," and he's right. "Some old bird trying to break into Woolworths."

"'S'not Woolworths no more," says Sal, "shut down when all the banks went collapsed," which Gav gets annoyed about, cos all the banks are still here, and anyway who cares.

But he's wrong about summat else, an' it's up to me to correct it. "She's not old, that's my neighbour, Honey... Helen."

"That's the bird you wanna...?"

"Give over, Gav. We've gotta help." Cos no one else gonna look after us, the government, like.

"What's the matter, lady?" calls Sal as we make our way across, cos Sal's soft hearted too really, you can have some sweet moments with Sal.

"Have a swig of this, luv, it'll sort you out," says Gav.

"Helen, luvee, is that you? Are you okay?"

Helen turns to look at us. I knew it was her, but she don't look too pleased to see us. "Get away from me, Dylan." It's the same voice when she yelled the other week. "You're just like her," she spits out.

I hold my hands up, "Hey, lady, just trying to help."

"You stink just like her."

Not a nice thing to say, I think, but I don't say so, like, cos I can see she's having a bad day.

"She didn't protect me," Helen says to Sal, more quietly this time. Sal is all lit up by the barber's shop, highlights the wisps coming out of her blonde dreads. "She said we always had each other. She didn't stop him. She just hid with her glasses of wine." Helen stops talking, like she has just seen the words drop out and can't get 'em back in, and instead she flings herself against the glass again.

So, right, I feel real bad about this, but she don't want me near her, and she's gonna make herself a mess, cos she's found one of our bottles lying on the floor and tries smashing that against the glass too, but only the bottle breaks and I can see red in her fingers. So, no lies, I really do not wanna do this, but I take Gav's phone, and I slowly thumb out 999…

HELEN

I wake up on a single bed against the wall. Am I back in the little box room I grew up in? I listen out for Bill and reach out for Ajax, but he's not there. And the smell of the room's all wrong. I force my eyes open. There's no Bill, and there's no Ajax. Instead I see worn hospital bedsheets and a second-hand nightie. Oh yes, the nightie that I'd refused to wear last night when I'd worked out what sort of ward I was in. I hadn't wanted to wear anything worn by mad people.

Sun is pushing through the blinds and I sit up, looking again at the nightie which is scrunched up into a ball, half boiled to death since last being worn. I could never have caught madness off that. Things seem better in the sunlight. I can even smell toast.

My room opens onto a large kitchen-diner. It makes me dizzy how cosy the blond laminate furniture makes it look, like you wouldn't guess where you really were if it weren't for the nurses in the glass office in the corner. One nurse turns and gestures to the toast, which is sitting on a plate on the kitchen counter.

I'm a little shy, but everyone looks so content, it feels okay to ask a question. "Is it okay for us to eat the toast?" I ask a girl at the dining table whose chin rests on her hand, as she stares off into space.

"Oh. Oh." It sounds like I must have interrupted her chain

of thought. She shakes her head as if throwing off an unwanted daydream and the curls around her face shake too. She's pretty, make-up-less, and her hair is styled in loose curls. I know from Lily that this is probably a wig or extensions. "Oh. No. I don't know. I can't eat the food," she tells me as if it is really too obvious. "I'm not actually supposed to be here."

"Not supposed to be here?"

"I'm just stopping briefly. There's been a bit of a mix-up." She motions down to her wheeled suitcase leaning against the chair.

I nod, because that seems less likely to give away the fact that I have no idea what she is talking about.

"They're taking me away soon," she adds.

The phrase seems to hook a man passing by. He is tall, with tattoos all along his neck, and a spiky hairstyle, at least where the hair has not already balded. He stops mid-step and lowers his face down to hers on the table, his stubble looking harsh and sharp close up, and mouths at her slowly, "They've taken you away, Anna," he gestures around the room, "*this* is away. They've taken you away and you are all locked up." He tuts and sighs. "*Every* morning," he complains to the window.

If Anna is scared, she doesn't show it. She seems to look through him, her head calmly resting on her hand. He tries to hold the stare for a few seconds, and she just moves her head so that she can look past him.

But one of the nurses calls out from the glass office and he straightens up, before kicking the table, dislodging Anna from leaning on her hand, and walking away.

"Are you okay?" I try to reach out to her, but she doesn't seem to notice anything that has happened.

Instead she looks at me, suddenly bright and clear, and says "What are you in here for?" as if I should reply, murder or GBH, and I stop staring at her suitcase wondering if it is really packed at all.

Why am I here? With the sunlight falling on the softly coloured furniture, it does not feel like I spent the night breaking bottles, and ending up in A&E. I was starting to pretend that none of those embarrassing things ever happened.

"Well?" She leans closer, a small smile trembling on her lips.

I can't say that I am here because I was crying in the street, because if you always went to hospital when you cried everyone would live in hospital, and no one would live in the houses. There wouldn't be anyone left to be nurses.

My mind starts to fizz: *And Bill is dead and Bill is bad. It should be good that Bill is dead, but it's bad to think that it's good that people are dead. Sometimes it's good to think that bad people are dead, but it's always bad to think that it's good that your dad is dead.*

"Well, what did you do?" Her eyes are wide and her cheeks are sucked in.

"I was crying."

"Crying?" She scowls.

And who is going to make it all better now? Who is going to say sorry now?

"Did you hurt yourself?" She comes closer still, like she wants to gobble up all of my answers. I know what she is trying to find out. The thing they said about Mrs Cauldwell when they took her away, when they sectioned her. But I came here willingly. Am I a danger to myself… or others?

I want to smash through the glass at Woolworths, however scratched and bruised that leaves me. I think of scrubbing my grubby fingernails until I have no more nails, no more fingernails. Is that the same thing? I don't answer, but I look down at my bandaged fingers. Anna doesn't notice.

"Or, did you hurt someone else?"

Lily.

I hurt Lily and the unhurt Lily is impossible. "Stop asking me questions!" For a moment I thought everything was going to be toast and sunlight. Why Lily? Why? Why? Why?

"Helen Kennedy?" a nurse calls, breaking the spell, and I breathe out so loud I almost cough.

Anna pulls away from me and turns her face so that I can see it, but the nurse can't. "They're going to test you," she whispers, "to decide if you are a strong person or not. And if you're strong, they'll set you free. Free as a bird." Her eyes spiral up to the ceiling as if watching a bird fly away.

"And if I'm not strong?" I ask Anna and my voice goes high at the end. I don't like Anna anymore; I just need some piece of comfort. But she straightens back up quickly, as the nurse has started walking towards us.

I shouldn't have eaten the toast. I shouldn't have stepped into the ambulance and its high-tech interior, making the crying-in-the-street thing official.

I shouldn't have chased Lily when she left Asda. I shouldn't have kept my birth certificate around to be found.

I start preparing my excuses for the System: I'm sorry. I didn't mean to smash the bottle; my daydreams, you see, my checking out, they let me hide from the past and they are beautiful.

Lily, why did you walk over my grave? Why wasn't your mum enough for you?

MARNIE

In the quiet couple of years after the ambulance doors were closed on me, I continue on my Thameside walks. They are the only thing that get me through while I avoid everyone but the grandbees, still too little to let heritage come between us.

Although perhaps they know about madness.

I can't even guess yet that Aisha will grow up wise.

Ingrid no longer visits me to uncover old stories or dream about lovers. Ingrid just doesn't visit me at all. Those days are over. But she still needs a babysitter, so she sends Aisha and Ryan up from the car without her. They reach my front door, looking bewildered by the new way of doing things, Ryan in a duffel coat and Arsenal jumper; Aisha all prim and proper in wellies with flowers on. "Aren't you all grown up, coming to see Grandma on your own?" I say to them, so that maybe they will forget that Mummy ever came in with them. Because the grandbees are good, the only good things left.

The System fills me with pills at St Thomas's and tells me that I should have a talking doctor, but there is such a long wait of silence and I think that the System has forgotten. Even when a letter finally arrives and I meet with the nurses and doctors, I just nod at them and their advice that makes no sense at all because they only know about my argument with Lily. They tell me to write a letter to Lily explaining my side of the story, not knowing that I can never ever tell my side of the story and even if I could, Lily would never read a letter from me. She would tear it into tiny little pieces and flush it down the toilet. And then spit on it. This part is genuinely obvious, and it doesn't need explaining.

The System doesn't know about the newspaper article that Lily gave me, and the so-called biological mother in Dudley with the Royal Albert teacups. I start to zip that back up on my own, just like I did before Lily came home as my grown-up stolen baby.

I avoid the sight of Lily and pretend to myself that she knows nothing and I hide in my habits and the bottles from the hospital until the images of Dudley start to get pushed back into my dreams. I'm sorry that Lily's hurt, but it's the only way. I look out at the flowing river from the waiting room at St Thomas's and think, time flows. That's all. Grey water moves on. After all, I still have my safety, the lock on my front door, and the grandbees.

And then, two years after the argument, after Dylan leaves the flat opposite, I discover that my life turns into yet another layer of the cake. I just don't realise that things are going to change straight away. In fact, when I come home fresh and clear from one of my walks and my solitude, I stumble into a shopping trolley, and assume it must be Mrs Cauldwell's, the way it stands on the mottled tiles at the bottom of the stairwell, like a flag, telling me that this space is hers.

Not Mrs Cauldwell again. I wince up the stairs, in case she is about to start throwing things.

But as I glare up, I see it's not Mrs Cauldwell. It's an old lady with a blonde rinse in her permed hair, wearing jeans and a tired-looking puffed coat. "Hello, dear," she calls down as if she is already trying to offer me friendship along with chocolate biscuits, like all the rest. She smiles without even realising that she might not like what she finds out about me. After all, I was nearly sectioned once, and maybe only not-sectioned because of "the pressure on beds", as the doctors said.

I shrug as she comes down the steps. "I'll help." I indicate the trolley, even though I don't make eye contact in case she thinks that I want to spend time with her in the stairwell. I don't want any friendship, not Lily's, not the old men at the Anchor and Hope, not this lady's.

"Oh, no, really, it's no trouble," she starts, but I have already grabbed it. It's overflowing with apples, and there is a box, maybe of cereal, jutting out towards the bottom.

She reaches towards the trolley at the same time. I look at her and she looks at me. She isn't letting go of the trolley.

"My, you're all out of breath," she says. I wait for her to loosen her grip so that I can get this thing over with. She sees me looking and raises an eyebrow. "You know what, sweetie? I'll arm-wrestle you for it."

I stop in my tracks and look at her standing there in her all-blue outfit. Maybe it's the thought of being arm-wrestled by an old lady in a quilted coat and trainers, and maybe it's because my lungs are full of air from my walk, but for the first time since Woolworths, I start laughing. In fact, I laugh so much that I have to sit on the blistering floor paint of the concrete step in my anorak to get my breath back between gulps of laughter.

I feel the flush of the laugh filling up my cheeks. How did I not notice that I had forgotten to laugh in two whole years? It must be the drugs. With all that sudden laughter, I would think that I would know that things are changing already, that I have a new friend, but I don't see that yet.

Mrs New At Number Seventeen looks at me smiling and doesn't seem to think this is weird.

"Just a thought, but you could do this laughing thing with chocolate biscuits and tea. It would be okay, you know." She leans forward and whispers, "And your bottom would be a whole lot less cold on a proper chair than on those steps."

"No," I say, with my voice getting higher as it comes out, because I've already tried excuses and they didn't work.

"Fair enough," she says with a prompt nod. But then she starts to sit down next to me. I don't look at her. Her coat presses against mine. I can smell mustiness and lavender as I try to ignore the rustle of the two fabrics meeting. Why is she doing this?

She shuffles about in her fake leather handbag with peeling plastic on the edges and pulls out a purse, unfolding the wallet side where people normally keep the credit cards. She shoves the photo from it in front of my face: two white women, my age, with greying hair and slightly podgy smiles. Both sit either side of a glowing Mrs New At Number Seventeen on a park bench pulling faces at the camera.

"My girls," she says proudly. I look again at the picture. She is very small between her two daughters and I'm taken aback by their ages. Even though it's obvious now I think of it, I'd imagined her daughters to be two versions of my Lily.

"My daughter's taller than me too," I say, forgetting that I don't want to talk about Lily. It's so hard to pretend that a whole person doesn't exist. There are all of these traps.

"Ah, now I can explain this," she says, stuffing her purse back in the battered handbag. "I put my girls on the rack to give them a head start in life. Tall people are more successful, you know. Some say my methods were cruel, but it will come back in fashion, mark my words," she says. "What's your excuse?"

I do a little laugh. "I fed her plant food that was meant for bean plants." Mrs Number Seventeen starts to giggle with me, but then I breathe in quick because I forgot for a minute that I probably did feed Lily bad stuff without knowing it because the flat was so dirty and the time was so confusing, while the fluorescent kitchen light would hum at me, and the clock would leer. Until they took my baby bee away from me for twenty years. And when she returned, she took the side of The Parents.

I hold my breath so that no choking sobs come out.

Mrs Number Seventeen gives me a long quiet look with her pale grey eyes.

"I have to get back to my flat," I tell her as coldly as I can, using the banister to pull myself quickly to my feet.

"Well, my name's Marnie and the nice thing is that I know that we are going to be friends," she says, also getting up, using her naked palms to push herself up against the dirty steps.

She is so, so wrong. There is nothing that Mrs Number Seventeen would want from a friendship with me.

AISHA

My best friend Gina calls me an ice maiden. It's kind of irritating, but I know she's right. In assembly, last term, Mrs Clarke announced that I was getting an award in assembly for "concerted effort in French" and Gina left the hall in fits of smothered giggles. "You're even an ice maiden when it's a good surprise," she hissed at me, turning her mouth down, as we filed out of the hall. Gina's white with a really long face, so turning her mouth down always makes her look kind of stretched out, especially when she's wearing school uniform.

I don't get why the boys fancy her, but I'm her best friend, so I shouldn't think that she's ugly.

Normally we meet at the bus stop for school, but not today. If I walk to school alone, no one can see me crying. I don't know why I want to cry, but the whole heavy build-up in my head just needs to crash out. I can't talk to Gina about Mum's new boyfriend, because then it would be public, which is what I'm afraid of, so I can't tell her about the rows we have about it either.

Before this set of rows, Mum would try and talk to me about stuff, but she doesn't really get me. Like she would say, "Any nice boys in class?" And boys are all right, as in, I mean I'm not a lesbian or anything, but, to be honest, there aren't really any nice boys in class, they are all sweaty and pushy and laugh at me for being good. Gina likes Neil Sanders and talks about him a lot, but I think that he plays up too much in class. I did think that Steven Palmer seemed quite smart and polite until Gina told me that he'd pushed his hand up her skirt as she left geography class. Gina was crying. I don't get it. I don't want Steven to treat me like that, but I can't help wondering why is it that he wanted to do that to Gina and not to me? It doesn't make sense that I wonder that, does it? Gina wears trousers to school nearly every day now.

And I don't get Mum either. I tried to talk to her about why she never talks to Grandma anymore and she just said they fell out and ate her packet of crisps more aggressively.

"About boyfriends?"

Mum looked at me out of the corner of her eye. "No, she wasn't judgemental about boyfriends." Then she made a small laugh to herself. "Unlike Maurice and Jenny." Mum used to come home from storming rows with Maurice and Jenny. I mean, all she does is row with people. Out of the blue, she would make sudden announcements in front of the TV about how unreasonable one of Jenny's suggestions was, or how they had no moral high ground. She'd mentioned my dad. She'd said, "I know you love your dad, but it would be weird if we all started living together now, wouldn't it?" as she walked around the sofa, viciously rearranging the cushions.

"So, did Grandma do something terrible?"

"I don't know." She shook her head sadly. The crisp bag in her hand was completely scrunched up now. "She wouldn't tell me about where we came from. Do you know what I mean?"

I shook my head. I didn't get why Mum was always talking about heritage. I've been learning stuff in school that makes me think that the important thing is about people. I'd like to study psychology sometime.

Mum threw out one hand, exasperated, but I could tell it wasn't because of me this time. "She wouldn't tell me who she was. It's like she doesn't care about us. Don't you think we have a right to know?"

Her voice started to get higher. That could be a warning

sign, so I shrugged. But there must be more to it. Apart from anything else, why did Grandma start to go a bit strange? She doesn't brush her beautiful red hair properly anymore. I still find things in the flat that are in the wrong place, and dangerous things, like hob rings have been left on. But I love Grandma. I move the things to the right places, or turn the hob off, and say nothing so I don't upset her. And it's okay that she doesn't play with us like she used to with old-fashioned games that could even tear Ryan from his PlayStation, or listen patiently to our stories from school with snippets of good ideas to solve our problems. That's all probably because we're a bit older now.

"So she didn't see her mum, and you don't see yours."

Mum stopped her angry stare into the middle distance and smiled. "I suppose I see what you mean," she said, shoving the crisps back into the larder. She went to walk out of the kitchen, before turning back with a half-smile. "You are a funny, serious little thing, you know that?" which made me feel kind of warm.

We don't talk like that since the new boyfriend.

***

When I get into my form room, Gina comes over to sit on my desk before I even have my coat off. "Thought I would see you on the way in today?"

I shrug.

"You heard the gossip? About Kara in form F? She's run away and left a note and taken all the money from her parents' account."

"Really?"

She smiles at my shock. "The police are looking for her. They have to. She's a minor."

"Well, and she took money that wasn't hers."

Gina rolls her eyes at me. "Maybe she had a good reason. It was probably the only way that she could get away from her mental dad." She suddenly turns her mouth down. "Um, sorry," she says.

I say it's all right, but what I want to say is, come right out, Gina, and say what you really mean, because I know what she's getting at. Yesterday, one of Ryan's friends came up to me in the dinner queue and shouted out in front of everyone that Grandma was mental.

Grandma wasn't really mad. She was just going through a bad time, that was all.

I just wish I could talk to her like we used to talk, and I could tell her about all the stuff going on at the moment: Mum's boyfriend; Ryan coming home from his dad's with the smell of drugs in his hair.

"Seriously, though," Gina continues. She's digging into her bag. That usually means that the lipstick compact is about to come out. "You got rehearsals tonight?"

My heart sinks. Rehearsals. I don't want to be at home. I really don't want to be at rehearsals. Sometimes the only quiet place to be is at Grandma's.

HELEN

The grandbees. That's all I wake up for nowadays. At least I have them as I start ducking and diving from all the other people. Aisha's face has started to curve into Lily-shaped cheekbones. She is pure and innocent, nostalgic of the happy-ending days when Andrew was still around. They've given her a part in the school play and I've been invited, with the glossy flyers with cake stands and ladies with parasols and Aisha's name on the line-up list. And Ryan's misbehaviour will always make me laugh. They both jolt me with joy, hurtling towards grown-up-ness.

Today, I have made them hot chocolate to warm them up. I squeeze squirty cream from Asda on top of the hot chocolate and add tiny marshmallows that remind me of jewels. I have bought my grandbees gingerbread men that are not exactly gingerbread men, but gingerbread cat faces, with Smarties as noses and streaks of icing for whiskers. I want to warm my grandbees up from the cold outside. I want them to be happy. That makes me happy.

"Did you brush your hair like that on purpose?" Ryan asks suddenly, peering up at me as he sits down at the table.

I put a hand to my head. I don't know when I last looked in a mirror, but I probably haven't bothered to brush my hair for a long time. There are more important thoughts crashing through my head day and night: *Just admit it. I've caught you out. You were hiding my family from me. Just you admit it.*

They're going to test you to decide if you are a strong person or not. And if you're strong, they'll set you free. Free as a bird.

But something is very wrong with the grandbees. Aisha has not taken her coat off even though it's a warm coat with a pink furry inside and tight cuffs around her wrists, the glint of a green stone bracelet squeezing out from underneath. Ryan's eyes are downcast. The grandbees are uptight despite my love and I am not sure what has happened to make them like this. "Drink up," I say and Aisha sips like I am a con artist, like I am trying to persuade them to drink sleeping pills so that I can steal all of their stuff and leave them to wake up in the dustbins. Does she know about my sleeping pills, my anti-anxiety drugs, my antidepressants, all stacked away in the bathroom?

Or maybe she has just grown too old for gingerbread cookies on saucers.

Ryan looks more keen as he starts to recognise the pleasure of gingerbread scooping up the whipped cream.

Eventually he looks content enough to say, "Mum says we have to come home early tomorrow."

"You're not staying for the weekend?"

"Aisha was supposed to give you the message." He looks in Aisha's direction accusingly and she doesn't even look up. "We've got to go back as soon as Mum gets home from work. She *always* wants us to be at home when there's a new boyfriend around," he adds, as if he is saying, I always have to wear those horrible boots in the rain.

Aisha recoils.

"Is Mum's boyfriend nice?"

Only Ryan answers, shrugging. "Yep," he says cheerily, then steals a glance at Aisha and adds, "*I* think he's all right." There's a faint emphasis on the "I".

"What do you think, Aisha?"

Aisha looks up at me with a worried expression on her face. She doesn't answer or look happy. I look away and pretend I never said it.

After a while, Aisha has drunk only half of her cup. "Grandma, please can I go and do my homework now?"

"Of course, love."

"Can I use the bedroom where it's quiet from the television?"

"You do what you need to do."

She takes the hot chocolate and leftover gingerbread to the sink. I am left with Ryan. Aisha closes the door.

I've hardly had time to ask Ryan how his day was when a loud sob escapes through my closed bedroom door. Aisha is crying? I look down at my own plate, hoping that perhaps it's one of the neighbour's cats begging for food, but as it persists, I know I can't pretend it's not Aisha.

I do not know how to look at Ryan. I do not know what to do. I know he is looking at me, and after a few moments I can't help meeting his eyes. "I shouldn't have asked about Mum's new boyfriend?"

Ryan shrugs as if to say it's not that. He regards me over his hot chocolate. I can tell from the slurping that it's nearly finished. "It's because Aisha's friend Gina says that you have gone mental and that you had to be taken off in a straitjacket," he whispers under his breath.

That's not fair! Things just got a little tough and that was a couple of years ago now. How do they even know about it? "That's not true, Ryan. Do you see a straitjacket here?"

He looks carefully around the living room, just in case. It is empty and clean since the day I lost my bee the first time. There are not many places to hide a straitjacket. "No."

"You see. This is all just silly rumours." I take his plate away, trying to hide the croak in my voice.

"Grandma, my Smartie! I haven't eaten my Smartie."

I return the saucer with a thump. At least if he is thinking about Smarties, he is not thinking about straitjackets.

He picks up the Smartie. It is blue. With his teeth, he picks off the top of the shell. "Don't go mad again," he says, before swallowing the Smartie shell.

"I haven't gone mad."

Ryan cannot even tell that my tone is trying to correct him. "One time is okay."

"I haven't gone mad."

"Joey in my class, his sister went bonkers and then everyone forgot. Except for me, because I am his best friend." He leans back in his chair and looks around the room, as if double-checking about the straitjacket. "Joey told everyone else it didn't really happen. But he told me that it did really. And I stayed being his friend."

I look at him with my not-mad face, but I am interested in what he is telling me. Even Aisha, now crying in my bedroom, might forget?

"You *can* pretend if you know how. Like I pretend not to be mad at Luke when he *keeps on* spoiling football. I curl my fists but hide them behind my back and it does work a bit."

"Well done, Ryan. You're a good boy."

"It's the same with being mental. You have to pretend that you're not mental. You have to be a bit boring, like a normal grown-up and talk about money and business." He leans on his folded arms on the table, the Arsenal jumper wrinkling at his shoulders. "Well, and also, don't laugh too much," he adds. Ryan is ten. Beep Beep Bop.

"Look at me, Ryan."

He does as he's told. His eyes are framed by long dark lashes that make his expression appear even more serious.

"I have never been in a straitjacket. I have never even seen a straitjacket apart from in a museum once." I want to add that I wasn't even sectioned, but Ryan wouldn't understand what that means.

"I believe you." He pushes the saucer towards me. "Finished now." Then, as an afterthought, "Please don't tell Mum that thing I just said about Luke."

"I won't."

Ryan nods as if to say that we understand each other now.

I look at the white wall dividing my bedroom from the kitchen. I want to run into my bedroom and tell Aisha that she has been told lies; that her school friends are wrong, there is no straitjacket.

But I would only look madder than I am already.

I glance down at the flyer for the school play, but Lily will be at the school play too. She will be there, not talking to me and hating me, her head full of Royal Albert teacups and Dudley council houses. My tummy erupts with butterflies.

***

It's Mrs New at Number Seventeen's fault that I see Kingsley again.

"Hello, dear?" calls a cheerful voice with a slightly Northern twang through the door, still wanting to pretend that we can be friends. I know who it is straight away. I think about not opening the door, but I can't help it. "I was wondering if you could help me." She doesn't pause, even though I immediately want to decline. "Deptford Market is cheaper than the supermarkets and I thought I would give it a go. But the bags can get terribly heavy, going from stall to stall, and I would so appreciate some young arms to help me." She lifts her shoulders up as if demonstrating the effort involved in carrying heavy shopping. Her padded jacket wrinkles up as she does it.

I think, "I am busy." But I know it's not true really.

"You're not too busy, are you?" Her voice is generous, acknowledging I might be busy, but assuming I'll pretend I'm not. I wince. It's like Mrs New at Number Seventeen knows what I'm thinking, which I suppose is more than I know. That makes my head crumple up and that makes my forehead wrinkle, and when my forehead wrinkles, it is obvious that there is something wrong even if you can't read minds.

Mrs New at Number Seventeen must be no more than five feet tall. It feels unfair to be so affected by someone so compact.

"I suppose I can help…" but I do have suspicions. I have suspicions because this neighbour telling me she needs help carrying the shopping is the same neighbour who raced me to take the shopping trolleys up the stairs a couple of weeks ago. She must want to talk to me. I am not in a mood for talking.

We walk up the graffitied alleyways to the market and reach the fish stall, where there are mountains of ice bunched up with fish laid upon them. On the floor is a pile of ice with an ungutted octopus the size of a football on top of it. It has huge oval eyes. The eyes stare into the distance. The octopus looks at Deptford High Street in the same way I have looked at Deptford High Street each time that Lily has fallen out of my life.

Mrs New at Number Seventeen is asking me something about Aisha's school play. I don't even remember telling her about the play.

But I'm hardly listening to my new neighbour.

And as I glance up from the ice, there he is: Kingsley, at the other end of the High Street, moving in our direction along the cobbles. How can he be here after all these years? This is my home, not his. Does he know that me and Lily don't even talk anymore? Should I run?

Mrs Number Seventeen's chirping voice interrupts my thoughts again. "You are going, aren't you?"

I put a hand to my head to try and focus. I can't think about both of these things now. If Mrs Number Seventeen were not with me, I would turn around and hide back in my flat, phone my grandbees and make sure that they are safe, miles from here.

I have to turn my back before he recognises me, the loony who was there the night of his arrest. I pretend that I have just seen something interesting in a cardboard box under the long green canopy of "Housewives Cash and Carry", but it's hard to look interested in light bulbs.

Mrs Number Seventeen gives me a quizzical look. She turns to see where I have turned my back to. I know that Kingsley won't know who she is if he sees her, but when she looks straight at him, I feel like she is shining a deep glowing light over us, over my recognisable red hair. Faded but still red. I hover closer to the shade of the canopy.

"Now, who's that, then?" she asks, slowly.

I wince.

She looks back at me. Then she nods, as if there is something really important inside the "Housewives Cash and Carry" and gestures me indoors, following in her blue jeans. I stand there, blinking from leaving the sunlight, trying to see if there is anything useful amongst the smells of meat and sawdust. Marnie starts looking in the box next to the door which is full of control pants as if that was the real reason she wanted to come in.

She waits. But I am not going to tell her why we have to hide.

After a while, she says, "So, you're not going to the play?"

I shouldn't have told her about the grandbees. I forgot that it's hard to talk about grandchildren without mentioning the step in between. I can't be explaining to everyone that the System took Lily away from me, or about turning mad. But I do say, "I can't go. Aisha's mum, Lily, hates me."

"Oh no! That can't be nice for you, pet." Marnie moves away from the underwear, which is a relief, because I wasn't sure she knew what it was. I risk taking a glance out of the window, because it is bright inside, and Kingsley would not be able to see in.

"Do you miss her?"

"Yes…" But whenever I miss Lily, I remind myself that she did go on about the past a lot. It was never going to work out for us, not really.

"To be honest, pet, I really know how it is. My eldest, Nina, she's got quite a temper." She sighs, tapping at a box full of flip-flops, green-marker-penned up with *Only 99p* on the side. She has perfectly manicured nails, glinting in glossy burgundy, like jewels attached to the ends of her old body, because Becca in the flat downstairs wanted to practise manicures. They clash with her old-lady hair and navy outfit, but it's okay really, it suits her littleness. "But grandchildren are the best bits of the whole family thing. They are easier to get on with than the ones in between. Let your daughter talk to you if she wants. Don't let her break up you and Aisha."

I nod. I can feel a lump in my throat, but I know she is right. Even though Marnie doesn't know that Aisha is so upset with me that I've texted her to accept a ticket to the play and then hidden the phone down the back of the sofa in case she never replies. I know that if I don't go, Aisha will never come back to me.

I look outside of the shopfront again.

She leans back. "I think we must be safe now, pet?"

I nod again, because I don't want to talk about Lily and Aisha anymore.

But Kingsley hasn't passed. He is just closer, has stopped at a blue pointed bag stall and his hands are waving all around the place, although I can't see the person he is talking to. I turn around to Marnie, as if she can rescue me again, but as I do so, I see Kingsley jolt backwards.

I take a step back too, has he seen me? No, because he jolts backwards again, and this time loses his footing and falls to the floor. A set of pigeons get panicked and scatter into the sky. Kingsley looks angry. I try to see the man who pushed him, but he is behind the canvas and I can only see his arms waving out. I want to warn him, you shouldn't make Kingsley mad.

Kingsley gets to his feet, slowly, batting away one pigeon that dares hobble closer on gnarled red feet. I wonder what he will do, and this time even Marnie is standing watching, just as silence is settling onto everyone around us too, like snow in the summertime.

Kingsley looks around, but doesn't spot me in the crowds, and then something catches his eye.

It is something that I have seen in Deptford High Street before, the fluorescence of a police car. This time it is just sitting there without sirens and conversation about "quite a commotion on the High Street". I can't even tell if there is anyone in it. But the sight of it seems to change Kingsley's body language and there isn't going to be a fight. "We'll sort this out with the lawyers," he yells, and with a second's glance at the car again, he turns away. The small group of onlookers tries to look like it was never looking. "Ryan!" Kingsley calls, with one hand outstretched.

Ryan? Oh no.

And Ryan comes out of the newsagent's opposite, his hand digging deep into a paper bag, before pulling out a long red and blue jelly sweet. Kingsley grabs his arm, and I take a step forward. I feel Marnie's hand on my shoulder.

"Are you sure you want to go over there?"

I look again, and Ryan has dropped his interest in the brown paper bag. He hangs next to Kingsley and it shocks me. Ryan is like a full coloured shadow of Kingsley, his arms hanging to his sides like his dad's. And, actually, Ryan does not look too upset. Even though Kingsley is walking like his steps are steaming, Ryan is just catching up behind.

Why are they here together? Lily's gone back to him? Maybe this is why Aisha is not happy about her mum's new boyfriend. She's gone back to Kingsley who put my bees in a women's refuge.

No, of course not. Kingsley just has the right to see his son. It's one of those things the System makes happen, even if you think it's not right.

But Lily always had that look in her eyes, since Kingsley. She has it even now, years later. Andrew knew it too. There was always that look that only ever came back if we talked about Kingsley. And there was always something dead when he was away.

Marnie is looking up at me. I glance one more time at the

pair walking away, and I don't know how I am going to figure things out.

"Thank you," I say to Marnie. I thought she was irritating, but she looked after me. She was clever. I don't really have the words to go beyond thank you. "He's someone... someone I don't want to know anymore."

She has this small smile like she understands. Then suddenly, with a giggle, she says, "Hey, could you get me a ticket to the play? It sounds like a hoot."

My head shoots up. She does have an infectious laugh, and even though I don't know why she would want to come, I can't help but smile. I can go to the play and find out. I can see if Kingsley is at the play with Lily or if my bees are safe. "Okay," I say in a voice that I hope doesn't sound too keen, and then I realise that she can't come, not unless I tell her the truth, and I look at the strange old lady who rescued me from Kingsley and I take a deep breath. "But I need to tell you something before the play. I haven't quite told you the truth."

Marnie gently nods, so I know she wants me to carry on talking.

"My daughter. I named her Lily when she was born. But I didn't do it properly. Officially she's called Ingrid. She is not my Lily; she is their Ingrid."

Marnie sighs and puts her hands in the pockets of her jacket, frowning as if she thinks it's all a storm in a teacup. "Oh, pet, I think that you told us the name that means something to you."

And when she says that, I realise I can't remember why it really mattered. Lily and Ingrid are just the same person, and suddenly I realise that now I've explained it out loud, I can even think of Lily as Ingrid. It's a relief. It makes a sort of distance from all the chaos she's caused.

"I always like the bit of our conversation when you crack a smile." She looks at me with one eyebrow raised. "I'm so glad I have such a nice next-door neighbour."

***

At home, I hunt out my phone to text Aisha for another ticket and I find the garish green light flashing to say I have a text. The text says: *Booked your ticket for you. Love Aisha xx*

I sit on my thin blue bedspread with the phone resting on my knee and cry, like I have not cried throughout all the time I was pretending not to be mad. I cry because my little grandbee forgave me and gave me kisses in her text.

***

We are in the bathroom getting ready for the play, Marnie, Becca from downstairs, and me.

Becca has also been adopted by Marnie. She has a pretty petite face. Her eyes are eyelinered deeply, the way that many Indian girls often do their make-up, and she has gold earrings that drop below her jawline. "Becca's the wonderful mum of three beautiful children," says Marnie and I think that I've seen them playing, fine-boned like Becca, like they would break as they argued by the swings.

Becca asks me if I have ever thought about having a bob, "It would really bring out your cheekbones." She has the strongest south-east London accent I have ever heard, stronger than the bees. It's as if she has grown out of the ground of Deptford, between its cracked paving stones, rather than come here as a baby refugee from Sri Lanka.

But the way that she says bob reminds me of the sharp lines that will make me look smart and not like a lady who was almost sectioned, which is not a good look to wear to your grandbee's school play. So, I hide all the bottles from the chemist at St Thomas's before Becca and Marnie come in and let them into the bathroom, Marnie and Becca from downstairs, my friends.

In the bathroom, they both make a mess. There are red sprinkles of hair on the white painted tiles of the floor and patches of water and spilt shampoo making pearly puddles on the side of the bath. "In fairy stories they give away locks of their hair," I say sadly to the ginger tufts lying, soggy and spiky near the plughole. My hair always reminded me of copper, like fresh new 2p coins.

Becca can't help letting a small laugh out, pushing one of her own jet black curls over an ear. I join in.

"Do you think Ingrid will like my hair like this?"

"I'm sure Aisha will," Marnie nods approvingly and she sharply twists up the packet of biscuits that she is wandering around with, as if that's the best thing done with worrying about Ingrid. Marnie is quite dotty, but at the same time she is very certain.

They make me look in the mirror. For a moment, I'm thrilled by the sharp and funky lines, but after that I'm not sure I recognise myself. I won't be able to daydream of wearing the green embroidered skirt walking in the hills with my red hair streaming out behind me anymore.

"We can't leave it like that," says Becca. "We need to balance the highlights a bit."

Marnie glances at me. "Balance out the highlights," she mouths while Becca isn't looking and bites into another cookie. Marnie doesn't do highlights; she wears a pale blonde wash that slightly colours her grey permed hair.

"It's not…" I need to ask this question as Becca is halfway through the make-up, "Well, what's that thing people say about sheep?"

"Sheep?" Becca scowls. "Why do you think you look like a sheep?" She looks at me. "Is it the eyes?"

"Helen means does she look like mutton dressed as lamb?"

I look at Marnie because she makes the comment so quickly and she looks a bit guilty. But I'm starting to realise that Marnie is my friend, like a lullaby, a reason to forget the fears sometimes.

I look at my reflection again, and I feel a fresh blast of freedom. I have control, I can change who I am, I don't have to be held down by who I was yesterday, or thirty-five years ago when things were really bad.

MARNIE

Bit of a pity retiring from counselling. Bit of a pity all round. I loved the job, and then when I lost the mental stimulation, I got the mentals. Well, not that I really agree with that sort of terminology. The truth is that I got confused with bills and had to sell my dear little flat in Clapham and move here to Deptford. But I'm a lucky soul really, with my new warm home. Onwards and upwards. A tiddle-bit of damp in the bathroom did no one any real harm.

Nina wasn't happy about it all, though. There was a stony silence over the phone the day I fessed up. Bit of a growler that one. She didn't have one of the best starts in life and to be frank, that was my fault. I was drinking a lot when she came along. But I know she was only angry that I was in this situation and didn't know how to say it any nicer. "But I have lovely friends here in my new home," I told her. "I'm going to see The Importance of Being Earnest *with heavenly-Helen and brilliant-Becca."*

She cleared her throat. "I know what you're up to, you know. Now you're retired, you're trying to find non-paying clients and call them your friends."

Nina always says it just how she sees it, but it only took me a couple of moments to come back to her. "Like you can talk. There's always waifs and strays sleeping on the carpet when I come up and see you, and don't you try telling me that they're only the garden gnomes."

She did actually manage to giggle at that one. "It's my upbringing," she protests. Like I said, no leg to stand on.

***

As we open the double doors to Helen's granddaughter's school, I see Helen pull back as she breathes in. "The smell…" she starts.

"Wood floor polish," I tell her with a nod, but I can see that it has brought back some bad memory, poor pet. Of course, your teenage years are the worst if there's something not quite right going on at home. But it's best not to pry. I've seen so many Helens with the same problems that I can see what's gone wrong from the off. She's still got to work through it all by herself. She's smart, she's spent long enough looking at houses and trees instead of reading books and having debates that an understanding of the ebb and flow of the world will have sunk into her bones even if she doesn't have the proper words to explain it.

By the time we reach the assembly hall, her fists have tightened up and she's stopped talking, I take her arm to remind her we are grown-ups here now, that that past has long left us, and she seems to snap out of it and remember why we've come. "I wonder if Lily is here yet?" she says instead.

It's all so sad, this situation with Helen and her daughter. What people don't understand is that we can only change what happens now. Helen's daughter would be a happier person if she learned to forgive. I know it's so old-fashioned to say it, but Helen would be too. There's no magic pill, but forgiveness can go a long, long way. Oh, well, there we go. We all have to make our own choices, find our own paths. It's my job, well it used to be my job, to help some find the path, but they still had to choose to take it. "How can you love your neighbour as yourself if you don't love yourself?" I would ask my clients.

Some of the believe-themselves-unlovables would giggle shyly, but others, they would look at me with dark, cavernous eyes as if I don't know what I am talking about, how could I possibly know how awful they really were? But, hey ho, that's what I'm here for – was there for, before I retired.

Oh, I miss my job.

The little lad I recognise from that day in Deptford market marches up to us in the same football shirt he wore when I last saw him and points out where Helen's family are sitting. Helen makes him shake my hand, and he glows when Helen makes him shake Becca's hand, pretty little thing she is. "I'm going to be in all the plays in year nine," he adds, presumably for her benefit and I try not to chuckle. Fortunately, he doesn't notice. "Look – Mum's new boyfriend, over there," he calls out, instead. We all look over. Oh-so-subtle we are not. And see that "Mum's" new boyfriend is a skinny man in a roll-neck top, everything seamless, from his boots to the top of his neck, like that man from the computers in America.

I see Helen look over to him first. And then she looks at the woman in the red dress behind him.

HELEN

Ingrid sees me looking, and I pull my eyes away guiltily, but she is as startling and beautiful as the day she first arrived in my flat. Her dress drapes elegantly around her curves, somehow more relaxed than how she would have dressed up in the days with Kingsley. So maybe that is a good sign. There's more of a swish to the skirt. Her hair is swept up into a braid all around her head, showing her silver drop earrings. She looks like a statue, she looks like a Greek statue, calm and serene and nothing like the woman who staggered away from me at Asda.

I try looking back as she takes her seat, carefully laying a soft charcoal wrap coat on the back of the chair next to Ryan. Her nervous, shy smile has gone and there are lines around the edges of her mouth. For some reason, the new boyfriend is no longer in the hall. There is not even a seat for him. I take in the full view of bee standing here. I'm offering to forget about the photocopied newspaper article scrunched up in the Quality Street tin, the things it made me do, the medication the System still tells me to take. Maybe Ingrid will forget that she feels damaged like her foster brother Goodness, with a scar from the back of her ear to her eye, and maybe she won't ask me to talk about April.

I meet her eye.

She doesn't smile. She nods. I haven't forgotten that Ingrid is arch. If she made eye contact, she meant to.

I smile. It is a shy smile. I've never looked at myself in a mirror when I smile like this, but I wonder sometimes if it looks like a smile at all. At the same time, I make my head hard inside, just in case.

Maybe that's what Ingrid's nod feels like to Ingrid – more of a smile than it looks to the outside.

Thank you, Aisha, for inviting me to the school play, I think. And now I know you are safe from Kingsley.

The lights start to dim, in the hall that they would have held assemblies in, where I wished that the noise in my head would go away, that the lessons would explain things that were happening to me, that they would tell me that everything was okay; never explained why we couldn't accept gifts or lifts, or even talk to strangers. I could tell that there was something that was secret that the grown-ups knew about and wouldn't tell you. And that meant that what was happening to me might not be so normal after all.

Every day I just wanted them to take me into a room, and never let him near me again. Like April should have, I think with fury. That woman who Ingrid thinks is harmless, with her eyes that always slid away from the important things to find out where the next glass of wine was coming from.

I hadn't learned to make my own tune, my own Beep Beep Bop to crowd it out by then. But now I crush it all out, all for Aisha.

***

It turns out that Aisha has a really big role in the play. She is someone called Gwendolyn who wears a beautiful pale green dress. Gwendolyn has a scary mother who likes to tell her who she can marry and who she cannot. In the olden days, when people wore long dresses, it was okay for mothers to tell daughters what to do like this. This makes me snort at the wrong time and I can feel Ingrid getting annoyed at me, even from two rows away. But I can't stop thinking how funny it would be if I could tell Ingrid who to marry.

The characters all have flowery names, a bit like Aisha really. But I feel at home, because the actors are different races, just like my family, so it feels more friendly. Aisha holds herself really well. I don't know where she gets that from, not from me. But she looks like the ladies who would have afternoon tea in Edwardian times in the way that she stands with her slim neck and high chin and I think that's why they gave her the role.

The play makes me laugh, just like Marnie said it would, even though I had been sure it was about being serious. In the plot, it matters that Aisha's beau is adopted. They say that to lose one parent is unfortunate, but to lose two could be considered careless. Everyone laughs at this, but with Bill dead and April forgotten, I am a disaster of lost parents, so it doesn't feel very funny. Things are only okay in the play when they find out who the man's family really is, and when the men are allowed to use their proper names, the names that their parents gave them. Then people can have their happy endings that they thought that they would have at the beginning. This is not going to make Ingrid think good things. I feel a chasm open up inside of me. Marnie squeezes my arm again, but, of course, I never told her why Ingrid was so furious.

***

At the end, when the lights come on and the audience claps, I look over at Ingrid and wonder if I can go over to make a joke about how different the play was from our lives, how funny it would be if I could tell her she had to marry Andrew again, but I don't think Ingrid would laugh.

I wonder about going over and telling her that I have seen Kingsley in a fight. But I don't want to discuss Kingsley with

Lily in case that light in her eyes comes back. Anyway, it wasn't a fight, just a scuffle.

"Would you like another wine gum?" asks Marnie and just then Ingrid stands up to leave. As she breaks away, I feel like I am losing her with a snap, but I can't think of what to say to make Ingrid stay and be my bee again. I'd offer her anything but Bill. I glance at Becca and Marnie, but I have to leave my new friends. I have to get close to her. Ingrid is *my bee*.

I reach the foyer and stand looking around me, daughterless and confused, as parents and children with proper family links between them file out in dark coats. Someone in this mass of children's long limbs and loud shouts must be the one who told Aisha I had gone mad. I feel disoriented, waiting for someone to call out my insanity underneath my glossy new haircut. But as the faces come near, they are clear and happy, and I can't imagine any of them being so cruel.

Becca and Marnie have followed me out. Becca is using her phone to work out the best bus stop to use to get home, tapping intently with two thumbs onto a green screen.

"Wait a second," I hear Becca say in her wide-open vowels, "the reception's rubbish here," looking around at the ceiling as if she can tell where there is good reception by the look of the air. "It's loading, but real slow."

Then suddenly, as we wait, not a stranger's face, but Aisha's face, comes into view.

She is walking quite fast towards me, still wearing her green dress with a daisy pattern and a little high jacket. She looks upset, trying not to trip on the long skirt, but it is not a Grandma-is-mad type of upset.

"Aisha, you were so funny."

She looks at me. "Grandma, I need to talk you," her voice is croaking.

"Okay…"

Becca calls outs suddenly, "Here it is… number forty-seven. Oh… We are gonna have to run."

Marnie raises her handbag to her chest.

I look at her, "I've got to stay." Becca raises her eyebrows but is ready to run, even in her glossy black heels. "Really, I'll be fine, but I might be ages."

Marnie nudges Becca, "Let's make a run for it." She nods meaningfully towards Aisha.

I turn to Aisha as they go. Aisha lands on one of the green chairs with a thump, her downcast face staring at the grainy carpet.

"Aisha?"

"I can't go home," Aisha tells me and her lip starts to tremble.

"What do you mean?" I sit on the chair next to her and lean with my arm around her shoulders. She has to go home. It's the only safe place. I think that I must act like Marnie, who somehow gives you enough time and space to say what you need without being nosey.

"I'm so embarrassed. How could she do that to me?"

"Do what, love?"

"Come here, like on a date, with Mr Laterly." She is finally defeated by having to say this and puts her head in her hands. Even when she was crying in my bedroom and I was in the kitchen with Ryan, she did not crack a tear in front of me. That's not happened since she was seven and she tripped on the steps to my flat and came through my front door needing a hug and a sticking plaster. I'm worried that in her stage clothes everyone can see her.

"Mr Laterly?"

"Chester." She can see that I still don't understand. "Mum's boyfriend, Chester, is my drama teacher, Mr Laterly. It's so embarrassing. And everyone will think that I got the main part because of this."

I suddenly get it. Mr Laterly, Aisha's drama teacher, is the man in the roll-neck jumper. Ingrid is dating Aisha's teacher, publicly.

"They'd have been flirting with each other at parents' evenings. How could they? Who would do that?" She looks up at me. "Can I stay at yours, Grandma? They will both be at home. I don't want to see my drama teacher in my house with my mum. It's so gross."

I want to protect my grandbee, like in the olden days. I feel such a warm glow, like my happy-ending days, but I'm a little bit scared of what Ingrid will say.

"Please?" She must be able to see I'm not sure. "If you have an old T-shirt I could borrow; I can sleep in that and my knickers. That's what I would do if I stayed late at a friend's."

I take a sharp intake of breath. "Be careful staying at other people's houses."

"What do you mean?" she asks and looks at me full of innocence. The quick tears she let go have left lines through her pinkish blusher, and her foundation is streaked. I don't know why they put so much make-up on her. Her skin is fresher underneath the make-up. The real precious Aisha is underneath and the tears let it show through.

But I can't explain what I mean and think about her plan instead. Aisha actually needs me. I could make things better for Aisha and maybe Ingrid would like me a bit more for that. "Well, okay, but you must text your mum, to tell her where you are."

Aisha nods and smiles. She seems to have forgotten about her friend telling her that I went mad. Or maybe she hasn't forgotten, but she doesn't seem to mind anymore.

***

"Did your mum reply to your text?" I ask Aisha. She has changed back into her own clothes and we are walking to the bus stop in the very cold, which turns our breath into clouds. It's a nice feeling in the cold with a warm feeling for someone you love. We are surrounded by small, low council houses, whose cosy lights are gradually turning off in the night. Aisha's school is behind us and its metal gates are closed and locked on its memories and shudders of my old days.

"Mum just said, 'Whatever'."

I look at her in the light of the bus shelter. Aisha has kept on her false eyelashes. They are pretty, but she is fourteen now and it scares me how grown-up they make her look. "Whatever"? I was a terrible mum. Would I have ever said, "Whatever"?

We hold our arms around ourselves to keep warm as we wait for the night bus. We even laugh at ourselves doing it until a car pulls up from the other side of the road. Just a resident from the council estate, I tell myself. But no one gets out. I try not to panic, as I begin to realise that the car is definitely paying attention to us.

I try to move between Aisha and the car. But as the window rolls down, I see Ingrid at the steering wheel, the amber light catching the shimmer of powder on her cheeks.

"Oh, hello." I feel the rush of when we made eye contact in the school hall, but I feel guilty standing here with her daughter, as though I have stolen her. "We looked all over for you."

Ingrid ignores me and looks at Aisha. "What do you think you're doing?" she spells out the words slowly.

Aisha looks up and glowers at her mum. Her face is full of unsaid words brewing that she knows she can't shout out in front of me. I am here and Chester is sitting in the passenger seat. After a while, Aisha says, "You said it would be okay." The way her voice turns up at the end turns her into a little girl again.

"Oh, did I now?" And Aisha says nothing, as if she is being buffeted by the icy glare of Ingrid's stare. Ingrid holds her stare for a couple of moments, before narrowing her eyes. "We'll talk about this at home. Get in."

Aisha turns to look at me. I can't tell if it's with disappointment, or if she's trying to say sorry, and I watch her cross to the back door with her costume swinging beside her in a carrier bag.

I had so wanted to be a safe place for the grandbees when they need me, even if it's Ingrid they need to be safe from.

"You have to learn that the whole world does not revolve around you," Ingrid mutters under her breath as the car door slams shut. I peer in at the dark shape of Chester to see if he agrees, but he just looks embarrassed.

Ingrid hasn't looked at me the whole time. I thought that we made a connection just a couple of hours earlier and now I have offended her through Aisha. Even now, she looks at the top of the leather steering wheel. She moves her eyes as far as the wing mirror and says, "Don't expect to babysit anymore."

"What?"

"If they're old enough to go off in an evening with nothing more than a text message, they're old enough to look after themselves." She makes a move towards the window control, but then pauses, looking back at me. "So they don't need you."

She can't take away my life so simply. To take away my grandbees is an impossible thing. But taking away my bee was an impossible thing, and here is my bee already winding the window up and the image of Lily is replaced by my own reflection. Does Ingrid mean I will never see my grandbees again? I already feel the dread of Aisha's absence and if this is the last time I see her, I want to keep the image of her in my mind, the way she needed me in the cold night. And then the image of the red tail lights pulling away to the roundabout. And then nothing, as I sit in the bus shelter alone.

I only have Marnie left now.

***

Marnie sometimes drops cards or notes by without knocking, but they're not like Mrs Cauldwell's cards. They have silly jokes that make me laugh, lifting me out of the fog of the drugs that St Thomas's have had to top me up with since the school play. This is Marnie's way of reminding me that what happened with Ingrid and the grandbees is not all my fault.

Because, true to her word, Lily has stopped me from seeing the grandbees. Over the months and years, I text, I phone, but there's silence. Marnie tells me to pop by the house, but that's an impossible thing, and Marnie doesn't push it.

"I shouldn't have come between Ingrid and Aisha," I say. What a mess. No daughters like their mothers.

But Marnie is having none of it. "It's all so sad. Your daughter would be a happier person if she learned to forgive." That word, "forgive". It keeps coming up. Then she catches my eye. "She wasn't fair to you, pet. If she can't get over the past, she's best not worried about," she adds instead.

I don't tell Marnie that the drugs make my mind swoop like I'm on a big dipper, bringing up the past, bringing up Lily, taking me through every joyful and crashing step again. Maybe I should tell the doctors and they might give me new things to take, but sometimes I forget that Lily has gone, and that is so beautiful, I don't want the potions to take it away, to stop me from checking out. I do still love Lily. I do still love my bee.

There's a letter underneath today's gift from Marnie, a fridge magnet that says *You'll always be my friend, you know too much* in pink letters drawn like graffiti, even though things are really the other way around between us. The letter's addressed with crazy looped writing, so I know it's not from one of my bees, it does not give me false hope and there is no disappointment when I work out who it's from. Dylan.

I read it just like I used to read Mrs Cauldwell's notes, curious even though I knew I did not want to know what she had to say. It's long and rambles on about cleaning up and not missing AA meetings, which is a good sign for him, but I still find it's like a dirtiness because I don't know why he wants to tell me all this, about his new business "fixing up electronics that he buys at Charlton boot sale", not until I get to the second page and there is the reference to Deptford High Street.

I hope I am forgiven for calling an ambulance on you when we last saw each other. I didn't call the police. I'd never do that. They just turned up. But it's not a day I want to remember to even get as far as forgiving. *I wanted to write because the thing is, I have found it very hard to forget what you said to me on the street in Deptford...*

No. Not this. I stamp the top half of the page down so that I can't see the words anymore. I'd hoped Dylan had forgotten the detail of that night as the cider started to fill up his veins, forgotten how I had accused him of being like April, with a glass always in hand when she should have protected me. But after a few minutes I can't help lifting the page back up slightly to find out why he's writing. *What I've learned in my personal journey is that sometimes people who have been through what you have been through, they find it easier when they forgive.*

This time I slam the white page closed, pulling it with my fists to scrunch it up into a ball. What I've been through? What does he think he knows? Him and his personal journey. He can't inflict it on me.

I don't finish the letter. I click on the hob to burn it, just like Ajax, but when it's disappeared into a flame, the flat is still uneasy. Who does he think he is? And *who* does he expect me to forgive, anyway? There's no one for me to forgive. I have blocked everyone who hurt me right out of my mind.

It's not like being confronted by Lily, but everything is stoked up again, and I'm already dizzy, full of pills. I have to stop myself going down that path again. I know what I need to do. I need to move the tin of my birth certificate and Lily's cuttings out from behind the sink. It just doesn't feel safe there when Lily knows it exists and could tell other people. What if she met Dylan? What if she told him where to find my secrets?

Amongst the Cif, the bleach and the sharply folded J-cloths, it takes me a few sharp shoves to dislodge the tin from behind the U-bend where it's wedged and it nearly cracks open when I do. I sit back on the floor for a second to try and reorient my spinning head. There's a slight ring of rust around the lid, across the picture of ribbons and old-fashioned ladies with tall hats, but I don't want to look too hard at it. When I get my bearings again, I drag a folding dining chair over to the kitchen units, without letting go of the tin. I mustn't let go of the tin, the coldness of the metal creeping through my T-shirt. If I put it down for even one second, someone might find it. It's so hard to remember everything at the moment. So I have to climb the chair with the tin still in my hands, trying to steady myself against the kitchen units, with my free hand.

That's when I slip. At first, I think it's okay because I can hold onto the handle of one kitchen unit, but the door just pulls away from its hinges with a jerk and I fall and everything is in slow motion as I go. I can see the chair wobbling out from under me. I can see the tin burst open onto my clean white kitchen tiles, and I think what a terrible day it became when I opened that letter from Dylan.

Then there is a sharp crack against my shoulder, and everything goes white for a while.

I lie on the tiles, trying to think through the pain, trying to breathe enough to pick myself up with my good arm and get help, thoughts of the day coming through me in waves, and mixing with time and history and names of drugs that end with "zines" and "lines" and "mines". In the corner of my eye, I can see Ingrid's letter, fallen out of its tin, with its violent blue sentences telling me about her visit to Dudley. I hate Dudley and April and the past and the letter, and that's when it hits me, through the pain in my shoulder and the cold of the floor tiles, this is what Dylan was trying to tell me: I have not forgiven April, my mum. April Webb is bitterly, hopelessly, crazily unforgiven.

I didn't even know it.

THE GRANDBEES

The System is always trying to look inside of you. They tried the morning after I last saw Lily and woke up in a mental ward, and they try years later, now that I have broken my arm and shoulder. They have machines for seeing inside of you in a room in the clinical white rectangle of St Thomas's hospital. The System dresses me in hospital clothes and they look at my insides from another room with its own Beep Beep Bop. It's just another thing they do when they are not passing me white paper bags of rattling bottles. Sometimes the X-ray helps the doctors see things inside that they never knew about before. Maybe they see more than fractures. Maybe they see deep secrets.

I freeze up my deep secrets just in case.

I shudder as the nurses tell me that I can put my own clothes back on and make my way out of the windowless room with a black and white poster that tells me that I don't need to be ashamed if I leak a bit, and I wish there was a poster that told me that I don't need to be ashamed of all sorts of other things. But there is no such poster, so maybe I should carry on being ashamed.

When the door to the X-ray closes behind me and I am back in reception with the daylight pushing through the metal-framed windows, I know that I don't have to think about secrets anymore. I am still holding my worst secrets down, despite Lily's investigations all those years ago. No one has found those secrets.

"Hey, Grandma."

I jump and turn around to the teenage figure leaning against a column, who I had just walked past. It still surprises me to see her, thinking that the day Becca sent her to find me was one precious memory to keep and play with. "Aisha?"

She's wearing her school uniform of a yellow shirt and brown cardigan, which is not quite the regulation brown. She wears a necklace made of large red triangular stones. It's too garish for the uniform, as if her real personality is trying to burst out from under it. She comes over to me, pulling one headphone out of her ear. "I got signed off school."

"I'm so glad to see you." I really am.

"It went all right, though?" she asks. She looks worried by just how pleased I am to see her.

I blink. I can smell bleach from the mop in a cleaner's hand in a corner of the hospital reception. The speckled floor shines where it's wet, and phones chirrup in the reception area. The sharp smells and sounds take me out of my memories and wake me up to where I am. "It was fine," I pause, because I realise it sounds like I am saying it's all right in the way people do when they are not going to tell you anything deeper. "It really is fine. Just checking that the fracture is healing and that no other damage is done."

Aisha looks relieved, then she looks sheepish. "I need to talk to you about something." She breathes out slowly and looks to one side. "I'm not sure you'll be all right about it."

"Okay?" I can't think how Aisha could ever upset me. Is this about the kids throwing stones? She swings her school bag from her shoulder, and pulls out a white A4 envelope, before pushing it into my hands. There is something about its scruffiness, the not-quite-straight seal down on the gum and the wrinkled edge from Aisha's bag, that tells me that it's not a get-well-soon card.

I look at Aisha. Her hands are back in her pockets and her head hangs down. "I just wanted to say, firstly," she indicates the direction of the canteen with her head and starts towards it, "it was Mum who signed me off school."

I have never told Aisha that Ingrid hates me. That would be bad for Aisha and I know how to keep secrets. So I don't know what to say to Aisha, because suddenly my need to hear why Ingrid cared enough to write a letter to school is echoing in the canteen, bouncing off the till and the bright bossy chocolate wrappers. I look at the TV in the corner with no sound. Does Ingrid still hate me? I smell hospital-cooked pizza and wonder, does the letter to Aisha's school mean it's all okay? My mind goes in strange swirls these days.

"I think she might come and visit you sometime." She pauses to pick up a tray and puts an egg and cress sandwich on it, without glancing at the label. She is staring at the melamine tray as if she is trying to find the right words. "But not right now. She has a lot on. Think she's had a few appointments with Ryan's dad, or something."

"Kingsley?" Him again. "Why's she doing that?" I can't help my voice going high at the end. Why am I hearing this man's name so often? Maybe that is because there are still questions and guesses and suspicions that make you want to hide. I can't meet Aisha's eye; I'm scared that some facts or guesses will spill out.

Aisha shrugs. "I don't know. It's just that..." She looks out into the distance behind me. She is not going to say what she is thinking. She has secrets too. Different ones, I think. She turns back to the rows of sandwiches. "I'm so sorry, Grandma. I know that Mum rowed with you, but I don't know why me and Ryan stopped visiting much later. That was wrong."

"No, Aisha," I start. "I made friends with my neighbours."

"Yes. But you shouldn't have needed them. *We* should have been there."

"You've spoken to your mum?" It seems better to admit that we fell out so that I can put my energy into moving us away from Kingsley and all the horrible things I don't want to remember about him. I hug the envelope to me, rather than pick up a tray of my own, not wanting to take my attention from Aisha.

Aisha seems to shake herself out of her sad mood. "You know, I think that Mum's not so angry anymore."

"Really?"

"But she did explain what happened."

I hold my breath.

"She doesn't know about, umm… the building next door," she adds, like we should probably keep it that way. "But the other stuff, like what you argued about. There just seem to be so many broken links," she says sadly, putting her hands in her pockets and adopting her teenage hunch again. She looks up and nods at the envelope that I'm holding. After a second or two, I realise what is inside of it and I feel disgusted. "Your family's contact details."

I have been holding it close to my body, not knowing how contaminated it was. It must take so little paper to hold such small information, but now it's heavy in my arms.

"It's just in case," Aisha continues quickly. "I don't even know what happened that you don't talk to your mum." She peters out for a moment. "But I thought one day you might want to talk to her again."

It feels unfair on poor Aisha, to return the envelope to her, but I can't stop myself from shoving it quickly into my Asda bag for life. I know that it's the same woman, the same house, the same fear of Bill. Can anything about April have changed?

I look up from my bag to Aisha's anxious face. Despite her uniform and loud necklace, the seriousness makes her look so grown-up. I remember Aisha complaining that everyone is hiding things from her, but that was about Kingsley, not this. Is she looking for the answers to different questions now? I could tell Aisha every last poisonous drop of the abscess that has been hidden inside for so many decades. And I must not do that. I never should do that. Aisha does not know enough of the world. She would go chaotic.

Instead I pick up a tray for myself and fill it with Coke and Lucozade and Victoria sponge slices in plastic containers. She watches me, and gently puts the egg sandwich back on the shelf. We go to sit down.

"Grandma?" She pulls a chair out next to me.

"Yep?" I'm relieved that it sounds like we are going to change the subject.

She takes a while to find the words, pulling and releasing one of her curls like a spring. "Why wouldn't you tell Mum about your family?"

There is a long silence. It is hard to come out with any words at all with my drug-fried brain. "She never asked." I'm not lying. It's not Ingrid's style to ask straight like Aisha just did. She asked around the subject. She dropped hints. She searched through my underwear when I had a suspected heart attack, and even yelled at me for telling her nothing, but she never said, "Where are your parents? Who is my father?" I could not have told her the truth when it was nothing like what she was expecting, nothing at all. If I had, she would have been angrier.

"Would you have told her if she asked?"

"Maybe not."

Aisha is quiet. I am scared. Because her world is so black and white. There is wrong and there is right.

"Don't you love us?" she asks quietly.

Her hand is frozen, half grabbing at another curl. How could she possibly think that I don't love her? If this was Ingrid, I know she would be trying to manipulate me, but Aisha is more direct. She looks back at me with waiting, fearful eyes. Is this what my grandbees have been worrying about all of these years? Is this why they stopped seeing me?

"Maybe I don't tell you because I love you?"

"Oh," she says, letting her hair go and reaching instead for the ring pull on her can of Coke. She adds nothing else. I scoop slices of Victoria sponge with a plastic fork, listening for her explanation. But she doesn't say anything, just sips at the drink.

I have to ask as I press my fingers into the last crumbs of sponge, "What does 'oh' mean?"

"Well, I just hadn't thought of that."

Suddenly the worry is all over. How can it be possible to know that Aisha trusts me with such a small insignificant word as "oh"? But Aisha does trust me after everything that has happened.

Then I remember something with a thump. "Did you tell your mum about the kids throwing stones at you the other day?"

Aisha looks sad, and I see her swallow, but I think she agrees, that she will tell her properly this time.

***

On my dining room table is the white envelope that Aisha gave me, full of the past, full of what broke up my time with Ingrid for good, and almost got me sectioned when Ingrid said she'd found her, *that* poor woman alone now, the childless mother now widowed.

I realise that I need to ask Marnie a question. It's a difficult question, but I need to know the answer. When I knock at her door, Marnie gestures me in and to sit at her table. Now that I am here, I don't know how to start on the serious stuff.

But I forget. This is Marnie. She just fills the room with safe chatter, rich and warm. "Well, poor Becca," she begins as she fills a brown teapot with Yorkshire teabags, more than two. "Her eldest is being bullied at school. Can you imagine? And her being the eldest, the youngest is getting quite upset that they will start on her next. She's spoken to the form teacher, and she doesn't seem too bothered, seems to almost be telling her that it's Yasmina's fault."

"They're probably jealous because she is so pretty," I say.

Marnie stops for a moment. She was taking the milk out of the fridge to pour into a glass jug on the side. "Yes. She is pretty. Becca's parents are Tamil, I think. They had a bad experience in Sri Lanka and had to move here very quickly, no personal possessions."

Like me. I left everything behind and shelter now in a concrete flat that looks so ugly from the outside, but provides safety and protection on the inside.

Marnie sits down. Everything is laid out neatly on the table. Doily with biscuits, no plate. Chipped jug with exaggerated curves and cubes of sugar in a white bowl with a blue stripe. I tell her things myself. I tell her how I have seen Aisha again after all these years; that it's not just that she seems to want to know about my past, or even her past, but she seems to want to know me. Whenever Aisha asks about the broken shoulder, I say I fell off a chair trying to sort out some of the stuff on a high shelf and she tuts and says this is why she should never have lost touch with me. I feel safe, like I really can ask. While Marnie is concentrating on pouring the tea, I gather my bravery.

"Can I ask a question?" I eventually manage.

"All questions are permitted from now on," she says, dramatically putting the teapot back on the mat. "Might not answer them," she adds with a nod and a scrunched-up nose. But I think she will be all right with my question.

I shift uncomfortably on my seat. I look around the room, my head whizzing with the fact that I have started. Here and there are stuffed toys and teddy bears and lots and lots of stacked opened envelopes with their contents replaced as if they are organs that should never have fallen out. That is what life is about, things that have fallen out that need to be put back in again.

I have to work out how to ask a question that won't tell Marnie everything, that won't make my whole true story fall out, not just the Ingrid bit, but the Bill bit. It's about that letter I got from Dylan, after he had cleaned himself up and thought he knew everything there was to know about everyone, especially me, who had shouted out so much on Deptford High Street.

Dylan had his fingers on a piece of thread and if he pulled at that thread, like he tried to, by telling me to do this forgiving thing, the whole sorry truth could unwind and fall out. I don't want to fall out.

So I ask, "Do counsellors tell people to forgive people?"

Marnie takes the question as if I am asking her what is the best thing to do if my pasta sauce turns lumpy on the hob. "Well, they don't really tell people what to do. What makes you think that they do?"

"Someone once, who was in this flat before you said something; I think he had a counsellor, and he said that things are easier when you forgive."

"He's right about that," says Marnie, even though she doesn't know anything about what I have to forgive. She seems to think the statement will cover everything. Should I apply it to April, even to Bill? I cannot start on forgiving Bill yet.

Suddenly I want her to ask what I need to forgive because I just don't seem to be able to keep hold of my bees without this. That is why I am letting Marnie see inside. I feel dizzy, light-headed. I wonder if I have asked my question right, but when I think over it again, it feels like I am making a big fuss about nothing.

I eat one of the chocolate biscuits. I crunch it in small bites around the edge and then finish it off properly. The sugar seems to fill my veins and restore what energy the letting go of little bits of secrets has washed away.

Marnie does not react at all, so I can see the counsellor in her. And I can see the reason why she came and asked me to help with the shopping even when she really did not need help with the shopping.

"How do you know if you have forgiven someone?" I look at the doily for a distraction, taking in its clever curves and holes in a way that I wouldn't normally.

Marnie shrugs. "When you stop feeling bitter, I suppose. When you stop asking for things to be repaired."

Bitter. I don't know if I feel bitter about anything. I don't feel good, I know that. "Sometimes there are too many feelings to know if you feel bitter."

"I know." She is totally still.

Bitter is the feeling somewhere in my stomach right now when I look at the biscuits, feeling sick. Am I bitter elsewhere? I could be bitter about Ingrid for leaving Aisha's dad, when they were happy, for finding Bill and April. I sip my tea. I have left it a bit late. It is lukewarm.

And yes, there is a bitterness about April too.

Outside, an ice cream van starts playing his tune. Then I remember something. "You forgave me for being unfriendly when we first met."

Marnie does a little giggle and reaches for another biscuit, as if she had forgotten and now it's a funny memory. I realise Marnie's giggles are never laughing at me, they burst tension, like popping bubble wrap. With Marnie's help, I wonder if I could just about work this thing out.

I have decided that I want to start with forgiving Mum. Because this makes sense. And forgiving Mum does feel good, like a heaving nightmare lifting off me, like taking away a huge amount of worry about why and what if, and what did I do wrong for all of this to happen to me.

"I miss counselling. I miss helping people," Marnie says, looking at me sadly.

***

"Hello," says the person who has just called me on the other end of the phone.

There is a second's pause. Is it that I recognise the pause, or was there a breath in the pause that was familiar? Because I know exactly who it is, although I daren't say anything until I hear it.

"It's Ingrid," says the voice.

I try to hold my breath, to sound cool, as if I am pretending that I'm not scared. Ingrid doesn't wait for me to answer.

"Aisha told me what happened with these kids throwing stones."

"I'm sorry."

"And I will sort it out. This is a hate crime, and they won't be getting away with it."

I don't know what to say.

"And thank you," she adds. Then she clears her throat. "I'm sorry your day was ruined. We were thinking of going for a picnic this weekend?"

***

Now everything is changing. I'm being driven up Blackheath Hill in a ten-year-old convertible Mercedes and the Sun has started to come out – forcing its way through the leaves of the trees. There's a huge queue of traffic, which lets you stop and gawp at the large, elegant old-fashioned houses, hidden behind red-brick walls and shrubbery. If I lived in one of those houses, I could have a bedroom for me and a bedroom each for Aisha and Ryan, and a bedroom for Ingrid, and more for every one of her beaus.

And the reason, I have to say, that I am thinking like this is because Ingrid is sitting right next to me driving, streaks of grey in her ponytailed hair. And she's smiling. Like she is doing something good.

I thank Aisha, and maybe even the broken shoulder? A good thing can come from a bad thing. The bird wasn't worth the mention, but the bee was beautiful.

I can feel Ingrid smiling next to me though. I can hear her breathing as I try to calm my own breathing down. I'm still woozy with drugs. Aisha made me sit in the front, which was a bit intimidating because I am now sitting right next to Ingrid in her long lace T-shirt and leggings. Does this mean I'm forgiven? Has the past all been forgotten? I stare at a scrunched up sweet wrapper in the glove compartment. Maybe Ingrid doesn't actually hate me. She's just been unhappy with me for a very long time.

"I got 86 per cent in my maths test, Grandma," Ryan says as the traffic gives and we can go forwards again.

"Well done."

"Mr O'Bryan says that if I had gone back and checked my answers, I could have got even more."

"Will you do that next time?"

"No, I'm just saying. I could have got even more."

"I bet you and me would have had 100 per cent in our maths test if we'd checked our answers, wouldn't we, Helen?" says Ingrid, raising a well-groomed eyebrow. She is even cracking jokes. I sneak a look at her from the corner of my eye because she is driving and hopefully looking at the road so she won't know I've done it. I need to calm down. I thought that we could make friends when we went to the play together, and look how that turned out.

***

"Do you want to watch YouTube videos on my iPhone, Grandma?" Ryan asks as we settle down on the picnic rugs in the park.

I look at Ingrid. "He can watch TV on his phone?"

Ryan shuffles to kneel next to me and starts to show a film of a crocodile being eaten by a python, while Ingrid starts unpacking food from M&S carrier bags that flutter in the breeze. Ingrid's nails are unpainted, and I wonder if she still gets manicures that are like stories all on one fingernail anymore. I wonder if I should say sorry for everything that happened, for avoiding her, for making her stagger away from me by Asda's, but she looks calm – like that history is all part of who she is, but it's okay really.

I try different words in my head that might be right, but Ingrid turns to me instead. "So, things have been tough lately?"

I nod.

"Aisha's spent ages choosing food she thought you would like."

I smile and pick up a chicken wing. "That sounds like Aisha."

Ingrid stays by me, doesn't move away, so I know it's okay to make casual conversation. "How's work?" I ask her, because I don't want the conversation to stop.

"Oh, yep. A story in that." She places her knife on her empty plate. "They're making me redundant," she says, matter of fact.

The System is dropping Ingrid? But Ingrid is made for the System, with her calm elegance and control. The one thing I always relied on was that Ingrid was able to look after herself.

Even if I never saw my bee, I could know she was safe. What will she do now?

"Well, not a bad story. It's okay, really. I've got plans." She winds the plastic seal off a box of mini Swiss rolls and pops one whole into her mouth.

"But you have children to look after. Why would they do that to you?"

"It's just these austerity measures." She brings her hand to her mouth, removing a little shimmery brown lipstick. "Relax. I'm fine. They pay you off."

I can feel my voice getting higher. "But you still have to live."

I see the old irritation flash in her eyes. "It's fine. Really."

I try to arrange myself in a not-worrying pose, remembering how often I've worked on it in the past: meeting Andrew at dinner; meeting baby Aisha; meeting Lily when she came back with Aisha from the women's refuge. Which I had forgotten about, actually, and I shudder.

"Please, Helen. Look after yourself. I'm not just being nice. I have it all sorted. Please trust me."

I think that we have been there for a couple of hours, even drinking Prosecco out of cardboard cups with pictures of ribbons along the edge, when Ingrid's phone rings. She walks away from us to take it. I look over at her from my seat. She looks so sophisticated, having the conversation on the phone in her sun hat, blinking her wide oval eyes.

"It's Kingsley, on the phone, with Mum right now," Aisha says, nodding her curls towards Ingrid. "I saw the name flash up as he called."

"Oh." I keep forgetting that they need to talk to each other, Ryan's parents.

"Why 'oh'?"

"I thought, the way she looked, that she might be talking to a new beau, not an ex."

"Yes," says Aisha.

"You know I saw him in Deptford market a couple of years ago," I tell her. "With Ryan." I glance over to where Ryan is sitting. He is balancing eating a chicken drumstick whilst pressing buttons on his phone by the monstrous, half-dead trees, the width of my little round dining table, with curling bark racing off in all directions.

"Oh, yeah. Mum said he'd hunted out his old business partner there, the one who'd tried to get him in trouble for something, ages ago."

"That would explain it."

"He's just won a case against him, and actually made a lot of money out of it. So he acts even more like the 'big man'. He's bought some snazzy place in North Greenwich and buys Ryan expensive things, like that phone."

"Do you mind?"

"Not really." She pulls at some tufts of grass. "I don't care about things. I care about people and doing the right thing."

She's not lying. I lower my voice to a whisper. "Why do you keep asking me about him?"

She says nothing for a while, pulling more tufts as if she's preening a pet. Then she shrugs. "I dunno."

See. I am not the only one to have secrets.

***

I go back to Marnie with another question, about how Ingrid always seems to think I am having a go at her even though I am forgiven now, how I always say the wrong thing, how maybe this was why the social services took my bee away from me, they knew I would be so terrible as a mum.

The walls of Marnie's flat are no longer yellowed with Dylan's cigarettes. The paint is quite fresh. In the hallway and kitchen, there are things hanging on the wall that aren't just pictures, like there is that famous picture of the *Hay Wain*, but with a clock in the corner where the sky is, which I like because it means that you can have something that is pretty and useful at the same time.

She smiles and squeezes my arm. "She sees you as her real mum," she says.

"I don't understand."

She turns her chin up slightly before explaining, "That's how daughters are with their mums. Because you're close, you see the worst of her. She trusts you, pet. See?"

I frown at Marnie.

"Believe me, I made the mistake of reading Nina's diary once when she was a teenager. Shouldn't have done that."

I still don't understand, and I wait quietly for Marnie to explain, because that's how she works. She pauses, just in case, and then explains, like she knows that my silences are just questions I can't work out how to ask.

"I mean, she hadn't exactly plotted my death..." she pauses before sipping at her tea, "but I was left with no doubt that Nina had the celebration party for my demise already planned."

"No!"

"Things weren't good when she was little," she says mildly. "I was drinking a lot. I made a lot of mistakes."

But surely Marnie cannot have made mistakes as bad as mine?

"It's families, Helen," she says in a soft voice as she pours more tea. "I'm not saying it's right, or nice, but we want more from each other than we can give sometimes. We're angry when they are not perfect, or can't read our minds because they normally give us so much. Don't worry. It's easier with the grandchildren. I always got on with the grandchildren better."

Worry? Why would I worry? Ingrid views me as her real mum? This is beautiful, this is amazing. After all these years I thought she hated me, and actually she was just being a delayed teenager.

"You remind me of marmalade," I say. And it's true, because it's a bit like her name, and marmalade is comforting and homely. But after it popped out, I wonder how I thought that it was okay to say that. I pretend to be really interested in the crumbs on my plate.

Marnie smiles at me. "Helen, you're the one the with red hair. You're the one like marmalade."

And we both have a good giggle at that. Which is what she always told me we would do when I met her.

***

I call Ingrid when I get home, after Marnie-Marmalade has helped me again.

"What do you want? I'm at work," Ingrid barks.

"Nothing, just saying hello," I say.

She seems confused. Her voice softens and she says, "Is there something wrong with the medication? Do you need any help?" But I say it was nice to hear her voice and I will catch up with her later.

She sees me as her real mum.

***

Aisha hugs me right in the middle of the hospital waiting room in front of all the people who are still ill and try to look like they are not looking at us. She hugs me because they have taken off my cast, leaving my pale and floppy skin out in the daylight. Aisha's hug is a formal hug. Aisha is not a hugging type of girl, but you can see that she thinks it's important. It's the school holiday, so she's wearing skinny jeans and a thin jacket. She refuses to talk to me about what happened to the bullies, because she says that today is about me. She says, "I've saved up some money to go out and buy you a cake and coffee to celebrate."

She takes me to one of those posh coffee shops that everyone says they love, which are all brown and red leather inside.

Aisha buys me a frothy coffee and a slice of cake made of red sponge and icing. I am touched by this gesture. She is a good girl, Aisha. My heart is racing from the freedom in my arm, and the hot rich coffee makes it beat faster. I feel light-headed. Aisha says that my cake is called red velvet cake, and I can see that it must be made with red dye, which seems a bit silly because that can't possibly change the taste, even though the taste is really, really good.

She has something on her mind. Earlier, in the waiting room, she flicked through the pages of a women's magazine, swiftly and firmly so that I knew she wasn't reading it properly. Those magazines are only trying to sell you stuff anyway. And Aisha doesn't believe in buying that sort of stuff. Now she plays with her millionaire shortbread, staring around her at the people with slim silver laptops or tapping into their phones. I want to tell Aisha to be happy now. She and Ryan and Ingrid and me had a good time together in the park. I even called my girl Lily-Ingrid in my head, so that she is kind of mine and kind of her own Ingrid. And Marnie and Becca, my neighbours, are my very good friends. I think of a sailing boat leaning its sails across a calm blue sea.

***

But what I am forgetting with all the rich milky coffee swirling inside of me is that this is what is called The Calm Before The Storm.

Here is something I have started to understand: Marnie says that even though good things can end, bad things can come to an end too. So even though there is another storm coming and things will be bad, they are not The Way Things Are. So I need to brace myself.

The storm is coming here in this coffee shop right now. It is coming in the form of Aisha, who empties a sachet of sugar into the stiff cream of her hot chocolate and says, "I really need to know why Mum left Kingsley."

"Why, what's going on?"

She pauses before putting her spoon down. She's shaking. "Please tell me."

I can't tell her. And I certainly can't tell her in public, in front of the baristas and chalked-up drinks menu and piles of croissants.

But her face is determined. I lean across the table; her head has fallen to her hands. I quickly glance around to see no one is watching and touch her arm. "What do you remember?"

"That I hate him. I hate him because of Mum, and I'm scared of him."

"Okay." I stall for time. "Why do we have to talk about him then?"

She looks up at me, her face streamed with tears, but she is trying to hide it from the other tables. "Can't you guess? I thought you worked it out at the park."

"Pardon?"

"She's going back to him," she leans in to whisper to me, one hand clutching one shoulder. "They're getting back together. She's asked us to pack up back home and move in by the end of the week now that my exams are just over."

"She's going back to him?"

Aisha is looking at me when she tells me. She can see that this is the most terrible thing I can think of. Her brown skin seems to have gone grey. How will I not be able to tell her the truth now?

"There is something, isn't there?" Her set jaw says she is more determined now.

I don't know enough. I only know what I believe. I remember with a sharpness the days before Lily fell out with me, when I still hoped that she would get back with Andrew, before he had a brand new family of his own in another country. And the night that he was trying to look after Aisha with a broken rib.

"What happened?" Aisha prompts me again.

I think back to that night that Lily was in the women's refuge. I worked out what had happened at Ingrid's when I went to Andrew's new flat. Should I have done something more? But I couldn't prove a thing. "What happened" sent my mind round and round in circles, trying to convince myself that I knew enough to go to the police, and when I couldn't, I tried to convince myself that it really wasn't that bad. Until it was better to leave the whole experience buried with Bill and April, something that couldn't hurt us anymore anyway.

I start to lose myself in the memory of that night.

"Grandma?" Aisha prompts me.

I realise I have been staring into space. Teenage Aisha and I are still in the Costa coffee shop in the glass circle outside Charlton's M&S. She is so different and so much the same as the toddler on the sofa that night at Andrew's.

Aisha carries on. She can see that I am frozen with fear about the right thing to say. "I remember being at the top of the stairs," she says.

The stairs that come all the way down and turn a neat corner into the living room, leaving room for the front door and toilet.

"And I remember that I was supposed to be in bed, but that I wouldn't brush my teeth, so he came upstairs. And I remember that he was already angry, and my heart started beating, and that I told myself not to be scared and to think of Daddy coming home."

"And...?" I wait, my heart thumping.

"That's it."

"That's it?"

"Well, then I remember that I was at the hospital, and I was sitting on a hospital bed with a doctor shining a light in my eye and asking me to look in certain directions. And I was kind of thinking that this was okay now, even though I hurt all over my body. I knew that I had a bad feeling about being there, but that being there was not the actual bad thing which was over so that I didn't have to think about it anymore."

"Do you remember anything else?"

"That the bookcase at the bottom of the stairs wasn't there when I went back to the house. Seeing that made me feel really bad again. But Kingsley wasn't there either, so I figured he took it with him." She stops talking for a while, and then she says. "Your turn."

"I think you know more than me." I've given up on my coffee. It sits, half-drunk with dispersed foam on the side of the table.

"But there is something that you know?"

"Not *know*," I try to explain. But suddenly I realise I do know, and I've known it all along. I think about Andrew telling me that Aisha had broken ribs. How could that not mean that Kingsley was the one to injure her? Just because you can't prove something, doesn't mean you don't know it. I thought I could not be sure, but now I am. How do I tell Aisha?

I remember that night that Lily called me from the refuge, and how I told her more strongly than I've told anyone anything in my life that she's not to go back to him. "I pressed your mum to tell me why she left Kingsley so suddenly. She wouldn't say. I was sure that her broken arm was because of him, but she never even owned up to that." I pause and look towards the jars on the coffee bar to be sure no one can hear before I say it. "You had broken ribs, I think, but no one could prove that you hadn't just fallen. And in the end, Lily made sure he left, so what was the point in proving anything, putting you through whatever the police would put you through to find out?"

She lifts and thumps her hot chocolate glass onto the table, and looks outside towards the main road and the pebble-dashed houses, biting her lip. "You've been letting Ryan go to visit him when you knew all of this?"

"No. It wasn't like that."

She turns back and raises her eyes at me, waiting for the explanation.

"Well, not exactly. Your mum, I think she knew what she was doing. She stopped him going for long periods of time. She knows her own power. If she got scared for Ryan, Kingsley knows what she would have done."

Aisha looks down at her drink, which she is hugging with both hands. She does not understand why I could not know this, even though I did know this. Sometimes the everyday with your grandbees can seem like a beautiful dream with the wind blowing in your hair. It's not the complete truth that you are playing happy families, but it only takes a few tweaks to reality. You just keep the best bits in your heart and throw the rubbish out.

I don't know why Aisha would hate me for not telling her this. But Lily hated me for not telling her stuff, so maybe she does. "And she wants to go back to him," she croaks.

I get up and try to put an arm around her, but she stands and runs out. She flees from the scene, squeezing past the cramped chairs and tables, not caring. I know how that feels. I've done it myself.

***

There are too many bits of grit, too many dark stains. They have all accumulated even though I have been trying so hard. They have all built up and I'm not sure I can keep them under control anymore.

It's Marnie I need at times like these. I knock on Marnie's door when I reach home. She will know what to do. But there is no answer. I wait quite a long time actually, turning back occasionally to my own open front door, hugging my arms to myself, not sure when to give in and go back. Marnie would normally be in about this time, but only silence plods around the stairwell.

I'm disappointed. Marnie is so wise. She doesn't belong in these two blocks of the road with me and Dylan and Mrs Cauldwell, where there seem to be more ill people than the other flats further down. Maybe the System are remembering when Marnie drank too.

Recently I told Marnie this, the not belonging with us bit. Marnie smiles.

"There is always a wise old woman tucked away where you don't expect."

I nod respectfully, and she giggles. "I am joking."

"Oh. Okay."

We are in her flat, around her doilies and empty teacups. "How do you think that a person becomes wise? She has to live through the tough times and see how they turn out. She has to tumble through the agony of thinking that it will not turn out right, and then see how things are when the dust of the tragedy has settled."

She says it as if "tragedy" isn't really the end. "Really?"

"But even you tell me 'here is the reason you must never give up', when you tell me about Lily coming back to you." She is carefully laying out a circle of Rich Tea biscuits, each overlapping the other. There is a half-sliced walnut cake on the counter, ready to come out next.

"I don't understand."

"You never thought you would see Lily again. But the reality is that each generation brings a different flavour, a different perspective, and undoes the things that you thought were set in stone. You only know that when you've lived it."

This sounds so true; all I can do is think about it for a while as I stare out of Marnie's windows to the car park below. When Ingrid had fallen out with me, I had assumed that the one thing that was fixed in my life was properly broken again. I did not realise that it was just a passing bad time, just as there had been a passing good time and that the times will just carry on passing like the layers of a cake.

"She'll never be properly my friend. She'll start asking who her father is again. And I can never tell her that."

Marnie has started slicing the cake. She pauses, knife in hand. "I suppose if you tell her a little bit, she'll just get angry that you can't tell her more?"

What would happen if I told Ingrid a little bit? The littlest bit is the worst bit. "Ingrid's father is a very, very bad man, worse than Kingsley."

Marnie pulls a sympathetic face. "Yep, I agree that you shouldn't tell her that bit."

"I don't know anything else."

Marnie comes to place our plates on the table. She doesn't tell me this is ridiculous, that I must know more than this.

"She won't be happy, but I don't even know if he was West Indian or African. I didn't know how to tell where people were from back then."

"If that's how it is, that's how it is." Marnie does not react at all.

"I always tell her not to get into unmarked cabs on her own," I add. Because the System warns women about getting into cabs alone in case bad things happen to them, the same bad things that happened to me. So this is the one good thing that can come out of not knowing who Ingrid's father is, that I can warn Ingrid not to get hurt in the same way. I want to believe that this makes up for not being able to tell her anything else.

I know that it doesn't make up for it really.

"That's kind of you." This seems to be enough for Marnie. It's like she knows even when I've never told her.

Marnie is standing on a chair to reach the teapot. She never lets me do this for her. Marnie gets everything, doesn't she? There is a question I really want to ask her. But I'm scared. I'm scared of the answer. I'm scared that Marnie might not be my friend anymore. But when I think about it, it is too late for that.

When she is down on firm ground, I can't even wait to ask her. Because I have decided.

"Marnie?"

"Yes, pet?"

"Was it my fault?"

"No, pet."

But maybe she doesn't know what I am asking. Maybe she thinks I am asking about Ingrid falling out with me. I'm not asking about this. "But they both did it to me. Bill did it to me, and Ingrid's father did it to me. It must be something about me. There must be something wrong with me."

"The only thing about you was that you had no one to look after you properly."

"Don't you think that might have been my fault that no one looked after me though? Like maybe I wasn't nice to look after."

She brings the teapot over to the table and puts it down like she is upset. It spills a bit of tea from the spout. But I know that it's not me that she is upset with. I just know that she is still my friend. "What? When you were a little girl, a young teenager? How could that be your fault?"

I see what she means. But it doesn't stop me thinking of every little thing I did, everything I might have done or not done that could have stopped it from happening. I should not have run away from home. I should have run away from home earlier than I did. I should not have trusted anyone. I'm quiet while I think about these things, because I know already that Marnie will still say they are not my fault, even if I give her every detail. It doesn't mean that she is right.

Marnie must know that I am thinking this, because she goes to her sideboard and gets a piece of paper out. She draws a circle on it. She says, "Helen, think of everyone whose fault it is and give them a space in the circle according to how much it is their fault. Did you ever do pie charts at school? This is going to look just like a pie chart."

I did do pie charts at school. I used to get all gold stars in maths before Bill started on me. So I take Marnie's pencil and paper and I try to plan it out before I draw, with Marnie moving politely away as I work. And when I draw, I put in Bill's fault which is really big, and Mum's fault, even though I have started to forgive her, and Ingrid's father's fault (also big), and the teachers who didn't help, and the people who saw me hiding in the shadows next to shoe shops, or on the benches at Southwark Cathedral, and did nothing, and then it's my turn to be part of the diagram. And when I look at the chart to try and add my fault, there is not enough room with the pencil's width to make a space that can be my fault. My fault is too small to draw.

Marnie folds the piece of paper up and puts it into my hand. I realise that I have never told her what "it" is, but she still knows what to say.

"Thank you for being my friend."

"Ah, really I am a daft old bat."

"Oh." That was something that Ryan had said loudly about her when he was bringing the chicken wings up from our day in the park. I really had hoped she hadn't heard. "I am so sorry about that. Twelve-year-olds, I mean, I just don't know where they get it from."

"Don't worry, pet. It's all part of my wise woman disguise." And she lifts a cardiganed arm across her face as if concealing it like Zorro.

***

It will be the money of course. That's why Ingrid is going back to him. She is losing her job, and Kingsley with his well-cut suits always had the money to dazzle her and control others. Aisha once said he was always talking about his law degree from Wolverhampton and how she could be as successful as him if she worked hard. Now with this settlement from his business partner, there must be more to show off about.

The bathroom door is closed, and I am leaning on the sink staring at the white tiles while I try to remember not to Beep Beep Bop, while I try to stay in the present and help my bees, so when I hear the phone ring, I think twice about answering.

It's Ryan. "Grandma?" I grip the side of the cold bath. There is something wrong. I can hear it straight away in Ryan's slightly high voice, not pretending to be a cool teenager anymore. Has Kingsley hurt my bees already? "You've got to help…" He garbles the last word so I don't know if it's a "me" or an "us", or something else I have to help.

"What's happened?"

"It's Aisha."

"Aisha?"

There is a pause before he whispers. "She's going totally mad."

"What do you mean?" Is she cleaning the house? Is she walking through stinging nettles next to the Thames, or maybe trying to break the windows of Woolworths? I have a flash of a memory – standing under the amber street lights, watching my teary reflection in the broken shop window, but in the image it becomes Aisha in her grey hoodie and green earrings looking back at me from the glass with sad, enlarged eyes.

"I can't stop her. She's running around the house emptying cupboards and things. Mum's not answering her phone. What do I do?"

Ryan has called me because I would know about these things. I am the expert in madness even though he never found a straitjacket in my flat. Poor Ryan, Poor Aisha. I have to get to her right away. "I'm coming now."

There is an uncertain okay-ness at the end of the line, then, "But, Grandma, you're an hour away."

"Is that a problem?"

There is a long pause. "Maybe she won't be here by then."

I can't imagine that. Where would she go? "Ryan, do you think you can make her stay for that long? Just until I'm there? Try to ask her questions, perhaps. Or ask her for help."

He agrees uncertainly.

"Honestly, Ryan, I will be right there. Trust me."

When I reach Thamesmead, the light is fading. I remember my other trips here, the trips that spilled over with happiness, before losing Ingrid the second time.

In the semi-dark, the carefully crafted new houses look more sinister. Despite the unloved cars in the street, it's not possible to see what is wrong in Ingrid's red-brick house just from looking at the front door. I suppose they built them like that, to look safe and normal. The System could build doll's houses, but it couldn't make the people inside of the houses be dolls, free of the family dramas.

Ryan opens the door before I can even knock it, releasing cosy light onto the pathway. "She's upstairs," he says. He has a thin blue hoodie pulled up over his head and streaks across his face from his nose as if he's been crying. "She's trying to leave. Come on." He jumps up the stairs ahead of me, two at a time, turning halfway with a pained face to make sure I am following, but I am still taking off my shoes to avoid dirtying Ingrid's floor, trying to work out how I am going to live up to my reassurances. When I catch up, I see Aisha in the bathroom at the top of the stairs, a Sainsbury's carrier bag in one hand, trawling through a bathroom cabinet with the other.

"Aisha?"

She turns, surprised to see me, surprised enough to slow down from what she is doing, but not so stupid that she doesn't give Ryan a really dirty look, straight from the Ingrid gene pool. She doesn't say anything and turns back to the bathroom cabinet, her burgundy pyjama top riding up as she reaches to the higher shelf.

"What are you doing, love?"

She keeps her back to me for a long while, but I'm not scared that she won't answer me, because she's just not like that. "What do you think I'm doing?" she whispers after a while.

"Ryan says that you're leaving?"

She slams the bag down onto the bathroom floor and turns to perch on the side of the bath. "Of course I'm leaving."

I wait for her to say more, to explain something so that I can help.

"I can't go to that place with Mum, and I can't believe that Mum would take us there."

She is sitting half-on, half-off a scruffy blue bath mat that is draped over the edges. She leaves me no choice but to do the same. From here, I see a large backpack under the sink, one of those ones that teenagers have with little ropes and canvas pockets, for reasons I can never work out. It lies half open, the lip of the top folded back revealing scrunched-up clothes. I look at it sadly, wondering if she has filled it with the same things that I filled mine with when I made my escape at the same age.

Ryan is still on the landing. "Ryan, go and put on your favourite film and enjoy it," I tell him through the bathroom door. He looks at me hopelessly, arms hanging at his sides, a strange echo of the days when they needed me, before they knew I was mad. "We need a bit of space to..." but I don't know what the thing is that we are going to do.

I turn back to Aisha as Ryan starts to go down the stairs, flopping down one step at a time with unlaced trainers. When I've made sure he's not going to trip, I swing the bathroom door shut. "You can't go away," I tell Aisha as firmly as I can.

She leaps back to her feet. "I am going away... I am going to look after myself and stop having to pretend to be a different person's daughter every other year. And I am going to be happy."

No. No. NO. This was what I said when I left. And then all these awful things happened. Beep Beep Bop. Bad things happened. But how can I explain? How can I tell her that these beautiful generations of Lily and Aisha started with such a terrible beginning? My bees will think that they themselves are bad things. You cannot run away Aisha.

Have I been protecting them from the worst ever thing? Or have I been saving up worse things for the future? Worse things have happened when the past could just have been explained and put to sleep.

I look at her desperate face, her young hopeful skin and upturned features. She is fifteen. How can I tell her what will happen if she runs away? How can she hear these things?

"I am going to get a job, and I will find somewhere to live. I'm nearly sixteen, I'm nearly a grown-up. Grown-ups manage to live on their own."

I look at her sadly. "Some of them don't," I say. Maybe I mean me. Maybe I even mean Ingrid.

She avoids my eye and slowly goes back to the bathroom

cabinet as if she did not think that what I said had any relevance to her. She takes a toothbrush. She takes a peach-coloured soap in the shape of a goldfish.

"But what about Ryan, Aisha? What will happen to Ryan?"

She looks at me, her eyes widen and she pauses for a couple of seconds. She opens her mouth to reply and nothing comes out. I have found a reason she will not leave. Aisha and Ryan might snipe at each other, but really they love each other, like mothers and daughters.

Aisha shakes her head guiltily before sinking to the cork floor. Her knees fold beneath her and her head tips forward. Her fingers run through the curls of her hair.

For a moment, I worry about what will happen next, how can I get her up from off the floor. Then I realise that poor Aisha sunk on her knees on the floor like a pool of water really means that I have won. She is on the floor because she knows she won't leave Ryan.

But I don't know how to comfort her, because I know that she cannot stay and she cannot go. I stand up from the bath and put my arms around her shoulders. She is moving like she is crying, but there is no sound and no tears, just dry convulsions as she reaches to catch her breath.

"What am I going to do, Grandma?" She looks at me. "I'm so scared."

"I know." I wonder if I should say the next thing. "So am I."

Somehow that makes her give a small smile. She moves a wisp of frizz at her forehead. "She can't really take us there, can she? There are laws, aren't there?"

I can't even nod. It's a lie. There might be laws, but it's the System that makes the laws work, and all they do is take away your bees. Can I make the laws work? "When's Mum going?"

"In a couple of weeks."

I stare into the floor tiles until I can think of something to say and I remember who has made so many things easy for me since I have known her. "Let me talk to Marnie. Marnie knows all of the answers."

Aisha looks at me. Her wide brown eyes tell me that she believes me. Or maybe she just wants to believe me, she really really wants to.

***

Ryan is sitting on the arm of the sofa when I come back down the stairs. And even though his film is on, he is looking at me as I put my shoes back on, not the TV. "Can I come back with you?"

I glance up the stairs to Aisha. I don't want to leave her alone in the house.

"Pleeease, she's going mad and I'm scared." He clings onto the arm of the sofa.

I nod glumly and go to make a note out to Ingrid.

"There's no point doing that," Ryan says. "She won't be back for *ages*." He goes to pull on his coat over his blue hoodie, forgetting it's still warm outside, and then he too pauses, looking upstairs, at where the noises of Aisha's movements are coming from. "How are you going to make her stay?"

"My friend Marnie will have some good advice."

"How will *she* know what to do? She's just a..."

I look at him.

"... little old lady."

"Marnie can fix anything." I'm not exaggerating. I haven't found anything she couldn't fix yet. She's been fixing me without me noticing for years and right now I want to grab the first bus to Deptford and race to her comfort and answers. "You should show her more respect."

He gives me a look that tells me that he doesn't believe me. It also says that he doesn't think that he should explain that he does not believe me. I am glad that not losing his big sister is more important to Ryan than not spending time with old ladies who smell of wee. He is a good boy really.

***

When we reach the flat, Marnie is still not answering. We both stand there knocking, next to the busy Lizzies and the rubbish chute. I give him an exaggerated shrug of failure. "We'll have to try again later," I tell him, and I am telling it to me too, so that I can calm my impatiently thumping heart.

His face falls and I feel a little bit glad that he had believed me about Marnie.

"But we need her to fix things," he calls out as I lift my key to open my front door.

"She will, Ryan. We just have to wait…" I turn around when I see him lifting the letter box and peering into it. "Ryan!" I want the ground to swallow me up. Thank goodness no one can see him. "Ryan, that's rude, put that down."

Ryan looks up at me, frustrated, letting the letter box tip closed again with its dull metallic creak. He leans his small fingers against it. "No, you have to look."

"Come into the flat, now." I walk towards the door and push it open.

But he's still kneeling. "Grandma, look, please. You have to look."

"Ryan, what's got into you?"

"She's in there, on the floor. I can see her. You have to look."

It takes me a few seconds to take in what he is saying. I kneel down onto the doormat, still the same doormat that Dylan used to have. It makes scratchy crunches on my knees. I put my hands on the concrete floor, despite the germs, to steady myself, and I peer through the letter box exactly as I told Ryan not to. Fluorescent light streams from Marnie's kitchen onto her hallway floor. And halfway between the kitchen and the hallway there is a body sprawled on the wood, deathly still. It's Marnie.

Ryan whispers to me in a quiet, hoarse voice, watching my face carefully for my reaction as he speaks. "Does this mean that we can't stop Aisha leaving now?"

WE HAVE TO FACE FACTS

I have my grandbees. My Lily-Bee came back to me, and she gave me grandbees, and we should all be happy now, but we are not. We cannot stop the waves rocking. They keep coming.

Some of the waves come because my Lily-Bee has the discontent. My Lily-Bee doesn't care about anyone when she has the discontent and this rocks everything, because you keep having to make new families and try and believe that they will be lasting families. They never have been lasting families so far. And you have to make bonds with people you don't like and you don't think will stop around, because they are your family now. But then, a bit later, they are not your family anymore. Even then, things might be worse.

But other waves come because I have secrets. And nobody trusts you when you have secrets. And maybe my secrets are what gives Lily-Bee the discontent, because she is looking for something I cannot tell her. She is looking for something that I cannot solve for her, so she looks in other places to find the things I cannot give her. She turns to the arms of different men so that she knows where she is going, even if she doesn't know where she comes from.

I want to hide.

But there is something I am missing in all of this when I want to lock myself away from all the colours of south-east London and scrub at the corners of the yellowed plastic window frames of the double glazing. The thing I am missing is that if I hide, I am exactly back where I was when they took my Lily-Bee away. The waves are hurting the grandbees more than they hurt me. What a confusion. I am only hurt because I love them, so I hide from them as if I have never met them.

That's not very smart of me and I don't need Marnie to tell me that.

I need to gather the pieces of this messed-up jigsaw and put us all back together. Even if we have never been properly together before.

***

I can stop Aisha leaving. I am sure of it. I have spent hours of each night at work thinking about what I have left now that Marnie is gone, getting distracted until the point when Margaret, my supervisor who normally ignores me, asked me if everything was all right, with her own mop in hand. I suppose I was being quite aggressive in making sure that the floor under the bakery baskets was quite clean. I nod without meeting Margaret's eye as I work out the answer. I need to go and see Ingrid before I do anything else. I need to start believing that I can make a difference.

"Lily-Ingrid," I call her when she comes to the door, in a ribbed jumper and gold hoop earrings, always so well dressed, even on a Saturday morning when everyone is out. "Lilingrid." She smiles at me. She knows what that means. Lilingrid means she is my bee and she is her own woman too.

"You could just settle for calling me St Petersburg," she says, leaning on the varnished door and I don't get what she means to start with, but then I say Lilingrid quietly to myself and get the joke.

I hope she knows that it means I love her despite what comes next.

"Sorry to hear about your next-door neighbour," she says with a half-smile. Just her saying that much makes me hurt all over again, but it's nice that Lilingrid is sorry.

I have chosen a time early on a Saturday morning when Ryan is at football and Aisha is stacking shelves for the holiday job I got for her at Asda. "Is there anyone else here?" I ask her, because who knows when she spends time with Kingsley. She shakes her head and opens the door for me to come in.

She motions for me to sit on the sofa in the front room while she goes to make me tea. We still cannot chat without tea. A smart work blazer is draped on the back of the sofa, which always makes me proud of my Lily with her posh job with the System. But I remember with a wince that she is leaving that job. I sit upright on the sofa and keep my jacket and sandals on even though I know this place so well, and they ask me to treat it like I am family. On the table is a set of GCSE textbooks in bold colours, neatly piled as if looking for a home.

Lilingrid brings two brightly coloured mugs out into the front room, asks me to pull out the mats from the coffee table drawer and places the mugs on top. She sits down opposite me, also leaning forwards as if nervous, with her elbows on her knees.

"So, this looks serious," she says.

"It is really."

I thought she might say something like, "If this is about…" and I'm glad she hasn't. Maybe that's because I have changed, I am acting differently.

"You're going back to Kingsley?" I look directly at her.

She leans back and sighs. "I knew it would be this. You can't stop me."

"No, I can't."

"So why are you here? In what way is this any of your business?"

"Have you spoken to Aisha and Ryan about this?"

"A dad will be good for them."

"He's not Aisha's dad."

She exhales, a half-laugh. "Now you sound like her, throwing it in his face any time he tries to encourage her to work hard at school."

I say nothing, trying to envisage Kingsley lecturing Aisha about homework.

She tuts. "Aisha wants me to be a nun. If I was a nun, she would not even exist right now, and neither would she have a little brother. Teenagers!" She throws her hands in the air.

I remember what Marnie said about mothers and daughters. I suppose that even though I find Aisha easy to be friends with, that does not mean that it will be so easy for Lily to be her daughter's friend. In a way, it's nice to watch Lilingrid being a mother with her exasperated sigh. "Better than the other way around?" I suggest.

"Sometimes, I think it would be better if she went out and let her hair down." She looks at me and shrugs. "But, yeah, it's nice to know she's not coming home at two a.m. knocked up by some layabout."

I smile. "Aisha is really scared of Kingsley."

Lilingrid draws her shoulders up. Her round eyes narrow. "What have you been telling her?"

I feel my heart quicken, I breathe deeply, I wait, I wait for her shoulders to drop before I answer.

"She remembers."

For a second I see fear in Lilingrid's eyes. Or guilt? But when I try to work out which, whatever I had seen is gone.

"I know things are tough right now with you losing your job, but will you really make them do this just for the money?"

"Money? Ha!" She stands up and moves to look out of the window with her arms crossed. There is a strange view from the window here: a patch of grass mostly obscuring the view of the shopping centre, a perfectly neat shopping centre, but a shopping centre in the middle of a housing estate nonetheless.

"I know money is important, I know that even if Aisha starts paying her way, you still have to look after Ryan, but is it worth…" I put my hands to my forehead. I don't know how to explain what I need to explain. I want to say, how can you do this just for the money? How can your bees' safety be less important than money? But I am trying to be nice, and I have never learned the words to talk about bad things.

Here I am talking about bad things, really bad things, without feeling the need to run away, run through the polite Thamesmead door and out into the sunny, windy outside.

She interrupts me anyway. "It's got nothing to do with the money."

"But you're losing your job. You said you had a plan. And then you took a phone call from Kingsley."

She looks pityingly at me over one shoulder. "I took voluntary redundancy. I'm moving to a PA role in the City. The pay is better there. The office is really posh, one of those grand old buildings where it's been all done up inside – all open plan, and the clothes all the other women wear…," She tails off as she sees my face.

"Then, why would you? Why would you go back to him?"

She sighs dramatically and slams her hands onto the sofa in front of her. "You don't know what it's like. You have no idea what it's like. I'm not young anymore. It's harder. I go to bars in Blackheath and the guys pass me by. In the office, they all chat up the young receptionists and talk about the kid in accounts. I mean it, the *kid* isn't even twenty yet. It's like I am invisible." She goes to look in the mirror over the fake fireplace. She puts a hand to her face, and fingers to the frown line in her forehead. "I am still pretty," she tells the reflection.

"You are," I assure her, her elegant limbs, and high neck, her high cheekbones and rich lips – even though this is not why I am here.

"But the young skinny girls and their hips and lips and gloss. It's like I don't exist even for the guys my age. And I'm so…"

"Lonely," I finish for her.

"I'm getting on for forty. I just want to be loved. You have no idea."

I have no idea what it is to feel like this woman who lives with her two children, who has one dad and two mums. Who had a loving husband, more than one. I really, really, really wanted Andrew to carry on being the man who made her feel loved.

But this is not my business. I am sure it's not perfect for her, but to tell me I have no idea? I must not get angry. Getting angry will not help.

"He's not worth it. You're not desperate."

She looks at her hands and I wonder what she is thinking. Maybe she is thinking that she is desperate.

"You have so much. You don't need him."

"I need him," she says simply.

"More than your kids?"

"Don't be stupid. It's not like I'm choosing between them."

But you are, I want to shout. I don't say it. I don't want to sound like I'm threatening her or scare her into doing something stupid. "If he hurts them?"

"That..." She pauses for the words, not meeting my eye. "That fuss was years ago. Why do you think he would do it again?" This is the closest thing to an admission she's ever made. My heart closes up all over again, because I know what has happened and hearing this makes the anger rise and I have to wait a moment or two before I can say anything else.

"Are you seeing him tonight?"

She brightens. "Yes. He's taking me to the West End. I've bought this great dress. It is made of really huge sequins that look like fish scales and fit around my curves." She holds her hands to her waist and looks down as if daydreaming about how she would wear it. "Let's just say, I think he will like what he sees."

"I always loved my clothes too," I say to her, sadly. "You get this from me."

She smiles. She doesn't understand. I don't mean that she gets just the love of clothes from me. I'm talking about hiding from terrible things, like staring at your pink nail varnish when your whole body is bruised. That's what she gets from me. And it turns out that she is more bruised than I realised. I had forgotten the scar that I had left her with.

"You're my daughter, Lilingrid. I'll always love you, and you're always welcome in my house."

"Thanks," she says casually. Because I don't think she knows why I'm saying it. She doesn't know that I can't let Aisha run out into the streets.

***

I leave Lilingrid the whole weekend just in case. Just in case she suddenly realises that something must change and I won't have to do a terrible thing. I have to be patient.

It's like Marnie said, you become wise when you've been in free fall for so long that you work out how to hold on to something to feel safe. Then you can help other people.

I miss Marnie. I miss Marnie-Marmalade so much.

When we found Marnie on her hallway floor, we called for an ambulance and everybody came. Ryan was a good boy. In the heat of the moment, he was the one who called 999 while my head was still going in circles about what to do. He forced me to sit down with sugary tea, just like Ingrid would have, just like she did when she first tried to push to find out more about her father. The police came, the ambulance came, and they did all their official things while the flashing lights kept lighting up my flat. They spoke on their fuzzy walkie-talkies, they took down our official details, they even broke down Marnie's door in a way that you would not think was possible. It was like cardboard, and one of the plant pots shot across the floor. But none of it meant we got Marnie back at the end of it.

All they said as they left was that she probably died of a stroke, but they could be more certain later. "It was probably instant," said the policeman who'd written down everything I told him. That policeman was kind.

"Instant" means she wasn't even there anymore when I knocked and got no answer on my way to Aisha and Ryan's. "Instant" means that she wasn't mouthing hopelessly for help when I passed by the door.

So "instant" is the only comfort I have about losing my best friend in her old-lady blue jeans when I needed her so much. Marnie's gone and I can only remember her words to help me protect my grandbees.

***

I phone Lilingrid again, late Monday evening, not knowing who will answer the phone. Ryan picks up. In the background I can hear the loud noises of an action film, shots ringing out, policemen shouting, "Now, now, now!"

"You okay, Ryan?"

"Yup." I can tell he is watching the film. If he were not watching the film, he would be more chatty.

"Is your mum there?"

"Nope. She's out."

"Know where she is?"

"Umm, think she's at my dad's. She's there almost all of the time at the moment."

I hear shattering glass and police sirens. "Are you watching a film?"

"Oh. Yeah."

"Aisha there?"

"Hmm. Think she's in her room doing something."

"Okay."

There is a reluctant, "You want me to go and get her?" as the film moves on to dramatic beating music.

"No, love. Don't worry about it. It was your mum I was wondering about." I take a deep breath. "Any news on when you're moving to your dad's?"

"Dunno. She took some stuff over today."

I try to breathe out without it sounding like a sigh. "Okay. Enjoy your film. Bye bye."

"Bye, Grandma."

***

When I phone the social workers, trembling, they make me an appointment with someone called Grace.

I want to Beep Beep Bop and run away, but if I run away, Aisha will run away and then the bad will start all over again.

But it's time to Face Facts.

The night before my appointment, I try writing everything down with a pad and pencil, not convincing myself anymore that what I saw back at Andrew's flat isn't important, doesn't mean a thing, doesn't mean anybody was *definitely* hurt by Kingsley. But after scratching two short sentences onto the printed lines, I'm too scared of seeing the words in solid writing. I scrunch up the paper and burn it on the hob, closing my eyes and taking deep breaths. If I can just get myself to the appointment, I will work out what to do when I'm there.

***

Grace is in her early forties and wears a creased navy suit. Her hair has been straightened into a quirky bob with a dyed blonde streak. She offers me a mug in her white office that smells of carpet and winces at a stain of coffee near the kettle, muttering about her colleagues and rubbing at it with a tea towel.

It's all as if she is a friend, which she is not. Grace is part of the System.

She leaves the dirtied tea towel on the kitchen top and comes and joins me. Her accent is a bit like Kingsley's, so she might be Nigerian too, but I don't ask because I get these things all wrong. Anyway, her tone is more friendly than his. Then Grace opens her notebook and says, "What can we help you with, Helen?" She lifts the pen from the table.

Here we are again, me and a social worker sitting talking about my daughter, nearly forty years since the first time, as if nothing has changed. Everything has changed.

I remind myself that the System owes me.

I croak through the facts and my tears, with her nodding

encouragement. Even though I am doing a good thing, I am also doing a bad thing, working with the System that takes babies away.

"I've bought something. It might make it easier to explain." I reach down to my Asda carrier bag, ashamed that it's not a briefcase when it's holding something so important. Grace leans back and I bring out Andrew's letter. He has written down everything he remembers from that night when Ingrid left Kingsley via a hospital and a women's refuge.

I pass it to Grace and she reads it straight away with me in front of her. And I feel kind of awkward and I don't know what to do with myself while she reads, holding each page directly up in front of her as if she is short-sighted, but it lets me relax and look around me, it lets me out of the tense little bubble that we are sat in. Grace has got facts that need to be faced now. Then she puts the papers down.

"This man, who is written about here, Ingrid is going back to him. She's taking my grandchildren with her."

"I see."

"The letter was written by the father of Aisha, the eldest. He wanted to take Aisha with him to his family in Jamaica, but…"

"But there's still the little boy," Grace finishes for me.

"Aisha would never leave her little brother in danger." I had told Andrew that and when I said it, he was quiet for a while. And it was a sad quietness.

"I wish he hadn't left the country. He would have rescued Aisha years ago."

Grace nods and doesn't reply.

I think to tell Grace that none of this would have happened if I had kept my flat with Lilingrid clean, but it doesn't seem relevant.

And Grace gets it. I can see that she gets it. She even seems to relax with me because she can see the purpose of my visit. Her questions become more precise and she leans into her notebook, jotting down all the bits that I think are important, or pausing to hold the pen to her lips as she listens. Then she puts her pen down and leans on her hands. "Has your daughter moved back in with him already?"

I shake my head and I look at Grace, knowing that she can help. She will rescue us. She is like Marnie really.

Grace pauses and puts her hands together, like she is going to tell me something really important. "So, what I need you to do, Helen, is to get in touch with us if Ingrid moves in with her ex-boyfriend."

"You don't understand. She will move in, unless you stop her."

She nods and smiles, pushing her bob over one ear. "Now, we can't stop people moving in with their boyfriends."

I'm put off by her deliberate firmness for a second, but she is wrong. The System has to help them out. "He's going to hurt them, beat them up or something."

Grace looks uneasy. I've stopped being scared. I'm angry. I realise that Grace is not going to stop anyone doing anything. I am not sure I care about Grace looking so uncomfortable. It wasn't comfortable for me to have to explain all of this to a stranger. Now she can't do anything to fix it. Today this could still be fixed. Tomorrow Aisha could be lost on London streets.

"Then tell us if they move in. We may be able to help then."

"It will be too late by then. She won't be able to leave him so easily."

"It's not like that, Helen." They all use my name in the System when they are telling me I am wrong, or taking away my bee. For a minute, it was easy to believe that Grace might be quite kind because she's not telling me that my curtains are dirty, and my saucepans will make my daughter seriously ill, but really she is just someone who has been trained to deal with people who cry. "We can't follow everybody around in case they commit a crime."

I take a deep breath, ready for a fight.

But Grace continues forcefully. "But we *can* help if Ingrid does go back to him. We would get in touch with Ingrid and meet with the family." She looks more confident now that she can tell me what would happen if the situation was completely different.

I stare at her in her blouse and ill-fitted trousers. I have wasted all my courage on this? This is about money again. Why does money always have to get in the way of everything, tripping everyone up and letting people down if they don't have enough of it.

She stands and I know I am supposed to do the same. But I'm not going to. It would look like I agree with her. "So don't forget," she says, putting her notes and Andrew's statement into her handbag, "to call us if that happens."

I am trying to think of something, anything, that will make her wait. "Aisha went to hospital with broken ribs!"

"I read that in your son-in-law's statement." Grace reaches in her handbag which is lying on the floor. She eventually pulls out a business card printed in green and black. I stare at it angrily. I don't know what I am supposed to do with that. I am not the sort of lady who receives business cards.

Grace gestures that I need to stand up and I can't carry on pretending not to obey, then she passes me the card again and I take it now because it's my only hope.

"This is the number you must phone."

More promises of fixing things. Don't make me laugh.

Back at home, I slide the business card under the bottom of the bowl from Turkey. That way I can see the bowl's ivy-like pattern unspoilt. But the truth is that this small business card will ruin all the beautiful things that Lilingrid has brought into my life.

***

I meet Marnie's girls after she dies. Sam is quite chubby, and cheerful-looking, although she seems to have lost weight since the photograph Marnie showed me. Her hair is slightly frizzy, shoulder length, more grey than blonde. When she knocks on my door, she mentions that her husband and Nina and Nina's husband are in the flat, clearing things right now. I can hear the clinking of washing-up and a mumbling of friendship. So I know they are loved because their husbands came with them. That is a good thing to know when they have lost their mum.

I wonder if they carry any of Marnie's wisdom in their genes, and I could ask them what to do to rescue Aisha and Ryan, but I wouldn't know where to start.

Sam invites me to the funeral. I am terrified and I want to say that I can't go. I have never been to a funeral before and the only thing that I have been to like a funeral was my baby sister's memorial, and that was when everything went wrong. Beep Beep Bop. Instead, I say, "Oh, did you know to tell Becca too? She lives in the flat underneath Marnie's."

Sam tells me that Marnie had a stroke, that she died instantly, which I already know. I want to tell her how the police kicked through the door like it was cardboard and Ryan told me off for referring to him as a little boy to the police, but it feels like missing the point.

Before they leave, Sam knocks again. "Listen, we can't take all this stuff," she indicates a collection of cardboard boxes in Marnie's open hallway, crammed full of Marnie's things. "And we just wondered if there was anything that you wanted to take, maybe something useful, or maybe a memento..."

I look at the boxes, brimming over with Marnie's personality. I can see the corner of the *Hay Wain* clock, pushing a rip in the cardboard where it lies on its side. It feels wrong to pick over the belongings of a dead person as if they're not coming back.

"It'll all be thrown away if it's no use."

I agree to shuffle three boxes into my own hallway, under the coats, to look at later. My flat is starting to turn out as cluttered as Marnie's.

***

Both daughters cry at the funeral in Eltham. Sam is dressed in a bright multicoloured crochet cardigan. I think that is so much like Marnie as I watch her walk slowly through the carefully planned garden of memorials. I can imagine Marnie wearing bright clothes to a funeral. She would be saying that she is being sad in her own way, sadness without wearing black.

The funeral takes place in blasting-hot sunlight. It turns out to be the hottest day of the year. Outside the red-brick building, I pass Nina and Sam a card with a picture of a sunset over the sea. I wrote in it that Marnie changed my life for the better. I wrote that she used to let me call her "Marmalade". I don't think that the card says anything that they wouldn't already know, but I hope that it reminds them of her. It reminds me what a good thing it was to know her. I cry as I write it. It makes me think how I will never cry at the funeral of April. I will never be there.

Is that wrong? Lilingrid thinks it's wrong.

Aisha comes to the funeral with me and sits with me solemnly on the velvet seats after hugging Becca. Becca looks really glam and dramatic in all of her clothes in black, accessorised in gold jewellery. Aisha has also found some smart black clothes from her wardrobe. I think that is so kind. She didn't know Marnie as I did, but she is kind of dignified and respectful. She does not mention Kingsley once and I don't mention the day I came over to Thamesmead.

We come out of the cemetery to the little cul-de-sac of white cottages. I say to Aisha, "How long now, before your mum moves to North Greenwich?"

Aisha just looks sad and I know that she thinks we should not be talking about such things here, at a funeral. So I can't tell Aisha that Marnie has given me the courage to take action. I cannot tell Aisha about Grace.

"Can I come over to yours in a bit?" Aisha asks suddenly.

I don't ask why. And this time I don't make her check with her mum first.

***

When I get home, the door to number seventeen is propped open and the smell of sawdust streams out, along with the sound of occasional drilling. Marnie's plants have gone. I like to think they are with the girls, but they are probably in the skip that has appeared in the road outside. The System is already preparing to place someone else there. No matter how many people I have known in that flat, it will always be Marnie's and now there is a huge space hovering outside my front door. The empty flat of Marnie is emptier than it ever has been.

***

Aisha is still in her black clothes when she reaches me. But when she comes through into my hallway, I can see that she has her backpack, the one that she was packing when I came around to stop her running away, and an old sports bag with the plastic peeling off the straps in the other hand.

I drop my "pleased to see you face" because I know what Aisha's bag means. I know that means that she has left. She has packed up and left Ingrid and Kingsley. She has even left Ryan.

I reach out to her in the hallway. "No, Aisha, no."

She looks sad and confused at the same time. Does this mean that I can make a difference to what she does next? She takes my arm in a clumsy way, and we hobble to the dining table. Her bags stay in the hallway. I wish I couldn't see them there, beyond the boxes of Marnie's possessions.

"Mum said that she would wait for me to go to the funeral today, but that we leave tomorrow."

I hold myself up with my palms on the table watching her

calm tearless face as she explains that she couldn't think of anything else to do but to come here.

"I know you care about Ryan, but this isn't really leaving him. I'll still be around. What I'll do is save up money from my Asda job for a cheap B&B."

"What sort of B&B, Aisha? Will there be locks on the door?"

She gives me the sidelong glance that she gives me when she thinks I am saying a barmy thing. Her hand is on the table curled into a tense fist, but then she nods. She does not cry. She does not complain. She just takes the chair opposite mine and sits still, her eyes in shade, and her lips in the bright sunlight from the window. She takes a deep breath, "Would it be okay to stay a couple of weeks while I save up?"

"Of course." That will keep her from getting into trouble for a short while. She doesn't ask me why my plan hasn't happened, why I promised her I could rescue her and I haven't. How can she not ask? Is she resigned to the fact that no one can help, like I was when I left my parents in the middle of the night, when I was alone on rained-out streets?

A breeze makes a tree outside shudder and rustle. Aisha doesn't look. I wonder if she might even stay here. Is that allowed? Is she enough of a grown-up now that it does not matter that the System says I am not allowed to look after any bees?

"Stay for good."

"No," she reaches out a hand to mine. With the shock of the human touch, I can't fight her anymore. "I'm not a kid anymore. I just need a stopover."

"Your mum will worry."

She looks at me then, straight in the eye. "Just like your mum worried about you?" For a second I feel like I am talking to Lilingrid all of a sudden, her icy judgement on my life preventing me from having an opinion on hers. Except Aisha looks totally shamed by what has come out of her mouth, holding her hand up to her face. "I'm sorry. I shouldn't have said that." She slumps back in her chair. "But you know she won't come running for me."

"She'll be angry."

"She's always angry."

And Aisha is right. Why should I care that Lilingrid will be angry? It won't make Aisha any safer. I squeeze Aisha's hand. "Please don't run away, Aisha. I am trying to sort this out. I just need a bit more time."

She gives me that dead look again. The look that says, I don't want to talk about this. The look that also has dread in the back of her eyes.

I let her use her old room, behind the door I no longer open, with its lonely pine furniture. The curtains are closed, but they are thin enough to let the daylight in. The memories of the nights the grandbees stayed here bunch up against my face like a soft pillow and baby talc. For a minute, I can forget that I am scared and that I don't know what is going to happen next.

Aisha peers in, and smiles. "It's smaller than I remember."

I tell her to settle in, without coming across the doorway. "Can you help yourself to something to eat? I have to go to work in a bit." I am pulling the door closed, but I am gripping the doorknob, not wanting to let it go.

"Sure, thanks. I really appreciate all this," she calls through the door.

She ought not to run away. It's in our blood, I'm certain of that now. Lily ran away to Kingsley, and then onto the next boyfriend; I ran away from Dudley and into more danger. What about Aisha? What is she running into?

I wait in the small hallway. I can't shake off the feeling that if I leave this girl who has escaped from her house, I might never see her again. I know how these things can happen.

I turn back and knock again on her door.

"Just a second." Aisha comes to the bedroom door. She has already changed into looser clothes, not quite pyjamas, but relaxed house clothes. Just seeing her looking so at home makes me shiver for the old days when my grandbees came and stayed every week, giving me back the Lily years I had lost. "I'm still here," she tells me with a cheeky smile. I feel all told off again, even though her eyes are truly sad.

She waits, but the words get stuck in my throat. If I get the words wrong, she might think that I can't let her stay for too long after all.

"There's a reason you can't go, Aisha..."

"I'm not going for a couple of weeks, so long as that's okay."

I nod, because even though what I am going to say is very important, I know she needs to speak too. "But if you ever find yourself in a place where me or Mum and Ryan can't help, then don't trust people."

"Don't fuss..."

"Especially not men." I bring my forefinger down to silence her. "They might say that they are taking you to somewhere warm you can sleep or they are just giving you a lift, but don't go with them."

"You mean, like, don't talk to strangers? I'm not stupid." She leans back against the doorpost and folds her arms.

I look at her under the bare light of the hallway. I feel a pit in my stomach. She's right. Aisha isn't stupid. Not like me. I was stupid. It was all my fault really.

She sees my face, "I didn't mean that to sound so harsh."

She can't hear what I am trying to tell her. "Don't go with them, Aisha. Really, really don't go with them. Please."

"Okay." She tightens her grip on the door handle, looking kind of scared, that what I say might not be so barmy after all.

"You'll think that you've found someone kind who will put a roof over your head, but he will take you to the middle of nowhere and will do terrible things."

She looks uncomfortable, but I need to make sure she understands the danger of just one small mistake. "Did you say you were on your way to work?"

"And there might be a baby who will never forgive you either. I really know this. I really know what I am talking about."

"That's kind of off the wall," she whispers to the carpet, but I catch a look from her that says that she can hear me now, that she can piece the story together from the backwards way it falls out. She uncrosses her arms and opens her mouth a little. "What are you saying?"

"Aisha," I cry and I realise I have been crying inside too. "If they catch you, there is so much pain. It's not just for a short time. It grips at you for years. Don't trust people, Aisha. Please."

Now Aisha gets it. I can see it in her face. Maybe she is not 100 per cent sure: she knows and daren't know at the same time. She looks down and starts playing with the drawstring from her trousers. Her breathing isn't right, trying to keep her ice maiden act.

I shouldn't have gone there. I had to go there. I had to stop her making the same mistakes.

I look straight at her downcast face. She won't be able to work things out while I look at her. It will slow her thinking down. "Promise me you will stay just a bit longer?" That's all I have, whatever promise I can wring out of her. Aisha has never lied to me her whole life. I hope she will not learn to break a promise just yet.

"Yeah," she says, pulling her face away so that she is looking back into the distance into the dining room. But I think she said it because she is still dazed enough to answer automatically, to give me the answer that she would have given me five minutes ago when everything was a bit more normal. "Yeah," she says, just like she did a minute ago.

***

Of course, I can't go to work. I grab my phone and run down the painted steps to Becca's, thinking: don't let me come home to an empty flat, knowing that you are nowhere anymore, Aisha, that you are under a bridge, that you are fighting off the unwanted attentions of men, being driven to isolated places.

I had to warn her, stop it from happening to her, but now I have started down a path, I feel light-headed and everything has fallen out of my control and I don't know what happens next.

Aisha is a clever girl. She might take a minute to put the facts together, but she will work out that her mum started in my womb after I was attacked by a man after I ran away from home. You can bury a thing like that, but it always comes back, growing uncontrollably in other people's minds. And when Aisha has put it all together, she will start thinking about what that really means for all of us and who we really are. Like *Bill is dead. Dead is bad, but Bill is bad.* But her story will be something slightly different… *The birds weren't worth the mention, but the bee was.*

Is she still standing silent and tense at the bedroom door? I only have that promise, wrung out of her, that she won't leave yet. Becca lets me use her living room to make the phone call. The room is empty except for a sofa, a TV and children's biroed pictures on ripped wallpaper. I am brave. I take the remote from the sofa and mute the cartoons and dial for Grace. I've stared for so long at the number on the business card, not daring to dial, that I know it off by heart. Aisha cannot hear me here. She cannot know I have betrayed them to the System. I call the social worker's office, and when I call, I am put on hold, and then asked to call back later. I say, no really, this one is an emergency.

"How can I help you, Helen?" There is something about the tone that tells me that Grace has been waiting for my call.

"Ingrid has moved in with Kingsley."

There is a pause. "We have to be very careful about this. Are you sure?"

I want to shout yes; I am sure. I have a fifteen-year-old in a sleeping bag in my spare room refusing to go back home. Ask her if she's sure.

I can see Becca in the kitchen, her three-year-old writhing in her arms as she tries to stop her coming back into the living room. She opens a drawer and pulls out a lollipop to distract her.

I wonder what will happen when they all find out what I have done. Grace hovers on the phone as if she knows I have something else to say. "I had to tell you," I say. "Aisha was going to run away. Who knows what would have happened to her?"

Because she is only fifteen, Beep Beep Bop.

As I come out of Becca's flat, thanking her, and trying to wave at her little ones, and I turn away from the door into the stairwell, I see the metal door at the front of the block is moving. It is closing as if someone has let it fall behind them.

Aisha has learned to lie very quickly.

I run to the door and pull it just before the catch closes. I squeeze through and look down the road both ways. Aisha is disappearing into the distance, in different clothes but with less baggage than she arrived at my house with. I tell myself that she cannot get far; this can't be proper running away. It is not running away for good. She half runs, half walks. Aisha without her composure.

I reach the High Street. It's harder to keep sight of her amongst the people buzzing at the market stalls. People are giving me strange looks, and I think maybe some of them might have seen me, all those years ago, crying on the High Street, trying to smash the glass of Woolworths.

Aisha is at the end of the road, beyond the green Londis on the corner, by the traffic lights flashing a green man. She dashes across the road towards the shops that are always shuttered. There is a bus from the right, slow and trundling in the steaming traffic, and another from the left.

When they finally pass, I can't see Aisha anymore.

I run up to the traffic lights, trying to strain my eyes along both roads and look carefully at the people obscured by the large signs. There is no one that looks like Aisha amongst the summery crowds. There are students giggling, there are mums walking slowly with parasolled pushchairs. There is no Aisha.

I look down and I realise that I am wearing my slippers still. And I'm even wearing a towel in my hair, wrapped in a turban, not as ready for work as I had thought. So, the strange looks I am getting are not because anyone recognises me from crying on the High Street.

Although I could cry right now, here in my slippers and towel turban. I could drop to my knees and cry to the pavement.

Which won't help anybody.

***

I am dizzy on Deptford High Street, dizzy amongst all the shoppers looking at my slippers and towel turban. I walk past the closed Woolworths, and remember the police coming for me when I was crying here. The police will come for me properly now. They will come to the flat with their notebooks, they will sit me down on my sofa and say that they have had a conference and it's not good enough, that I cannot look after my little grandbee. They will slam their fists onto the coffee table in frustration and the bowl from Turkey will shake. My grandbee will be taken away from me and given to better grandparents. I will not be allowed to look after her anymore, nor Ryan either. Because I am not just a bad mother, I am a bad grandmother.

But that doesn't make sense. The police won't come for me until they know that I have lost Aisha.

I will have to confess to Lilingrid, whom I last asked not to move in with Kingsley, so that she would not lose Aisha. I have to tell Lilingrid that I had her little girl and I lost her.

Oh, poor grandbee, come home, even come home to Kingsley rather than face the life I had.

I unwind the towel from my head, hoping no one is watching me too closely, and I slip it into a bin on the road. Then I phone Lilingrid's mobile as I walk along the cobbles, past the shabby green awnings and crates of dried-out-looking African vegetables piled up against the lamp post. My hair is cold against my head and I am glad it's still not fully grown back yet. The phone connects and starts ringing.

How far could Aisha have got by now?

It takes me by surprise when a male voice answers the phone. Could it get any worse?

"Yeah?" says Kingsley's voice. I wonder if he knows this is Lilingrid's mum. I wonder how she keeps my number in her phone.

I try my most normal voice. The one I had when I phoned social services and I have to raise it loud above the noise on the High Street.

"I would like to speak to Ingrid, please." Even though the voice I put on is a little bit posher than I normally speak, I know I still sound lost.

There is a slightly irritated sigh but no anger. I suppose that means that Lilingrid has not told him about my visit to her house and my attempt to stop her from moving in with him. "She was in the bathroom earlier. I'll just check."

I move quickly away from the stench from the butchers. Over the phone, I can hear footsteps and then I hear male and female voices until Lilingrid's voice comes closer. "Hello?" It is such a different sound from the bustle around me. She sounds contented, a woman in a relationship again. I imagine her warm and cosy from the shower, as if North Greenwich flats are full of fluffy bathrobes and wood finishes, like hotels on the television.

"Ingrid."

"Yeah, Helen, hello." I imagine a dust of talc being released.

I don't know how to start. I don't know how to break her warm and peaceful day.

"Aisha was here."

"Oh, that's where she is. She left a weird note. We got back late last night. Kingsley had seats at the ballet to get us away from all the unpacked boxes."

"Yes, but..." I have my other hand blocking up the ear that is not next to the phone.

"What? It's not a great time. Does she want something?

She's nearly sixteen. Does she really have to get you and me running after her?"

"She's run away." I know if I don't say it quickly that Ingrid will get bored before I can explain.

"Run away?"

"She asked to stay a couple of weeks, but then I—"

"She asked to stay with you a couple of weeks?"

"Yes, but—"

"And you didn't say anything about it to me?" Lilingrid is getting louder.

"I tried to tell you. I tried to say that she was scared."

"Send her over here right now."

"Ingrid, she's not here anymore. I'm trying to say... She's gone properly."

There is a long silence. I watch a lady in a headscarf finger fruit from the crate opposite me, lifting something pink-coloured to her nose for a while before putting it back and moving to the next crate. I am surrounded by people, shoppers, store workers, but not the one person I need.

Lily continues, a little quieter, "You don't know where she is?"

She was in my care. And I lost her.

I can hear Ingrid try to compose herself. "Okay, listen, I know that this seems really serious, but we don't have to panic yet. Can you tell me why you think she has run away?"

"She said that she was running away. She said that she would stay a couple of weeks at mine—"

Ingrid cuts me off, already losing her calm. "So what happened then? Why isn't she still there?"

I don't know what to say or how to explain it. "I'm sorry, Ingrid. I'm sorry."

"Just explain, Helen, and stop the apologising." She doesn't mean I'm forgiven. She means she wants all the information first and then she will start blaming people.

I take big gulps of dusty air, because there is no hiding now. I have sheltered against the wall of a gambling shop so that I don't have to shout over the noise of the road. A man in joggers swings out of the doors and charges off, throwing betting tickets behind him. "I told her about your dad. I told her the truth about your dad, and it was too much for her. She ran out of the house with her backpack and everything. I ran after her, but I lost her. I'm so sorry."

"What do you mean?"

I am drunk on my big gulps of air. I can't answer.

"Actually, never mind. I'll deal with this. Kingsley…" she starts calling to him as she hangs up on me.

I wish I could talk to Marnie.

***

Becca's front door is still open when I get back and she comes out of it in flip-flops and a strappy top, arms folded across her chest, as soon as she hears the beep of the door. "You alrigh'?" which is how she normally says hello, but she wears a concerned frown.

I like Becca, but she is not Marnie. I am not ready to tell her that I have lost someone else's baby, or how I lost her. I look to the concrete wall and shrug. "I'm just really busy, that's all."

She lingers as I climb the steps, but I don't have time to waste.

"Thanks for letting me use your room," I add, as I walk up out of her view.

Inside my flat, I turn on the light in Aisha's bedroom. Her "just moved in" belongings are scattered about the floor. There was a green sleeping bag unrolled on the bed, but it's gone now. I pull at the sports bag she has left against the bed as if it will help me find her, but there is not much in it. A jumper and a pad and pen. A lipstick. A nail varnish.

I drop the pen onto the bare floorboards and keep the nail varnish in my hand. It is burgundy, rich and glossy. There is a coating of spillage around the neck of the bottle.

Bad things happened when I ran away from home. But there were some good things: I had a nail varnish that was such an unbelievable pink.

I take the nail varnish over to my sofa, rolling it in my palm, staring at it until I can hardly see the colour anymore because the evening has grown dark. Wherever Aisha is, she won't even have this nail varnish to be her home and help her think of pretty things.

But a lot of bad things happened too, like the day that I had stinking period pain, like my sides were about to explode for two days.

What if those bad things happen to Aisha? How can we piece her back together from that? She'll never be the same again.

Should I catch a train to central London and all of its twists and secret corridors? I would never find her.

I try to phone Lilingrid again. The phone rings through, ring after ring, until eventually I reach Lilingrid's voicemail and hear her telling me to leave a message in a cheerful voice I've never heard her use in real life. Maybe it's her North Greenwich voice. I don't leave a message. I don't ask her to call me back. It wouldn't be enough to make things right.

I try to ring Aisha's mobile again, knowing that it will not connect, but just in case. The crackling voice of the lady who takes voicemails comes onto the line, and I wait for the beep where I am supposed to leave a message. I sigh in the message time. I leave Aisha a message that is a sigh because I haven't the heart to hang up yet, and that's when I realise I am going to have to go to North Greenwich.

***

North Greenwich is not like Thamesmead. It's full of flats rather than houses, but for some reason that is supposed to be better. They are built in bright colours, un-house-like colours, as if the builders confused the bricks with Lego. Cranes tower over them, glistening with red lights like jewels against the pale blue of the night sky.

I hover at the cold metal of the intercoms. I don't know how I'm going to explain to Lilingrid how much danger her daughter is in. I look up. The building is too tall to see the windows of the penthouse at the top. I press number twenty-two anyway and wait.

After a few moments, beeping, I hear the scraping of a voice. "Hello?" In the background are loud voices and music too.

"Ryan?"

"What are you doing here, Grandma?"

"I need to talk to your mum. Is she there?" I think about asking to be let in, but now that I am here, on his territory, I don't want to see Kingsley.

"She's kind of..." he pauses. "There's a big conversation going on."

There is a shuffle, and Kingsley's voice takes over, assertive. "Can I help?" which really means, "how can I get you away from here as soon as possible".

At the sound of the voice, I lose the air from my lungs, but I have to continue. "It's Helen, Ingrid's mum. Ingrid's biological..." I tail off. That bit's not important. "Can I talk to Ingrid? It's really important."

"She's talking to Aisha right now. Can I take a message?" Even with his normal American lilt, the words are flat and trampling, telling me that I have no business here.

"Aisha's here?"

There is a click and a whir and silence. The intercom has timed out. I stare at the buzzer, trying to decide what to do. A man and a woman come down the pathway giggling. The woman has long red hair, darker than mine, bubbling in lumps of curls, and the man has shocking blonde hair and a goatee. His arm is around her and she is clasping a bottle of wine to her chest. They both glance at me and giggle a little quieter, as he reaches for a key fob and holds it against the door to open. But they wait. I realise that they are holding the glass door open for me to go first. I look onto the carpeted stairwell, with magnolia walls. This is Kingsley's place. I shake my head and look away from them, saying "No thank you" so quietly I know that they won't hear it. Then they are gone, shrugging, the door gently folding closed as they walk up the stairs.

I click the buzzer again.

"Yes." Still Kingsley.

"She's here? She'd run away."

"She had not run away." He says each word slowly as if I am stupid. "There was no need to panic. I got in touch with her school so I could ring around all of her school friends and that's how we found her."

Look at Kingsley working with the System as if he's the model citizen, unlike his mad mother-in-law who needs to be spoken to in words of one syllable.

"Is that all, Helen?"

Is that all? Aisha is safe. As all of the panic falls out of me. I start to cry. "She's not hurt?"

There is another click with the time-out, so he can't shout at me anymore, but neither has he told me if Aisha is hurt or not. Does that mean that she is hurt?

I press again, more quickly this time, but it rings through for longer.

"Helen, please. It's not a good time."

"Lilingrid! Is Aisha okay? Is she hurt?"

"She was just at Gina's. Why would she be hurt?" She sounds genuinely surprised by the question.

Because you can be hurt when you run away from home, Lily. I came around to tell you that. I almost told you all of that.

I think that Lilingrid can hear my crying because her tone softens a bit. "You were panicking about nothing," as if I had not heard her panic too.

"Can I speak to her?"

There is an awkward silence. "It's not such a good time. And listen, please don't ring the buzzer again. It's been a long day, and Kingsley… well, we're all a bit stressed."

Oh, Aisha is so close, but I cannot reach out and tell her sorry and hug her, and tell her that everything will be okay. I try to picture Aisha in North Greenwich amongst the wood and the bathrobes. She is kind of safer than she was, but she doesn't fit, squeezed into the wrong place. She is surrounded by Kingsley, who is not her dad, and Lilingrid, who is upset with her.

"Did she tell you why she ran away?"

"Oh, she will do, believe me." Lilingrid does not understand what I mean, although she has accidentally admitted that Aisha kind of did run away and they are really annoyed about it.

I am just about to tell Lilingrid not to be too angry with Aisha, that it was just Aisha's way of dealing with the shock of the moment. Maybe I will even explain what it is that I told Aisha to make her so upset, when Lilingrid mutters under her breath, "It's not easy. She has to up her game. He's going to leave me if she carries on being such a handful."

I don't answer her. She knows I've been crying, so perhaps that hides how angry she has just made me. Then the click of the intercom turning off prevents me from trying.

***

I have to walk away now. I cannot even throw stones at the high window and its colourful balcony to wake Lilingrid up out of her madness. It's too high. But the main door is opening again. A woman my age in a crisp pale-blue shirt comes out. She is talking on the phone, so she does not offer me the door, but she doesn't shut it properly behind her either. I reach out for the door handle before it swings shut and walk straight for the lift. I can't be sure that she won't come back and challenge me until the steel doors slide firmly shut.

I pass white door after white door, overpowered by the smell of office carpet, feeling light-headed from the hum of the overhead lights. I could get lost in this labyrinth sameness, if I don't concentrate on the flat numbers. They are marked out by brass and I count them through to number twenty-two.

I have been banned from using the buzzer, but I can knock the door. And I am not going to let them intimidate me from protecting my grandchildren.

As I guessed, I can hear yelling inside. It is angry yelling, although it's not the sort of yelling that comes with punches. I think the yelling is about me, because I hear the phrase "stupid old bat", and Kingsley has never met Marnie, so he can't be talking about her.

I bang at the door anyway. It swings open. There are several people I can see at the door all at once, Lilingrid dressed all in black, who opened it, her face damp with tears, Aisha in the background, determinedly tearless, and Kingsley – at a safe distance from Aisha, but shouting nonetheless.

"Oh, Helen, please. What did you have to come up for?" starts Ingrid, trying to hide that she has been crying.

"Are you okay, Aisha?" I call out.

They both look down the magnolia carpeted hallway at Aisha and she walks down to the door to me, as if she is the only one who can resolve this. "I'm sorry I ran away on you," she whispers in the hallway. "I just…"

"I know. It's easy to panic." I squeeze her arm. "Are you going to be okay, though?" I whisper.

She nods sadly. In fairness, I cannot see that Kingsley has been violent today. She looks at me. "I'm sorry for the stuff that you told me about too. I did change my plans because you frightened me… In a good way," she adds when she sees my face. "I want you to know that."

I don't know what to say to her, because she knows about things that I alone should have to carry.

"So," announces Kingsley, straightening, leaning out of a panelled door that seems to go through to the kitchen. He has developed a paunch since I saw him last, and his hairline has receded. A lot. "We are all done here then. You can stop your interfering."

"Interfering?" I can't look him in the eye, I am so scared. I can't ask a reasonable question, like why it is interfering to want to know that my granddaughter is safe.

"Oh we all know why we also got a call from social services this afternoon, and have to entertain them later this week." Closer to him, I can see that he has flecks of white in his moustache.

The social services. I had forgotten about them. Lilingrid starts shaking her head, bringing her hand up to one cheek. It feels like they've had this argument already.

"We'll be explaining to them how *Lilingrid's* mother goes around scaremongering, accusing people of running away." As always, his words pop out with authority and significance, but I know I am in the right. "Preventing people from living with who they love," he continues, "when you're the one who can't look after her own baby!"

He is walking with each step towards the door, his voice getting louder and louder, and as he says the word "baby", I run.

I clatter down the stairs because I'm too scared to wait for the lift. Even when I hear the door slam and shake the whole building, and I realise that was all that Kingsley was going to do, I don't stop running. I reach the dual carriageway on the way to the cinema on the roundabout, and only then do I stop run-walking, only then do I look back at the windows at the top of the building, struggling for breath against a bollard, thinking: my bees are in there.

AISHA

I hate the flat in North Greenwich. I hated it even before Mum moved in, when I hadn't even seen it. Well, I like the views over to the hills, the maze of roads, and stationary traffic that twinkles in the light. And I like the spotlights in the bathroom. When we moved in, Ryan showed me the bathroom first. Of course, he had been here loads, long before me. He said, "Look at this," and flicked the switch onto the windowless bathroom, highlighting the mosaic tiles and mirrored surfaces. "Does this mean we're rich?" he whispered to me, wide-eyed.

I shrugged. "Rich in one way, I suppose," but when I tread on the soft carpets, I feel afraid, I feel we are receiving material things but we are paying for them with debts of anxiety.

Later on, during a Chelsea game, I asked Ryan if he loves his dad. He was sprawled out and leaning on one arm, and briefly lifted his face to scowl at me. I don't think that means that he doesn't. I don't love Ryan's dad at all, him and his law degree from Wolverhampton. I suppose I don't have to.

I have been in so much trouble for leaving home. It's like I've been a serious troublemaker. I'm so ashamed. But I just panicked. Every time I see the huge family photo of the four of us behind the two tall candelabra on the sideboard, I know that I am not supposed to be here. I think Gina was right, after all. Some people my age have to leave home and they do okay. I get that it went really bad for Grandma. I do get that. It's been giving me nightmares; more than the thought of living with Kingsley. When the day wakes me up, the nightmares go away again, I realise I am no longer in my Thamesmead bedroom, but in a double bed with a yellow duvet, and I have to get on with my life.

I am kind of trapped. It's bad here. It's worse outside.

I try to look forward to starting my A levels, but I keep remembering Grandma and it makes me so sad – the look on her face running away from Kingsley. I wonder if that is the look on her face in the past, when she was attacked? But I think in the end that it isn't. She was brave when she came here, braver than she would have been when she was my age, even though she was afraid.

Kingsley has been mostly all right with us so far. Well, not on the day they found me at Gina's. But at least he didn't hit anyone then. He threw a chair against the dining table after Grandma was here. It wasn't too bad, nothing broke, there is just a small chip on the leg of the chair. The glass of the table didn't smash at all, although the fruit bowl on the table slid off, leaving apples and oranges bouncing over the wood floor. We were too scared to pick them up right away. Then Kingsley went out for a long time and I could hear Mum crying in her room. She didn't even bother not talking to me this time. That's the sort of thing that gets me really scared.

When he comes back, he wants to tell me I need to concentrate to get through my A levels and get a good degree. Like him. I hardly need Kingsley to tell me to work hard. Mum is still looking at me. Even her jangly earrings seem to have stopped jangling so that she can hear what I say and so there is no way I am going to squeeze out the obvious answer to that – Kingsley, you are not my dad. "I will," I say, looking down at the laminate floor.

"It's my education that made me such a success," he adds with emphasis on the word "me". By success, he must mean someone who barks complaints down the mobile phone at his staff, and changes his car every year.

Maybe I am not being fair. Maybe Kingsley has changed. But whatever my head says, I am waiting for the moment that there will be an explosion.

Anyway, a lady called Grace in a grey suit comes around for what is called a "family conference". Grace is from social services. She actually comes to the flat. Her suit doesn't make her look sophisticated the way Mum's suits do on her. It's more like she is wearing it because someone has told her that she has to have a suit to visit families and she has lost weight since buying it. The jumper underneath is bobbling. I find it so embarrassing that she's here. I hope that no one ever finds out that social services were here. It's like I've been truanting or expelled, like the bad kids at school.

I googled "family conference" too. It turns out that the authorities have this weird idea that even the bad guys should sit and talk it all out together. Grace tries to make it seem all really friendly and normal. She's trying to be kind to us. Like she tells me that she likes my T-shirt which is just something I bought from George at Asda with my new wages and nothing special. The real problem is that we all know she is only really here because we are a dysfunctional family. That's what it said on Google. It's shameful. And I hate living here. I hate even sitting on this cream leather sofa which we constantly worry about damaging, but there should not be some strange woman in our house, or Kingsley's house, or whatever, asking our business.

Mum gets upset right from the start. She even starts crying while she's making a Nespresso for Grace, but the machine isn't quite loud enough to hide the noise. I know that might sound pretty normal, to be upset when there is a social worker in the house, but she's not normally like this. She's a strong lady and I'm proud of her being strong. Somehow being in this North Greenwich castle has made her happier but more pathetic at the same time. I've heard that phrase, "an emotional rollercoaster". Is that what she is on right now?

"I'm a good mother," she says, slamming the coffee onto the table. Me and Ryan join in and agree.

"Of course you are," says Grace. She is perched on the sofa, not leaning back, with her ankles crossed nervously in the strapped heels that she did not think to take off before walking in. For some reason, everyone turns to look at Kingsley then, who is staring at the coffee table.

When she has got Ryan to sit down and join us too, Grace asks us about school. I am scared she is going to ask us about running away, but she doesn't do that yet. She seems nervous. She repeats some of her questions. Grace asks if we are okay that we have moved in with Kingsley. She says it really casual as if it's just general conversation, but I know her game. I know she really thinks that this is all bad stuff that's going on here.

Kingsley is an intelligent man, and he knows her game too. He leans forward like Grace is going to be his best friend. "Basically, that mad bat of a grandmother the kids have has got some bee in her bonnet..."

"Mr Dryson, please would you let the children answer?"

"But you've seen this woman, right? Her squawky red hair and weird eyes. Freak show." He gestures each word with a forefinger aimed at the window, as if Grandma is out there somewhere on the horizon. "She's so nuts that they took Ingrid off of her when she was a baby."

Mum seems to shrink at the mention of her being a baby. Funnily enough, I feel sadder that Kingsley hasn't realised that Grandma's hair has turned grey while we were away from her.

"That may be so, Mr Dryson, but if I could just get the children to tell me first. How about you, Aisha?" and she turns to look at me, and I hate that.

It's none of her business, this strange scatty lady. And I think it's weird to be asked in front of Kingsley, despite what I read on Google. I turn my face away from her and look outside to where Kingsley had been pointing when he was talking about Grandma. I nearly lie. I don't want this person knowing anything. But as I look out to the tree-lined hills, I remember when I tried to run away, and I really nearly left Ryan behind, Grandma reminded me I have to protect Ryan too. After all, what will Kingsley be like after a while of having kids around all of the time?

I swallow my pride for Ryan. "I'm uncomfortable about it."

Both Mum and Kingsley shoot me a look, but they are all waiting for me to say why. I don't say why.

"Can you tell me why?" asks Grace.

But still I don't say why. And Mum starts getting involved now, raising her hands and telling me that I am stupid and selfish, as demonstrated by my running away last week.

That's when I get angry. I yell at Mum because I wasn't being selfish. I was just being afraid. I yell at Mum that I know that Kingsley broke her arm, and that I know that he broke my ribs when I was little. And isn't she worried about Ryan? And how can she let him talk about Grandma like that right here and now? "Why do you think that will be okay?"

I catch sight of myself in the mirror on the opposite wall from the family portrait and I realise I am standing up when I do not even remember getting up. I see that I am leaning over Mum and I want to shake her. In fact, when I am saying all of this my hands are all over the place and my heart is thumping.

I wonder if this is how it feels when you lose your temper so much that you throw a chair, or you throw someone down the stairs. This must be what "seeing red" is. But I don't see red. I see an open-plan living space with leather furniture, silver ornaments, and oak floors, and a small, scared family in the middle of it. I feel even more ashamed. But the people around me are all quiet and Mum is looking at the mosaic mat on the coffee table and biting her lip. And I look at Ryan and he looks sad too. All the violence he sees on TV and on computer games, but now it's in this little heart of a home in North Greenwich, and even though it's less violent, it's bigger than something that happens on a New York Street or a Galaxy Far Far Away, because here is real.

Then I look at Kingsley's face. It seems angry but also frozen. He doesn't say anything. It's like if he let one bit of the anger out just in words, then all of the anger would come out, pummelling out, and he would prove me right. And Kingsley is not stupid, so he does not do that.

I shouldn't have lost my temper. I feel like such a drama queen. It feels like I made a fuss about nothing. But there is no taking it back. Just as when Kingsley hit out, there are things that are done that cannot be undone. I cannot take back what I have said. I imagine I can hear a whir and a click in the air. I imagine that something new has been started now. Everything is going to change.

HELEN

When Marnie was alive, she would say that Lily was more like me than she would ever know. We were standing in the stairwell while she watered her doorstep plants. I asked her how she knew that, I asked her if she had seen something at the school play.

"No," she said, lifting the watering can up, and putting a hand to her back as she straightened out, "but she is your daughter. Half of her is your genes."

I'm not so sure about that. I have known Lilingrid a long time now, and she doesn't seem much like me, not really. There is that stuff about liking pretty things, but she is much more headstrong than me. She would never lose her bee because of the state of her flat, for instance. Somehow she would stop that happening. If there were social services threatening to do that, there would be a fight.

I have been waiting for the next phone call from Lilingrid ever since my visit to North Greenwich. Whatever social services will say to them, they know it was me that phoned them. But I don't get a phone call. She comes in person, sitting in the stairwell when I come home with the shopping, her long limbs making the most of the steps. Her high heel is rocking on the lowest one. She is picking at her cuticles with her pink fingernails. "Where have you been?" she asks me quietly.

"Getting the groceries."

"I've been sitting here for ages."

I knew that as soon as I saw her. "Sorry abo climb the steps towards her and lean back against tl blocks. I wait to hear it. I am here now. I will have facts after all.

I don't expect her to say what she says though.

She doesn't raise her voice, but she doesn't look me in the eye, either. "Why would you have my children taken away from me?"

I have to double-take and it's a few seconds before I can respond. "What?"

She turns her face to me, but still won't meet my eye. Her lips are a dark burgundy colour. Even though she's angry, her make-up is flawless. "Don't act all innocent. Kingsley was right. It was you that called social services."

"They wouldn't do that," but as I say it, I'm doubting myself. This isn't possible. I think for a moment through all of the thoughts and noise and the terror. No. It's not possible. My grandbees could not be safer in care than with Kingsley. The social services must have seen the same things in the news that I have. Lilingrid must be confused. I come past her towards the door, lifting the Asda bags to avoid brushing them against her. "Come in and sit down with me. We'll have a cup of tea." If I can calm her down, I can get some sense out of her. "Come and tell me what has happened."

She stands up. She's still dressed all in black, a long tunic over skinny trousers. "I'm not going in there with you. You took my children away." She is still not shouting, but it's like she is hard as baked clay and there is no softening her. That means she is angrier than when she is shouting, even when she was shouting about April.

"Ingrid! I never would. I know how that feels. I never would do that." I think about asking if it's Kingsley who suggested that, but I know that this one is between me and her.

She looks at me properly for the first time. Her natural hair is scraped back into a small bun, and the frizz has a softening effect around her forehead. It makes her look younger. She looks me in the eye and seems to believe me. But she has that same unhappy look on her face as the day that she knew that she could not fight Kingsley anymore. She wasn't angry, because she knew she could not win this fight. That is how terrible what I have done is. I have made things as bad for Lilingrid as Kingsley did.

I unlock the door without saying anything. Maybe if she believes me, she will come in after all.

"I never expected to see you at North Greenwich," she says, and her voice is far enough behind to tell me that she has not started to follow me in.

"I was so, so worried." When I look at her, I realise that she is almost telling me she was impressed that I was brave enough to come where I knew Kingsley would be. "I thought Aisha was in danger. I needed to explain to you why." She doesn't answer, so I push the door open a little more.

"So," she picks up the conversation again while I am facing away from her. She sounds almost casual. And then she stops before trying again with a tremor in her voice. "You were attacked, weren't you? That's what all this is about. That's how I was conceived."

I wasn't expecting the subject change and it makes me catch my breath. I let my hand with the keys in drop and steady myself against the doorpost. There is no point in Beep Beep Bop right now. I wish I'd stayed in Asda until they threw me out. And then I should have caught a train to London Bridge and hid in empty doorways. Like the olden days. Back where this all started.

"Yes."

"In London?"

"In London, by a man on a winter's night. Who told me that I was pretty and that he would take me somewhere warm where his mother could look after me, because she was lonely." Lilingrid doesn't say anything. She stands like a statue taking it all in and not reacting. "It was only when I was in the car that he turned nasty." The words stop then. Even though it was forty years ago, I remember the smell of the car seats, and the view of the car mirror with the air freshener hanging off it. Just the thought of the smell of the car makes me choke. The memories swing right back to the front of my mind, how the radio was playing Radio Two at the moment when I realised I needed to be scared.

But we are just having a conversation, about something that's gone away now. And the real thing that is left is Ingrid, and Ingrid is beautiful, my bee. I look at this Ingrid who would never admit that she had a broken arm, let alone that Kingsley broke it, asking me where she came from. She is looking away, taking the information in. I wonder if she wishes she didn't know.

"Did Aisha tell you?"

"Hardly. She's not talking to me, or I'm not talking to her."

"So how…?"

She shrugs. "I'm not stupid. I've been playing this guessing game for twenty years and now I worked out what secret could be so bad that it makes people do stupid things all of the time," she whispers to the floor with a scowl.

I want to ask her why it mattered so much, but I think I know: the heritage so that she can impress Kingsley; the "big family" so that she can bear losses like her little brother; even maybe that just this single mad old lady is a disappointment as a mum. Instead I say, "I'm sorry," for the bad stuff. For the secret, for the fact that the secret happened, for the fact it makes people do stupid things.

She looks up, but not at me. "And what has that got to do with not telling us about your parents?"

"Nothing. I'd run away. You knew I ran away."

"Did you not want to admit to being pregnant or something?"

"I was pregnant after I ran away."

"So what…?"

Oh, really. She doesn't understand and I can't explain all

this. We are going too far now. Surely I don't have to tell her about what Bill did to me too?

Marnie told me that Bill's and Lilingrid's father's actions weren't connected, even though they both did the same thing to me. She solemnly promised me that it was nothing to do with me, even though she never knew either of them. And Bill's gone away now. Why can't we just forget all about it?

Lilingrid waits for a while and then sighs when I don't answer her. She looks as if she is staring out into the distance through the reinforced glass over the stairwell, but there is nothing to see through the obscured glass. I think she is crying, but I don't know which bit she is crying about. Then she starts walking slowly down the stairs.

"Ingrid, wait. What's happened to Aisha and Ryan? Is it too late to fix it?"

She stops and turns slightly. "They're still with us."

"So it's all okay, then? Kingsley told them I was just a mad old lady?"

"No, it's not okay. Nothing's been decided." Her words are flat and factual. "The social worker is putting together a care plan. There'll be a conference when they have all the information." She says the words "care plan" and "all the information" more quietly, but with sarcasm.

My lungs are filled with a sudden punch of breath. The System loves its plans. The "treatment plan", for my breakdown; the "care plan" for my grandbees. I cannot believe I have done this. I have started a fire after all, a furnace. I thought they would just tell her that she would have to leave him. I have tried to protect them, but I have put them in greater danger. What will they do with my grandbees? "What does that mean?"

She doesn't answer for a minute. She turns further away from me and stares at the breeze blocks. "Let's see how happy they are away from me. Maybe they'll end up with someone like Maurice and Jenny."

"Maurice and Jenny looked after you okay."

"Oh, they cleaned and cooked all right and helped with the homework. But no one was ever enough for them. They always had to find a harder kid to fix." She laughs gently to herself. "The grass isn't always greener," she almost sneers.

But we both know that being brought up by Maurice and Jenny would be the least bad option if they're taken away.

I step towards her. "Leave him, Ingrid. Leave Kingsley. They won't take them away if you do that." It's me who is shouting. Ingrid hasn't shouted at me once. I'm the one doing the shouting.

She still doesn't answer me. She starts back down the stairs.

"There was no other way I could have saved them," I call as she moves out of sight. "What else could I have done?"

Faces appear above the railings from the flats above, leaning over towels that have been pegged to the banister as if this was a garden and not a dirty, dusty council stairwell. A skinny boy with just boxers on dashes away as I look up, but a bald head yells down to shut up. I glare up at the voice until I hear the beep of the door opening and closing. I want to run after her and put my arms around her, my bee whose life I keep on ruining from the moment she was born, from failing to tell her about her family and now even taking her children away.

But Lilingrid is an adult. That means that I should not chase her out as she leaves. I can't tell her I will fix it all for her. I cannot call her mother and I can't call the police just because someone has run away from me.

***

Above the cupboard with the tea and mugs, I have hidden an envelope. It is the white envelope that Aisha brought me in hospital, when she told me that I might be angry with her. It is the envelope with April's details in it.

I can't reach above the cupboard without a chair, so I pull

one over from the dining table. Its legs squeak against the tiled floor, and I level the back of the chair against the cupboard. I climb up and pick up the envelope, and climb down and sit straight back down on the chair. I don't move it back. I hold the envelope on my lap, squeezing my stomach down on it, with my head in my hands. How did things come to this?

My flat is so clean, and there is a beautiful bowl on the dining-room table. It feels so nice and sunny in here, but nothing at all is right. I thought if I stood up for things, I thought if I started facing things in the eye, then I could fix them, but now I have made them worse. Lilingrid is defeated by me, and that is worse than being hated by her. She says the bees will be taken away from her, just as my bee was from me. Each link in the chain of our generations has been broken. Did I start this?

And here is another thing to face. This looks like the only link in the chain that I have any control over now.

Taking control is like a rolling ball. It just carries on rolling. I have started to take control, so now I carry on doing it. I open the envelope and I look at the address and number for a very long time. It is still the same address. I don't know about the phone number. I look at it. And I cry a bit, although I don't know which thing I am crying about, and I look at it again.

Then I put the number back in the envelope. I'm not ready. But I don't put the envelope back on the cupboard, I put it next to the Turkish bowl. And as I do so I realise that it's not me who started this and broke all of the chains. It is Bill. There might be some broken corners that I can fix, but it's Bill whose fault it is really, who makes my Lily-Bee cry in the stairwell, who did things to me that made me run away from home, who has to be so big and horrible a secret that there is a barrier between me and everyone I love.

I am still sitting there, thinking that Lilingrid must be mistaken, they cannot be taking the bees into care, when I hear slow, heeled footsteps on the concrete floor, not a stiletto click though, so I know straight away that it's not Ingrid returned.

I have left the front door open. Whoever is there still knocks though, and I go to the hallway, where I see a face peering around the corner.

"Oh, Becca." It's not like seeing Marnie, not someone who can take all the broken pieces and put them together again when you didn't really think that was possible. Still, I am ever so fond of the face I see framed by two long gold chandelier earrings.

"You alrigh'?" she says, leaving the vowel to drift on and on, but I think that she means it as a question this time.

"Yes, I'm okay. My daughter was just here and..." I don't know what to add. I wonder if Becca heard the conversation. If Becca heard that conversation, she would know nearly all the bad things there are to know about me. Although she wouldn't know about the mental hospital and she wouldn't know about Bill.

While I try to work out what to say next, the softest of sounds comes from number seventeen. There is TV in the distance. We both turn our heads towards the door. I want to Beep Beep Bop and believe that the noises are Marnie moving cheerfully from room to room. I want to Beep Beep Bop, you know.

But Marnie is dead. I look back at Becca and I can see we'd both been thinking the same thing, but the sun is still coming through the reinforced glass.

"Do you want some company?" she offers.

She is so kind. "I do, yes I do. But, Becca, just let me put something away in my house first."

"Yes, I'll just get the kettle on then." She returns down the stairs. She looks happy that she can help.

***

Grace is coming up my stairs, and my grandbees are following her. This time the social worker is bringing bees to me, instead of taking them away.

Grace is calm and professional. This is quite nice of her, because when I could not get her on the phone to ask what Lilingrid was talking about, I did shout at her receptionist. She had a prim, patronising voice, so she shouldn't have been working in social care anyway. I shouted that they do not care about my little bees at all. I thought maybe Grace was hiding from me and was stealing the grandbees, and I never ever should have trusted the System after all.

Grace shakes my hand, which she never did before the children were with us. Grace says that we have to talk as a family and this time I count as family. No one can tell me I'm only biological family because Grace says that I am proper family. She is calmer than the other times I have seen her. But Aisha and Ryan don't meet my eye; Aisha in her skinny jeans and batwing top; Ryan in his hoodie.

We sit around my dining table, and I make my grandbees' favourite drinks and a tea for Grace. Grace talks in nice easy words and smiles a lot, and sometimes puts a hand on the shoulder of one of the bees. It's nice. I don't expect a lady with a business card to do that. She says we need to have a chat

"Because Dad broke Mum's arm," says Ryan with a knowing nod.

"Well, we don't need to talk about that bit now," she says to him. Then she turns back to me. Today she wears a white blouse buttoned right up to her neck, and it bulges awkwardly over her chest. "We have to talk about what our next steps are," she says. She is not taking any notes this time, but she has some papers in her hand. I am trying not to look over and read them.

But now that the conversation starts to get serious, I get confused. She starts to use words like transition and facilitate. I let the words rush over me, and try to think what I can make out of all the formal words. In the end, I think she is saying that everybody, absolutely everybody, Ingrid and social services and me and even Kingsley, we all want what is best for the children. Which I agree with, so I don't know why it is being said so seriously, unless it's all a trick to take the grandbees away. And then, out of the blue, while I am still trying to concentrate on what she is saying, she says, "What do you think, Helen?"

But I am really confused by now, so I don't know what to say. She looks at me very intensely, and after a long silence, she starts to frown. Even the bees look disappointed. I start to realise that it's really important to explain something to Grace. "Grace, a long time ago, they took my Ingrid away. I'm not allowed to keep any children."

Grace loses her professional look for a minute and gives me a soft smile. "You were very young, Helen. That's very different from where we are now."

My head is spinning. But I don't want to check out, I want to stay here in reality. "You mean, I am allowed to look after children now? Does that mean that I could take Aisha and Ryan?"

Grace nods and smiles. "That way things can be as normal as possible, and the children can still see their parents."

I look at my grandbees. They don't have to go into care. They don't have to live with a violent man. They don't have to sleep under bridges unprotected from bad men. They can come home to me.

"But are we too much for you, Grandma?" asks Aisha, reaching out to touch my hand. "I'd feel so much safer here than with them, but we would be so much work for you."

"Oh, Aisha, I'd like it if you and Ryan came here. I'd like that very much."

***

Now there are three of us on the sofa in the two-bed flat in Deptford. Ryan sleeps in the proper bedroom, and Aisha in the one that once was a living room. This sofa is a three-seater sofa and we are all watching an Agatha Christie film. Well, Ryan is playing on his iPhone, and Aisha is reading an A level text, and I am eating nachos, but we are all here together on the sofa for three.

Lilingrid hasn't spoken to me since the family conference took place at the social services. They'd invited me too in the end. But I have a plan to make things better between us. She still sees Ryan and Aisha at the weekends. She takes them out to the cinema and to McDonald's. They've even been go-karting up in Charlton and Aisha says, after the first few difficult months, that they've started to get on better than they ever had before.

I tell my grandbees that they mustn't hold a grudge against Lilingrid because we all have reasons for doing things that we can't always explain and sometimes we don't even understand ourselves.

Ryan is okay. He is quieter, but he is still such a boy. Sometimes when I see him trying to do wheelies in the car park, skidding out the way of a reversing car, I count the years that I will need to live to keep him alive until he is a grown-up. Every time I feel an unexpected pain, I worry that a stroke like Marnie's is going to take me away before Ryan is old enough to look after himself.

In the Asda staffroom, Aisha asks what we do if we see Lilingrid with a cast on an arm or a limb and my heart sinks before I can think of an answer. I tell Aisha that we will do what we can. If need be, Lilingrid can come and live with us in my flat in Deptford until she can find somewhere else. Then there will be four of us, not three like there are now. But Lilingrid is a grown-up and we have to let her do her own thing now. We just help when we can.

The three of us sit together on the three-people sofa. But three is not a good number. You can never say, there are three of us, we will always be okay, however much you love each other. Things will happen that you don't expect. People will become tied up in our lives, whether we like them or not. You must find others. You must not be scared. You must keep things going and jump in and protect those close to you and you must let new people in.

The other nice thing is that Aisha has been a bit quiet since she joined sixth form, but she keeps having little smiles to herself when she thinks I am not looking. Ryan says that his friend's brother says that Aisha has a boyfriend. Aisha gets really annoyed with him and tries to tell him to tidy his room. Of course, Ryan pays no attention to that, but it's enough to annoy him that she thinks she can tell him what to do that it diverts his attention from Aisha. And then, when the tiff dies down and I have to tell Ryan to go and do his homework, Aisha has that little smile again.

Or maybe she is smiling because she is planning her trip to Jamaica. We went to open a bank account together. She saves every penny from her Asda job to go and see her dad.

But I have a plan. I have a peace offering for Lilingrid and I think she will like it. I want to make her feel better, because it is a terrible thing to lose your bees. I am Beep Beep Bop scared, but I have faced Beep Beep Bop scared and got to the other side, even without Marnie. And here I am, warm and happy and with the pieces of my life almost forming a complete whole. I have started to see the picture that is my broken jigsaw, and there are only a few more pieces to add here and there, for a bit more detail in the sky, and a bit more detail in the helm of the boat.

I am about to leave the sofa in front of the television and go to the phone. I had to move the phone to the kitchen because sometimes the bees need the TV when I need the phone. I am going to pick up the phone and I am going to dial Lilingrid. And if Kingsley answers, I shan't be scared, I will ask calmly for Lilingrid and hope that Kingsley doesn't recognise my voice. How could he from the few conversations we have had?

This is what I am going to say when I have taken a few deep breaths, even though I know it means that I will also have to explain why I ran away from home. "Lilingrid, last week I phoned my mother to tell her I'm still alive, and that I'm sorry. I'm going to Dudley to see her soon. Do you want to come with me?"

ACKNOWLEDGEMENTS

Thanks to my Mum, Clare Morrall, for bringing me up to write no matter what, for writing great books that inspired me, and reading at least two drafts of the book when I agonised about whether I was going in the right direction or not.

To my sister, Heather Morrall, for setting the bar with her novel *Shrink*.

To Brian, for making me buy a laptop so that I would actually get on with the writing, as opposed to daydream about it, putting up with me forgetting to cook as I wrote and typing furiously through several whole TV series (including subtitled ones) and asking every couple of hours… "So what's happened now?"

To my agent, Philippa Sitters at DGA, for her continued support in helping the novel reach publication, and understanding why this novel is what it needed to be.

To Lauren and Lucy at Legend Press, for believing in my novel.

To the readers who are also writers, Zoe, Kairen and Milly, who offered valuable feedback.

To Charlton Congregation, for cheering me on, regardless of whether reading is their thing or not.

IF YOU ENJOYED WHAT YOU READ,
DON'T KEEP IT A SECRET.

REVIEW THE BOOK ONLINE AND TELL
ANYONE WHO WILL LISTEN.

THANKS FOR YOUR SUPPORT SPREADING
THE WORD ABOUT LEGEND PRESS.

FOLLOW US ON TWITTER
@LEGEND_PRESS

FOLLOW US ON INSTAGRAM
@LEGENDPRESS